She hadn't been needed in a long time

For the past three years Delaney had kept herself carefully separate from everyone in her life. If there were no expectations, there could be no disappointment.

Tonight she wanted to help Diesel's kids.

But as Sam continued to watch her, a different kind of need built in her...until all she could think about was Sam.

Tonight she wasn't craving a drink. She had a different demon to battle. This wasn't an unfocused lust she could dismiss. She had feelings for Sam. She could blame it on the adrenaline, but there was nothing impersonal about it. Nothing easy to dismiss.

She wanted him. Diesel's brother. The man trying to persuade her to do the impossible and tell the world who she used to be.

She finally understood the meaning of irony.

Dear Reader,

We all make mistakes in the course of our lives. If we're very lucky, they're small ones and they hurt no one but ourselves. But some of us make life-altering mistakes that go beyond mere blunders or missteps and change lives forever—both our own and other people's. How do you make amends for the kind of bad judgment that ruins lives and destroys families?

Delaney Spencer made a lot of mistakes during her years as a member of a famous band, but none worse than falling in love with its star. Three years after his death, she's still trying to atone for her past and put her life back together. Until her lover's brother tracks her down. Sam McCabe needs something Delaney has, but giving it to him would push her back into the life she's worked so hard to escape.

I've been fascinated by Delaney and her past since she appeared in the first Otter Tail book, *An Unlikely Setup*. Sam McCabe is absolutely the last man she should fall in love with—but the heart has a mind of its own.

I love to hear from readers! Visit my website at www.margaretwatson.com or email me at margaret@margaretwatson.com.

Margaret Watson

Life Rewritten
Margaret Watson

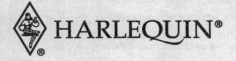

TORONTO • NEW YORK • LONDON
AMSTERDAM • PARIS • SYDNEY • HAMBURG
STOCKHOLM • ATHENS • TOKYO • MILAN • MADRID
PRAGUE • WARSAW • BUDAPEST • AUCKLAND

Recycling programs
for this product may
not exist in your area.

ISBN-13: 978-0-373-71673-9

LIFE REWRITTEN

www.eHarlequin.com

Printed in U.S.A.

ABOUT THE AUTHOR

Almost twenty years after staring at that first blank page, Margaret Watson is an award-winning, two-time RITA® Award finalist who has written more than twenty books for Silhouette and Harlequin Books. When she's not writing or spending time with her family, she practices veterinary medicine. Margaret spends as much time as possible visiting the area that inspires her books, the Door County, Wisconsin, cities of Algoma and Sturgeon Bay. When she's not eating Door County cherries, smoked fish and cheese, she lives in a Chicago suburb with her husband, three daughters and a menagerie of pets.

Books by Margaret Watson

HARLEQUIN SUPERROMANCE

*The McInnes Triplets

This is for Cathie Linz, Lindsay Longford, Susan Elizabeth Phillips, Suzette Vann and Julie Wachowski.

Thanks for always being there when I need you. You are all *very* special.

CHAPTER ONE

SWEAT DRIPPED INTO Delaney's eyes, making them sting, but she had to finish the song's complicated drum solo. As the cymbals crashed and faded, Paul strummed a chord on his guitar, the rest of the band resumed singing "In the Air," and the pub exploded with applause.

The microphone stands jiggled as people stomped on the floor. Evenly spaced, the silver poles formed bright bars in front of her, caging her and the drums. Protecting her.

The applause steadied Delaney, made it easier to lose herself in the music. Tonight, she needed that. It had been three years, but she'd never played publicly on the anniversary of Diesel's death.

It was harder than she'd thought it would be.

The lights blazing down on her turned the faces of the audience into dark shadows, but they didn't hide the figure at the back waving an open cell phone in the air. That streak of color, the twenty-first century version of a lighter at a concert, jerked her back to reality.

People were watching her. She shouldn't have let herself get carried away with that solo. She should have reined in her passion for performing, her craving to drum. She should have played a bland, unmemorable riff.

But Diesel wouldn't have wanted her to be bland. He would have insisted on her best.

An ache of misery rose in her throat. She should have told Paul she couldn't make it tonight.

She should have stayed at home and mourned privately.

But she'd convinced herself that performing would help. That the heat of the lights on her face, the sweat running down her chest and pooling between her breasts, the ache in her arms would soothe her. The power of the music pouring through her body and into her fingers, her voice, should have allowed her to forget everything else.

Instead, it brought all the memories flooding back.

Diesel, flashing a grin as they played together, completely in sync, perfectly attuned.

Leading the cheers as she finished a drum solo.

Lying dead on the bed in their hotel room.

The band finished "In the Air" and segued right into "Can't You See." No drum solo in this one. No vocal solo. *Thank you, Paul.* She wasn't sure she'd have been able to sing right now. She took a deep breath, wiped away the sweat with her sleeve and tried to bury her grief.

Two songs later, Paul stood his guitar on its rack and nodded to the other band members. Fifteen-minute break. Hank set his guitar down and headed outside to smoke. Stu, on keyboards, fiddled with his controls and amplifier for a moment.

When she'd been with the Redheaded Stepsisters, she'd coordinated her drinks with the sets.

First break, first drink. The music always heightened that emptiness inside her. The one only vodka could fill.

Delaney leaned against the window behind her and let the craving wash over her. If she closed her eyes, she could taste the ice-cold Grey Goose. Feel the heat as it slid down her throat. Tonight more than ever she would welcome the oblivion it could provide.

The thirst was always worse on March 20.

Fingering the AA medallion in the pocket of her jeans, she slid off the stool, set her drumsticks on the embroidered seat and wove through the cords and mics and guitar stands toward the bar.

"Great set, Delaney."

"Loved your drum solo."

"Can you guys play 'Landslide' after the break?"

Damn. Someone always asked for that song. She forced a smile at Ian, the professor who showed up almost every Friday night. "I'll talk to Paul. He does the set lists."

As she headed for the bar, Quinn saw her coming and poured coffee into a mug. He set it on the marble surface, and she picked it up and inhaled the rich scent.

She wished it was vodka.

"Made it fresh," Quinn said as she closed her eyes and sipped. He'd ground it fresh, too.

"Thanks, Q."

"Nothing but the best for our star." He nodded at the packed room, people sitting at the booths and tables and standing three deep at the bar. "They're getting here early on Fridays to make sure they have a table, and that means we're selling more food and drinks. Everyone wants to hear you."

"I'm not the star," she said sharply. "They want to hear the *band*." There was a wet ring on the marble surface of the bar. As she held her coffee, she concentrated on soaking up every drop of the condensation with a napkin.

"Don't fool yourself, Delaney. We never had crowds like this until you started playing with Paul and the guys. So would our *star* like something to eat?"

"Maybe later," she managed to say. One of the pub's chicken pot pies would be good, but after Quinn called her a star, she could barely get the coffee down. "Okay if I use your office? I need to change my shirt."

"Sure, go ahead."

Delaney closed the door to the office behind her. The air

was cooler than in the pub, and she shivered in the damp T-shirt that clung to her skin. She shucked it off and slipped into a dry one from the bag she'd left there—a ritual between sets. Just like the sweaty one, the clean shirt billowed around her body and hung to the middle of her thighs. Paul had asked why she was camouflaging herself, but she'd ignored him. She needed room to move when she drummed.

More comfortable now, she sank into Quinn's chair to drink her coffee and try to manage the memories. Once they escaped, it was hard to shove them back into their box.

Three minutes before the band was supposed to start playing again, she left her sanctuary. On the way to the front of the pub, she veered toward the bar. Quinn had the coffeepot ready before she reached him.

"You're good," she said as she held out her mug.

"Some people think so." He glanced toward the corner of the pub, where his wife, Maddie, was talking to one of the patrons.

Delaney rolled her eyes. "God save me from people in love." Her stomach settled and she took a deep breath. This was exactly what she needed—to talk and joke with Quinn just like she always did. To remind herself that this was just another Friday night. "Don't think much of yourself, do you?"

"Maddie thinks I hang the stars, and that's all I care about." He pulled a beer and slid it to another patron, then added, "Lots of new faces in here tonight—probably the ice fishing tournament. You should sing a few more songs in the next set. Maybe they'll come back tomorrow."

"I don't need to sing more," she said, trying to keep her voice light. "Besides, where else are they going to go? The Harp is the best bar in Otter Tail."

"The best *pub*," Quinn said automatically.

"That's what I meant." She hid her smile. She'd spent enough time at the Harp to know how to distract Quinn.

"There are guys here from all over the country," he said, passing a basket of pretzels to another customer. "They love you. It's a huge potential audience."

Guys from all over the country? God help her. She sank onto a bar stool. "Our Otter Tail fans are plenty for us."

She thought about the custom furniture business she was nurturing, the friends she'd made in town. She felt safe in Otter Tail. She'd managed to bury her past, but if someone recognized her as Chantal, former drummer of the Redheaded Stepsisters, everything would come crashing down.

She could forget about her placid, peaceful life. She'd be lucky if she could stay in the small Wisconsin town.

Deep breath. Calm down. The chance of anyone recognizing her was slim to none. She wiped her sweaty palms along the sides of her jeans. "I think Paul is getting ready to start."

Quinn nodded as she hurried away. When she reached her drum set, she put the coffee on the floor beside her, then sat down and made herself think boring thoughts. Bland thoughts. That's what she needed to do for the rest of the night.

As she adjusted her snare drum, the door of the pub opened and a tall man walked in. He sat on a stool and talked to Quinn for a few moments, then leaned against the bar.

He checked out the decor and the other patrons before he looked at the band. Something about his eyes reminded her of Diesel.

Damn it. Everything reminded her of Diesel tonight. It had been stupid to try to perform.

No. She could do this. She wasn't going to let a stranger rattle her.

And despite that flash of familiarity, he *was* a stranger. She would have remembered if she'd met him before. His dark, wavy hair brushed the edge of his collar, and his narrow face was all angles and planes. He had to be a fisherman—the lines around his eyes hinted at days spent squinting in the sun.

Most women would be intrigued by that face. Challenged by the air of mystery and tension swirling around the man.

She didn't get involved with strangers, even ones with intriguing faces. She wasn't Chantal anymore.

Whoever he was, he didn't live here. His jacket was battered leather, and his jeans were faded and white at the stress points. She couldn't tell what color his eyes were, but they scanned the room, assessing one person after another.

The people in this town were mostly open, trusting, easy to read. Not this guy. No one from Otter Tail could slice through a room with his eyes like that.

When he focused on the band again, Delaney wanted to duck behind the bass drum and hide. She didn't want those eyes on her—as if he could ferret out anyone's secrets.

"Okay, are we ready to go? Any additions to the playlist?"

Paul's voice drew her attention from the stranger and Delaney was grateful. The four of them conferred quickly, agreeing on the next fifteen songs.

"And 'Landslide'—I got three requests for it," he added.

"Fine," she sighed. She'd managed to steer them away from songs that featured her. But it was too much to hope that she could get away without singing at all during the set. "Not the first one, though."

"Nope. Everyone needs another jolt of energy. We'll

save 'Landslide' for later." Paul strummed the first chord of "Rockin' in the Free World," and Delaney closed her eyes as her hands banged out the rhythm.

As she lost herself in the music, Diesel's laughing face flashed in her memory. She forgot about the man who'd just walked in. She forgot about her vow to hold herself back, to try to keep herself separate from the music and the rhythm.

All she wanted to do was get through the evening so she could go home and mourn privately for her lost lover.

THE WOMAN BEHIND THE drums couldn't be Chantal. Sam shifted on the bar stool and leaned forward, trying to see her more clearly. This woman was a petite blonde with short hair, no visible tattoos and a face of delicate beauty and strength. She had absolutely no resemblance to the notorious rocker with black, spiky hair tipped with pink, and tattoos covering her upper arms. She didn't have Chantal's self-indulgent expression and hard eyes, either.

His source must have been mistaken.

But the P.I. who'd directed him here hadn't been wrong yet. Every lead Sam had gotten from the guy had panned out, from the town where she was born to the name she was using now. Sam had paid more money than he could afford for the P.I.'s services, but if this woman was Chantal, it would be worth every penny.

He'd come to the little pub in this town with the stupid name, confident he would find her here. Certain he would recognize her the moment he saw her.

How could he not? Chantal had ruined his brother's life. Was responsible for his death.

The blonde sat behind the two guitar players, her face almost hidden by the microphone. The drum set concealed the rest of her body, but when she moved, her shirt flowed around her and he saw a hint of curves. Her arms were those of a drummer, toned and firm, but the baggy shirt was the complete opposite of the tight, provocative outfits she used to wear when she performed.

The three men played a few chords, adjusted their microphones and put their heads together for a moment. Chantal, if it was her, sat with her back against the window, sipping from a mug.

According to the gossip magazines, she'd always drank from a mug during a show. It had held Grey Goose, ice cold. Chantal had expensive tastes.

Sam wondered if the bartender kept her vodka bottle in the freezer.

"You here for the tournament?" the man asked from behind the counter, and Sam swiveled to face him.

"What tournament?"

"Ice fishing."

"Hell, no." Sam shuddered. "Sitting on my ass in a little shack on a frozen lake? No, thanks."

The bartender's mouth quirked. "Got it. Not an ice fisherman. Welcome. I'm Quinn Murphy."

He held out his hand, and Sam shook it. "Sam McCabe."

"Nice to meet you, Sam. What can I get you?"

"How about a beer?" He'd have to drink something or the bartender would wonder why he was here. But he'd have only one—he didn't want the woman watching Rennie and Leo to smell the alcohol on his breath. He'd told her he had to work tonight.

"What kind?"

"Whatever you have."

"How about a local beer? We've got a pale ale from a Green Bay brewery, called Hopasaurus Rex, that's good."

Hopasaurus Rex? He sure as hell wasn't in Miami anymore. "Why not? I'll give it a try."

As Murphy pulled a glass of pale gold beer, he said, "If you're just passing through town, you picked a good night." He nodded toward the musicians. "They're our most popular band."

"They have a name?"

"We just call them Paul's band."

"Are they local?"

"Mostly. The keyboard player comes in from Sturgeon Falls."

Sam glanced at the group and saw Chantal take another drink. That much hadn't changed. "How often do they play?"

The bartender studied him a little more closely. "Once a week, usually. This weekend, they're covering tomorrow night, too. How long are you going to be here?"

"Awhile," he said easily. "I've got business in the area. If they're as good as you say, I'll come to hear them again."

Quinn nodded. "They're that good." He filled another glass for a customer several seats down. "Maybe we'll see you around, then."

"Probably so."

Sam settled back against the counter. He hadn't wanted to come after Chantal. All he'd wanted to do was forget about her. Forget what she'd done to his brother. To his niece and nephew.

Sam had failed his brother, and Chantal was a reminder of that.

Guilt swept over him again, and nothing could make it go away. When child protective services in Miami had called to say the kids were alone, their mother in the hospital, he'd told the social worker he'd hire someone to take care of them. Her voice had gone from friendly and sympathetic to cold when she informed him he was the emergency contact their mother had listed. He had custody of them now.

He didn't have the time, the energy or the patience to take care of two kids. Diesel's kids. But Heather's breakdown hadn't given him any choice.

When the P.I. had called to say he'd found Chantal, Sam had still been trying to hire someone to care for Leo and Rennie. One prospective nanny after another had fallen through, and he'd been forced to drag them along with him to Otter Tail. What was supposed to be a quick visit, in and out by himself, had turned into an ordeal. Five-year-old Rennie got airsick on the plane and carsick on the road. Her ten-year-old brother had been sullen and resentful, and barely spoke to him.

The tiny motel room left Sam no escape from the kids. He couldn't even put them to bed and close a door. He'd better be able to get those CDs from Chantal quickly. He wasn't sure how much more up close and personal he could take with the kids.

Diesel's children needed the money those unreleased recordings of their father would bring in. The kids had to be kept out of the limelight and protected, and he'd chosen a private school for them that would do all that and more. They'd have the best education money could buy. And they would be shielded from the paparazzi and the constant attention their mother's erratic behavior received.

If he could do that for Diesel's kids, he would feel at least a little redemption for the way he'd failed their father. But in order to get them in that school, he needed a lot more money than he had.

Sam was certain Chantal—or Delaney Spencer as she called herself now—had those tapes. The least she could do was hand them over to Diesel's kids, since she'd destroyed their father.

The guitar players slid onto stools, the keyboardist ran off some chords and the noise level in the pub dropped. Then the band started playing.

The music was nothing like the Redheaded Stepsisters. It wasn't hard rock, pounding rhythm, angry lyrics. This group played covers from a wide variety of bands, and they did it well, Sam admitted grudgingly.

The drummer was good. She didn't overpower the other instruments and draw attention to herself. But it was clear she was talented. She didn't sing, though. And Chantal had always sung.

Several songs later, Sam felt the first stirrings of real doubt. Maybe the P.I. was wrong.

Then the keyboard player hit a chord, the guitar players let their hands fall away from their instruments, and the drummer set her sticks on her lap and pulled the microphone toward her. It felt as if the whole room held its breath.

Sam played with a cardboard Guinness coaster as he waited. Watching.

The drummer's chest rose as she drew a breath and launched into a poignant Fleetwood Mac song. Sam snapped the cardboard coaster in two. There was no mistaking that voice.

Chantal.

He'd found her.

CHAPTER TWO

HE WAS WATCHING HER.

The faces of the crowd were in darkness, but somehow Delaney knew the stranger's gaze was fixed on her. Had been for a while. Since "Landslide."

She hit the tom-tom too hard, let the cymbal crash too loudly, and Paul shot her a questioning glance. She closed her eyes for a moment to steady herself, then adjusted the sticks in her hands. Her voice blended into Paul's and Hank's in the chorus of "The Hindu Times," and she sang more softly. Thank God she wasn't the featured singer.

By the time the second set was over, she was convinced the stranger had bored a hole right through her skull.

She put her sticks down and bent to adjust one of the cymbals to give herself a few minutes. She didn't want to run into the stranger with Diesel's eyes. At the end of a set, people began moving around, and the pub would soon be crowded and busy. In the meantime, she was safe behind her drums.

God, she needed a drink.

As she finally navigated the tangle of wires and mics, she noticed the guy was no longer sitting at the bar. She took a deep breath and let her shoulders relax. It was late. He had left.

Several people said hello as she made her way through the crowd, just like any other Friday night. By the time she reached the bar, she decided she'd imagined the man's interest. The band was the entertainment at the Harp. Of course people were watching them.

"You guys sound good tonight," Quinn said, holding out a fresh mug. "People are staying longer than usual."

"Thanks." She took a drink, savoring the caffeine jolt. "Man, I needed a hit of this."

"You want a chaser to go along with it?" he teased.

"Yeah, give me the usual." She waited while he filled a glass with ice and lemon-lime soda.

"One of these days, you're gonna have to cut back." Quinn slid the glass to her. "You're developing a serious habit."

She peered into the soda, craving a different drink. "Yeah. I'm good at that."

Quinn went still. "Is that so?" He stared at her until the beer he was drawing overflowed the glass. "I am, too. Maybe we should compare notes sometime."

The AA medallion in her pocket was warm from her body as she rolled it between her fingers. It was familiar. Comforting. Should she show Quinn?

She looked up and saw understanding in his eyes. The acknowledgment of a shared flaw.

Delaney needed to feel less alone tonight. To connect with another person. She drew the green medallion from her jeans and set it on the bar. "Two and a half years. That's the only note I have."

Quinn removed a red medallion from his pocket and laid it next to hers. "Five years. You have a sponsor in the area?"

"Number one on my speed dial." She exhaled slowly. Okay, she'd told Quinn and her world hadn't crashed. It was okay. She could go a little further. "Anniversaries are tough."

"Yeah. I know." Quinn's hand covered hers. "If you ever need a face-to-face, give me a call."

She picked up the token, rubbed its edge, then slid it back into her pocket. "Same goes for you."

"Absolutely." He squeezed her hand.

She took a long drink of the tart-sweet liquid and set the glass down carefully. "So, who was the stranger sitting at the bar?"

Quinn raised his eyebrows. "Some guy passing through. I can introduce you."

"No!" she said, but he'd already turned away.

"Hey, Sam," he called. "Come here and meet the drummer."

So the guy hadn't left.

Before she could escape, the stranger materialized before her. His eyes were gray. Nothing like Diesel's brown ones. She took a deep breath and her shoulders relaxed.

"Hi," she said, holding out her hand. "I'm Delaney."

"Sam McCabe." He closed his fingers around hers. His hand was warm and callused.

"Welcome to the Harp." She managed to smile, even though being social was the last thing she wanted to do tonight. But people liked to talk to the band members. And part of her job was to keep the customers happy.

"You draw quite a crowd." He indicated the people milling around the bar. "Impressive for a town this size." He focused on her again, as if he was memorizing her face. "You're very good."

"Paul, Hank, Stu and I are good together," she corrected automatically.

"The bartender says you're going to be here tomorrow, too. Can I buy you a drink?" He was leaning against the bar, invading her personal space. She tried to back up, but bumped into a stool.

"No, thanks," she said, holding up her mug. "I'm set."

"How about a refill?"

"Afraid not. Any more caffeine and I'll be flying." She didn't want to lie awake all night, haunted by memories of Diesel.

"You're drinking coffee?" He peered into her mug. "I wasn't expecting that."

She backed up again, and the stool behind her scraped over the wooden floor. "What did you think I'd be drinking out of a mug?"

"Most bands are fueled by something stronger than coffee."

"You've seen too many movies," she said lightly. "Enjoy the rest of the evening."

She edged through the crowd, trying to put as much distance between them as possible. Voices rose and fell around her, people touched her arm and said nice things about the music, but all of it was a blur. She was aware only of her tight chest and the ache deep inside. The hair on her neck rose, and she knew he was watching her.

It didn't matter. She wasn't that woman anymore, the one for whom drumming had been connected with sex. That was Chantal, and she hadn't been Chantal for almost three years.

It had taken a long time to erase that woman from her life. No man, even one with intriguing eyes, was going to bring her back to life. Finding her self-respect had been a struggle, and Delaney wasn't about to toss it away.

"Hey, what's wrong?" Maddie hooked an arm through Delaney's and pulled her into a corner. "You're acting like the hounds of hell are after you."

That's because they were. Between her involuntary reaction to Sam and the memories of Diesel, her past was wrapping its sticky tentacles around her. "Nothing," she managed to say.

Maddie peered into her face. "Talk to me, Delaney. What happened?"

Her friend was too perceptive. And far too easy to talk to. Maddie might not be a reporter anymore, but she still had the instincts. If Delaney wasn't careful, she'd be spilling her guts soon. "That guy at the bar." She jerked her head in his direction. "The tall, dark-haired one. He's watching me and it's making me twitchy."

"Hallelujah and praise the saints. Finally."

"What are you talking about?"

Maddie draped an arm over her shoulder. "Honey, it's about time you got twitchy. You've been out of circulation way too long. That guy watching you? It's called flirting. He's interested. And I have to compliment him on his taste."

"Knock it off, Maddie."

Her friend frowned. "Why, Delaney? As far as I know, you haven't been on a date since I've been here. What's wrong with enjoying the attention of a hot guy?"

"I have my reasons."

"And they would be?"

"None of your business."

"Are you secretly married? Engaged?"

"Of course not." Stupid mistake.

"Then what's the problem? Flirt with the guy. Have a drink with him after work. There's no law against that."

Yeah, there was, and it was chiseled in stone. No relationships with guys she met while she was performing. Not after what had happened with Diesel.

"I have to say, you've got good taste. He's smokin'. A real man babe. And he's still watching you."

The shiver down her spine was dread. "*Man babe?* Women in your condition aren't supposed to talk like that." Delaney put her hands on either side of Maddie's protruding belly as if shielding the baby's ears. "What if the kid hears you?"

"He or she will think I'm talking about their daddy." Maddie seemed to be lit from within when she glanced at Quinn.

Delaney ignored the pinch of envy. She'd lost any right to be jealous of other people's happiness. And she was thrilled her friends had found each other. "You have to watch your mouth around kids. They pick up everything."

Maddie snapped her attention back to Delaney. "Since when do you know about kids?"

"I've known people with kids." Even saying the words brought a sharp stab of pain.

"Really? When was this?"

"Long ago and far away. In another life."

The uncomfortable moment stretched too long, then Maddie linked arms with her. "Let's wander back toward the bar. We can bump into that guy again."

"I need to change my shirt and get something to eat," Delaney said. "Flirting is going to have to wait." Hell hadn't frozen over yet.

SAM WATCHED CHANTAL DRAG a very pregnant woman toward the back of the pub, then disappear through a swinging door. She still had the mug clutched in her hand.

It had held coffee. He'd smelled it. Maybe Diesel's death had scared Chantal straight.

He could use that. Explain that Diesel's kids needed those tapes. Maybe this would be easier than he'd expected.

"You must be a big music fan." It was the bartender, Murphy.

Sam turned to face him. "What do you mean?"

"You've been watching Delaney all night."

Was the guy jealous? "She's a talented drummer, and she's got a beautiful voice."

"Yeah, she has a gift." Murphy smiled, but it didn't extend to his eyes.

"I haven't seen a woman like her in a long time." He glanced toward the swinging door, but the two women hadn't emerged. "Does she live around here?"

Murphy's token smile disappeared. "That's none of your business."

Sam held up his hands. "I was just making conversation." Damn, he must be more tired than he thought. That had been clumsy and stupid.

Murphy's expression remained guarded. "No problem." He nodded at Sam's almost empty glass. "You need another one?"

"No, thanks. I'm good."

Sam turned away from the bartender's too-perceptive gaze. The two guitar players and the keyboard guy were back at their instruments, and Murphy slipped out from behind the bar. He pushed open the swinging door at the back of the room and yelled, "Delaney, get out here and bang on some drums."

Delaney pushed through the door sideways. She was talking to someone behind her. Sam couldn't hear what she said, but when she turned around, she seemed relaxed. Comfortable.

Unexpected anger rolled over him. It looked as if she had a nice life while his brother was rotting in the ground, and Diesel's children had become feral animals.

Her shoulders tensed when she caught his eye. She held his gaze for a moment, as if trying to read him, then headed toward the front of the pub.

She couldn't avoid him for much longer.

HE SHOULD HAVE PICKED UP Leo and Rennie an hour ago, but he was still in the pub when the band sang their last note. Delaney had soloed on four or five more songs, and her voice was richer, clearer, more mature than it had been three years ago.

Everyone else in the pub thought so, too. The noise had dropped every time she opened her mouth. Now, as the musicians began to pack up, the volume rose again and people stood to leave.

It didn't take long for Delaney to zip her drums into a gray vinyl bag. Then she hurried to a room off the bar and emerged moments later with a jacket, purse and gym bag. As she shrugged the jacket on, Sam stepped in front of her.

"I enjoyed listening to you guys. Can I buy you a drink?"

She didn't even slow down. "I can't speak for the rest of the guys, but no thanks."

She smiled as she kept walking, but the gesture didn't extend to her eyes. They were weary and sad.

Did she know what day it was? Had she been thinking about Diesel all night, too?

Sam signaled Murphy for his tab and slid several bills across the bar. As he grabbed his coat from one of the hooks on the wall, he saw Delaney pick up the drum bag. He hurried to open the door for her, stepping into a frigid March wind howling off Lake Michigan. Pellets of icy snow stung his face. Who would choose to live in a place with weather like this?

Someone who was running away. Someone who wanted to hide.

But she'd been found. And he wasn't leaving until he got what he'd come for.

CHAPTER THREE

"CAN I HELP YOU WITH those?"

"No, thanks. I have them."

Delaney turned into the parking lot, and Sam followed her. She spun around, her breath streaming out in a white cloud as she steadied the drums on her knee. "Get the hell away from me. Don't you understand *no?* I'm not interested, Mr. McCabe."

He raised his hands. "I'm going to my car, okay?"

She waited as he headed toward the Jeep. When he pressed the remote and the lights flashed, she walked the other way.

She'd assumed he was trying to pick her up.

Of course she did. A woman who looked like her would get a lot of attention, and he'd been watching her all night.

Interesting that she hadn't taken him up on it, though. According to all the gossip columns, Chantal had been a wild child.

She was heading toward a beat-up truck standing by itself in the lot. As he slid into his car, her feet went out from under her and she stumbled.

She almost recovered, but she didn't let go of the gray bag and its weight toppled her over. She twisted to protect the drums, and landed heavily on her rear end. As Sam hurried toward her, he heard a cry of pain, which she immediately muted, but she still cradled the damn drums against her chest.

"You should have let go," he said, reaching down to take them from her.

"My butt will recover. The drums might not."

She held on to them for a moment, but must have realized she couldn't get up on the ice. Allowing him to lift the bag, which was even heavier than he'd thought, she stood up gracefully before he could help her.

"I'll carry them to the truck for you."

She looked as if she wanted to argue about it, so he turned and started walking. Her truck was an older model, dark blue Ford, dented in a couple places and sporting several rust spots. He was surprised. With the money she'd made with the Redheaded Stepsisters, she could afford any car or truck she wanted.

He started to lift the bag into the bed of the truck, but she stopped him with a hand on his arm. "Not there. In the cab."

She snatched her hand away too quickly, and he glanced at her. She fumbled in a large leather pouch slung over her shoulder. When she pulled out a set of keys and unlocked the truck door, her fingers were trembling.

"Are you okay to drive?"

"I'm fine." She grabbed for the door handle. "Thank you for your help, Mr. McCabe."

"Sam," he said without thinking.

She glanced at him out of the corner of her eye, brushed a trace of snow off the seat of her jeans and climbed into the driver's seat, wincing. "Have a safe trip," she said.

She slammed the door closed before he could tell her he wasn't going anywhere. He edged away from the truck as the engine cranked listlessly, then fell silent. Through the back window of the cab, he saw her bow her head, as if she was staring at the dashboard. She must have turned the key again, because the engine coughed a couple of times, then caught.

When he got into his Jeep, she was revving the sputtering engine.

She was still in the parking lot when he drove out, headed for the other side of town, where he'd seen an all-night fast food outlet. He'd swing through it before picking up the kids and going back to his motel. He needed fuel.

Turned out redemption was harder than it looked.

SAM MCCABE'S TAILLIGHTS disappeared around the corner. With any luck, he was on his way out of town.

Delaney gave the truck a little more gas and listened to it sputter. Had he really thought he could wait for her in the pub and she'd go off with him? A stranger? What kind of an idiot was he?

Chantal would have considered it.

She slammed the truck into gear. Chantal had been an idiot, too.

The heater hadn't kicked in, but the truck was running a little more smoothly. She pulled out of the Harp's lot, the cold burning into her hands, even through her gloves.

The headlights were so dim they barely illuminated the road in front of her. Murmuring soothing words to the truck, she cautiously pressed on the gas. The lights got a little brighter. She should have replaced the battery long ago.

Snow swirled around the windows, but it was tapering off. It would stop soon. In her two and a half years up here, she'd become an expert at reading snow.

County M was plowed, but the surface was still slippery. She crept along, watching carefully for the kind of ice slick that had ambushed her in the parking lot. She rubbed the spot on her hip. She wouldn't have fallen if Sam hadn't distracted her.

A dark shape scurried across the road in front of her truck, and she pumped her brakes. Damn it. Fluffy. She heard a yelp— Oh, God. She'd hit him.

As she pulled onto the shoulder, the dog struggled to his feet and hobbled toward the other side of the road. She scrambled out the door, the wind biting at her face. Ignoring the pain, she ran toward the injured animal.

"Fluffy! Fluffy, come."

The dog looked over his shoulder at her and began to trot, favoring his right rear leg. She'd scared him. Delaney crouched in the road and held out her hand. "Here, Fluffy. Come here, boy."

He paused, poised for flight, and watched her. His owners had moved out a couple weeks earlier and left him behind. She'd been trying to catch him ever since.

No dog should be abandoned, let alone in this kind of weather.

"Here, Fluffy," she crooned. "I have treats. You want treats, baby?" She'd find something for him to eat. Maybe she'd keep him. It might be nice to have a dog for company.

He took a step toward her just as headlights illuminated the road behind her. The vehicle turned into the parking lot of the Bide-a-Wee Motel, but it was too late. The dog was spooked.

Fluffy scrambled down the ditch on the opposite side of the road, then limped into the woods. Delaney ran after him.

Her feet and ankles sank into the snow, and cold water from the ditch seeped into her canvas Chuck Taylors. "Damn it! Fluffy! Treats, boy. Treats?"

She pushed into the forest, feeling her way past the trees, stumbling over logs buried by snow. She stopped after twenty feet or so and listened. Nothing.

She continued through the snow-laden underbrush for a

while, but it was too dark to follow the dog's tracks. Finally, aching from the cold, she tramped back toward the road.

As she crossed in front of the truck, she noticed a few dark dots on the icy pavement. Oh, God. Fluffy was bleeding.

She turned back to the forest again, listening hard. But all she heard was the wind rustling the dried leaves on the trees.

She couldn't just leave him. He was hurt.

Another set of headlights appeared from the direction of town. She moved back to the shelter of her truck, her toes numb. The vehicle began to turn into the Bide-a-Wee, then swung back onto the road and headed toward her.

She waited for it to pass, but instead it slowed and stopped beside her. A black Jeep. McCabe.

Great. The perfect capper to the night.

The window came down. "Delaney? Are you all right?"

"I'm fine, Mr. McCabe. But thanks for stopping."

"Are you sure? You look pretty cold."

Her hands were fisted in her jacket pockets and her shoulders hunched against the wind. She forced herself to relax. "I'm fine. I was trying to catch a dog, but he ran into the woods."

Sam glanced into the backseat, then back at her. "Need some help?"

"No. He's gone." She turned and got into her truck, waving at him.

She turned the key and heard only a muffled click. The battery was dead.

She waved at McCabe again, hoping he'd leave. But he got out of the Jeep and walked around to her door.

"If you have cables, I could give you a jump."

"Thanks, but I need a new battery. I'll call my service guy."

She rolled up the window, pulled out her cell phone, punched a button and waited.

"Wilborn," Jase Wilborn barked into the phone.

"Hey, Jase, this is Delaney Spencer. My car died on M, about two miles out of town. I know it's late, but could you come and put a new battery in for me?"

"Hey, Delaney." He sounded exhausted. "I can do it, but it might be a while. I'm at an accident scene, waiting to haul the cars away."

"Okay, Jase. I'll leave it here and call you in the morning." She snapped the phone closed, aware of Sam waiting in the Jeep next to her. She'd call either Maddie or Jen, her other good friend, to come pick her up.

As her finger hovered over the phone, Sam got out and walked to her window again. Reluctantly, she rolled it down.

"Do you want a lift home?" he asked.

She could walk, but it was at least another mile to her house. Her toes curled in her wet, cold shoes. "I'll give one of my friends a call," she said.

He cupped his hands over his ears. "Are you sure? My car is already warm."

No way was she getting into a car with a stranger. Especially one who'd tried to pick her up earlier. "Thanks, but I'll be fine."

"We won't be alone, if that's what you're worried about."

The windows of the Jeep were tinted and she couldn't see inside. "You were alone at the pub."

"There are two kids in the backseat."

She leaned closer to the window, but couldn't see anything in the darkness. She shivered again. How could she drag her friends out at this time of night? "Fine. I appreciate it."

She touched her instrument case. The cold wasn't good

for her drums, but she couldn't do anything about it. Sliding down onto the pavement, she closed her door.

Snow crunched beneath her shoes as she walked toward Sam, the sound as loud as gunshots in the complete quiet of the forest. She hunched into her jacket, her hands buried in the pockets, reminding Sam how damn cold it was. The sooner he was out of here and back in Miami, the happier he would be.

As she walked past him to the Jeep, he noticed for the first time how slender she was. Delicate, almost. And she was shorter than he'd expected. He'd always thought of Chantal as larger than life. Tonight, she was just a tired woman.

"Don't you want your drums?" he asked.

"Do you have room?"

"As long as you don't mind putting them in the back."

"Then yes, I do. Thank you." As she returned to get them, she said, "How did you know I didn't want to leave them?"

"You fell on your ass rather than let them hit the ground. I figured there was no way you'd want to leave them behind."

"No, I don't. The cold isn't good for them." She cleared her throat. "Thank you. This is thoughtful of you."

"No big deal." He opened the back hatch of the Jeep, and she set the large vinyl bag on the carpet. She hesitated for a moment, then pulled a small cylinder out of her purse and lifted the drums again.

"You said you had kids in the car." She backed away as she spoke.

"They're sleeping." He peered in the window of the backseat, reassured when neither of them moved. The two small forms were slumped over, held in place by seat belts. Both of them were huddled into their jackets, hats pulled low over their heads. They didn't like the cold, either.

She set the drums down again, straightened and dropped the cylinder back into her purse. Pepper spray? Mace? Had she thought he was a threat?

As she turned toward him, the light from the back of the Jeep illuminated her face, and he got a good look at her eyes for the first time. They were a clear, bright blue-green, with a black rim around the iris—like the water in the Caribbean, clean and translucent all the way to the bottom.

He'd read about her incredible eyes, but he figured the articles were exaggerating.

They weren't.

She must wear colored contact lenses. No one could really have eyes that shade.

"Mr. McCabe? Are you ready to go?" She was edging away, watching him.

"Yeah. Sorry. Just making sure the kids are okay."

She slid into the passenger seat and twisted to view the two children. She didn't say a thing, but she watched them for a beat too long.

Finally, she said, "I thought you were just passing through town."

"I am, I hope."

"So where did you leave your kids while you were at the pub?"

He'd been relieved when he found Millie. Thank God for the internet. "There's a woman in town who does overnight day care for the people who work at the canning factory in Sturgeon Falls. She watched them."

Delaney turned back toward him. "You left your kids with a stranger so you could go to a pub?"

The implied criticism made him bristle. "I had business there," he said, turning on the ignition. "Not that the kids are any concern of yours."

"It's cold and late." She didn't say anything else, but

she didn't have to—her expression was easy to read. He'd had a beer and watched the band. That didn't sound like business.

"They were perfectly happy with Millie."

"I'm sure they were."

His hands gripped the steering wheel tightly. "You must have several of your own kids to know so much about them."

"You don't need to be a parent. All you need is a little common sense." She pressed her lips together. "Sorry, Mr. McCabe. It's none of my business. My only excuse is that it's late and I'm tired."

She was right. He shouldn't be Leo and Rennie's guardian. He didn't want the job and he wasn't any good at it. But there was no one else. He was stuck with them. Their father was dead and their mother was a drunken drug addict.

The sooner this woman—Delaney…Chantal—gave him the tapes, the sooner he could pack Leo and Rennie off to the private school and get back to his own life.

CHAPTER FOUR

THE CAR WAS QUIET as Sam put on his seat belt. He shifted gears and stared out the window at the pasture on the other side of the road. It was covered by a smooth blanket of snow, broken only by the occasional dead weed poking through the white. Snow had collected in the squares of the wire fence, making them look like tiny windowpanes decorated for Christmas.

He hated Christmas.

The last time he'd seen Diesel alive had been Christmas Day.

"Where am I taking you?" He needed to get Chantal out of his car before he said something he'd regret. He wanted her on his side. He wanted those tapes.

"I live about a mile down the road."

The car had cooled quickly when he'd opened the rear hatch to load the drums, and he turned the heat to high as he eased onto the road. Delaney bent down to take off her wet shoes, then put her feet in front of the heater vent. Her socks were green, blue and yellow stripes. He hadn't expected her to have a whimsical side.

"You don't seem too fond of our weather," she said. "Where are you from?"

"Florida, where I've never had to worry about freezing my ass off. How about you? Were you born and raised up here?"

"No, I moved here a few years ago."

"Because you love the weather?"

A small smile flashed across her face. "I've learned to tolerate the cold. I moved here for a job."

"Playing the drums?"

The smile disappeared, and she rubbed her hands down her thighs, tightening the slightly baggy denim over her legs. "No, that's a sideline. Just for fun."

"You're good at it. Ever think about joining a bigger band? Getting more exposure?"

"I'm very happy in Otter Tail." She stared out the window, and he couldn't see her face. Was she lying? Did she miss the spotlight? Maybe getting those CDs would be easier than he expected.

"How long have you been playing the drums?" he asked.

"A long time."

"Yeah?"

"I started in my grade school band."

He knew she was twenty-seven, but he asked, anyway. "How long ago was that?"

"Don't you know better than to ask a woman her age?" Her voice was light and teasing, but tension hummed beneath the words.

"Okay, mystery woman. You came from nowhere and you're ageless."

"Exactly." Her gaze was uncomfortably intimate in the confines of the car. "You've asked me a lot of questions about myself. What about you? What kind of business brings you to Otter Tail?"

"Too long to go into right now. I'll tell you about it next time I see you."

"Next time?" She sounded surprised. "I doubt we'll see each other again."

"I'll be at the Harp tomorrow night." He glanced at his watch. "Tonight." ·

"Really? More business?" She looked over her shoulder at the sleeping children. "Will they be in overnight child care again?"

"I'd…" He caught himself before he admitted he'd forgotten about the kids. "I'll see what they thought of the place. If they liked it, I guess that's where they'll be."

"And if they didn't?"

"Maybe the woman who owns the motel will watch them."

"Myrtle Sanders? You better think twice about her. She's trying to quit smoking, and it's made her a little edgy."

There was no mistaking the contempt in Chantal's voice. "Thanks for the tip," he said.

"Why did you bring them on a business trip, anyway?"

"I didn't have a choice," he said curtly. He felt her watching him, but continued to stare out the windshield.

"That's too bad," she said. Clearly, all her sympathy was for the kids.

"Their mother is in the hospital."

"I'm sorry." She looked back at them again. "Poor babies."

Her words made him tighten his grip on the steering wheel. He'd assumed Leo and Rennie would be happy to be away from their mother, from her alternating neglect and smothering, her irrational rages. But maybe they were just as unhappy to be with him as he was to have them.

"They haven't had an easy time of it."

"Sounds like it." She reached between the seats and tugged Leo's hat more tightly over his ears. Her shoulder was inches away from Sam's. He'd barely have to move to touch her.

This was Chantal. A woman he despised. One small

gesture toward a child wasn't going to change his opinion of her.

He drove slowly, and the only sound was the tires crunching on the snow.

Her scent drifted across to him, a mix of cinnamon and orange and spices, with a hint of fresh wood. It didn't match her blonde, wholesome appearance but it was dark and mysterious. Complex. Like Chantal.

Seductress. Siren. When she'd been onstage with the Redheads, no one looked at anyone but her. The rest of the band, including his brother, had just been props for her charisma.

It had been the same tonight at the Harp and Halo. She'd mesmerized the audience effortlessly. The pub had stilled every time she'd sung. Every eye in the place had been focused on her.

She didn't look like Chantal, but there was no doubt in his mind that she was one and the same. The woman so many men had fantasized about. Tonight even without the low-cut black leather tops and skintight jeans, she'd been the sexual temptress who'd played the drums like she was making love.

She couldn't enthrall him, though. He knew who she really was.

"My driveway is up here on the right."

Her low voice interrupted his thoughts.

"All I see are trees."

"Slow down. More. Right here."

There was a small opening through the trees that led to a narrow driveway, but no reflectors or signs to indicate someone lived there. There wasn't even a mailbox along the road.

"No way could I have found that by myself."

"That's the point. I live alone in the country. I'm not going to advertise."

Her words hung between them as he turned into her driveway. An image of Delaney, her hair damp, her eyes closed as she sang, filled his head. She was passionate about her music. That's what drew people to her...that's what was affecting him now.

Not the sense of aloneness that cloaked her. The sadness in her eyes. The hint of vulnerability beneath her outward strength.

They emerged into a clearing with two buildings. A small, two-story house with a garage sat off to the side, and next to it stood a pole barn. The house was white, with black shutters and a bright red front door. Lights blazed both outside and inside the house and barn.

"Thanks for the ride." She opened the door and leaped out. Before he could follow, she had the hatch open and the drums out of the Jeep. "So long," she called over her shoulder as she headed for the barn.

By the time he reached her, she was balancing the drums on one raised knee while she unlocked the door.

"Want a hand with those? I promise to be gentle."

Their eyes met and held, and she froze. In the space of two heartbeats, that clear, brilliant blue darkened and he heard her sharp inhalation. She held his gaze for a second longer, then fumbled with the key again and the door swung open.

Lost in those amazing eyes, he wanted her. Just like every other man who'd ever watched her perform.

She was Chantal. That's what she did.

Before he regained his composure, she'd closed and locked the door behind her.

He glanced at the Jeep. He'd left it running so the kids would be warm. He might as well tell her now who he was.

It would be easier than having the conversation in front of the kids.

He knocked on the door and heard her footsteps approaching. When she opened it, he said, "I told you I came here to do some business. I actually came looking for you. I'm Diesel's brother."

DELANEY STILL HAD HER purse slung over her shoulder, and as she stared at Sam, it slid down her arm and hit the floor with a plop. She gripped the door, staring at him as her stomach churned. "What did you say?"

"I'm Diesel's brother. Half brother, to be exact. I came here to talk to you."

His gray eyes were hard as stone, and cold as the lake in March. He shoved his hands into his pockets, but not before she'd seen them tighten into fists.

The man who had just made her heart race and her palms damp was Diesel's brother? Fate was a cruel bitch.

"I have no idea what you're talking about." Her hand shook as she tried to close the door, but he stuck his foot into the gap.

"Suffering from amnesia? Funny, but it looked as if you remembered a lot of things tonight. How to play the drums. How to sing. How to…perform."

"Go away," she said, clinging to the door. Her carefully constructed life was breaking apart in front of her, one piece after another crashing to the ground and splintering into a million pieces

"Don't you even want to know why I'm here?" He shifted closer, as if to come inside, and she slammed the door into his foot.

"Go away or I'm calling the police." She fumbled in her purse for her phone. Her hand shook as she tried to dial 911 while leaning against the door, struggling to prevent him from opening it farther.

"You sure you want to do that? I'd have to tell them why I'm here. Who you are."

She'd punched 9 and 1, her finger hovering over the final key. He wasn't bluffing—he wanted her to finish the call. She snapped the phone closed. No police.

"What do you want?"

His shoulders relaxed. "A deal."

"What are you talking about?" Frigid air blew in the open door, and a snowflake landed on her cheek.

"May I come in?"

"Do I look stupid? No, you can't."

At her words, he hunched his shoulders and blew on his hands. He couldn't handle the cold. Too bad.

He nudged the door with his foot, widening the gap. "If I wanted to hurt you, I'd already be inside. I'll be a lot more reasonable if I'm not freezing my ass off."

He opened the door a little more, pushing against her weight as if it was nothing.

She'd have to listen to him sooner or later, but she was too tired to deal with him tonight. "Move your foot first."

He hesitated for a moment, then withdrew. She slammed the door and engaged the lock.

He'd go away when he got cold enough.

She leaned against the door for a few minutes, but she didn't hear his footsteps retreating. His truck chugged steadily in the background.

She bit the inside of her cheeks, trying to hold back the nausea. She'd thought she was safe. No one had recognized her in three years. Until tonight.

But Sam wasn't a random stranger. He was Diesel's brother. And he wanted something from her.

She moved to the side and glanced out the window. He

was still there, stamping his feet and blowing into his cupped hands.

He'd be thinking about getting in his warm car. About his two children sleeping there. He'd decide to wait until daylight to confront her.

Maybe not. The date of his arrival in Otter Tail wasn't random. He'd chosen the anniversary of Diesel's death for a reason.

Did he think the memories would make her weaker today? Easier prey? He had no idea who she had become. And what did he want?

She took a deep breath, then another. Closed her eyes and reached for the mental calm she'd learned from yoga.

It wasn't there. Even yoga couldn't prepare her for this kind of shock. She glanced out the window again. He hadn't moved.

She had to face him. She wasn't running again. She had roots here. Friends. A life. She'd have to find a way to deal with him.

Without a word, she opened the door and he walked in.

"Thank you." He shoved his hands into his pockets, and his gaze swept the room. "You have a lot of furniture."

"Yes, I do. You insisted on coming in to talk to me. So talk."

His expression hardened. "Diesel had two children."

"I know that." Leo and Rennie. They'd been seven and two years old when their father died. She'd never met them— she'd retained at least a shred of decency. But she'd seen plenty of pictures. Rennie had her father's bright red hair. Leo had been blond, with Diesel's brown eyes.

"They haven't had an easy life. Their mother is…a mess. They barely remember their father. They need stability in their lives."

"And you came to me for that?" She stared at him, shocked.

"Of course not." His rejection should have burned. Instead, it made her stand straighter.

"Then what do they have to do with me?" Poor kids. The whispers about Diesel would follow them everywhere.

"You have some CDs that Diesel made. Bootleg recording sessions of music he wrote that were never released. Music that's different from the Redheads' stuff. His kids need that music to be made public."

"What?" He couldn't know about those CDs. No one knew about them but her and Diesel. And Diesel was dead.

"I'm here to negotiate with you for them."

"There are no bootleg recordings."

He shook his head, as if pained by her awkward lie. "Can't you do better than that? You could try 'they were lost in a fire.' Or how about 'the record company has them.' Or even the popular 'you have the wrong person.'"

"This conversation is over." She opened the door. "Get out."

CHAPTER FIVE

SAM PUSHED THE DOOR closed. "This conversation is just beginning. I'm not going to take no for an answer." He leaned closer, but she stood her ground. "Those tapes are Leo and Rennie's legacy. If they were released, they'd make a lot of money. Money they need. The person who told me about them said, and I quote, 'they were friggin' brilliant.'"

"Someone's been jerking your chain, Mr. McCabe." Her fingers closed around the phone in her pocket. Maybe she would call the police. Take a chance on Sam telling them who she was. She had to get him out of here. "There's always gossip when a musician dies. Rumors of unreleased recordings."

"Jeremy Davies told me about them. He heard you and Diesel in the studio a couple of times. He didn't care what you were doing—he said the music wouldn't have worked for the Redheads. He thought you were putting some stuff together for a solo album." He edged closer. "He had no reason to lie to me."

Jeremy had heard them in the studio?

Maybe he had. Her hand shook, and she released the phone. She and Diesel had been high or drunk most of the time toward the end. It wasn't surprising they hadn't noticed their bass player hanging around. "I may not recall everything that happened while I was with the Redheads, but if I made tapes that were 'friggin' brilliant', I'd remember. Sorry."

She reached for the door again, but he stepped in front of it. "I'm not going away, Delaney. Leo and Rennie are…" His jaw worked. "They're troubled kids. I want to put them in a private school, but it will cost a lot of money. Money neither Heather nor I have. I need those tapes. It's the only way to shelter them from the media storm that surrounds their mother and the sordid parts of their father's life."

One of those sordid parts being her. Delaney lifted her chin. "I'm sorry for those kids, but I can't help them."

"Can't, or won't?"

"Can't. Even if there were tapes, I wouldn't give them to you."

He continued as if he hadn't heard her. "When you give me the tapes, you'll need to help with publicity and promotion. Interviews. We can do a tour with the remaining band members. Jeremy is on board, and I'll talk to Garrett and Steve. A reunion tour of the Redheads would boost sales of the CD."

"Publicity? A reunion tour? You're out of your mind." He wanted her to become Chantal again? She backed up until she bumped against a desk, gripping it for support. The edge was rough—she was getting ready to sand it. "That's not going to happen. Under any circumstances."

"You could make a lot of money from this project. Why would you throw it away?" He crossed his arms. "It was clear tonight that you haven't suddenly developed stage fright."

No amount of money was worth going back. "Do I look like Chantal? Do you see any resemblance to her?" Without waiting for him to answer, she said, "There's a reason for that. I'm not Chantal anymore. And I'll never be her again."

"You are Chantal." His voice was flat. "You've just changed the package."

"I can still play the drums and sing," she agreed. "I could dye my hair again. Get a new wardrobe, new jewelry. But I won't."

"Seems like you could use the money." He looked around the pole barn, his gaze lingering on the naked walls, the old, drafty windows, the cracked concrete floor. Then he glanced out the window at her tiny house.

"I need a lot of things," she said. "But nothing money can buy."

"Forget the money, then. You'd be onstage performing for big crowds again."

Her fingers hurt where she pressed them into the top of the desk, but she barely noticed. He knew which cards to play. In spite of her denial, memories of a Redheads' concert rose up inside her. She heard the driving beat, the pounding chords of their music. Felt the lights, saw the ocean of faces in front of the huge stage. Smelled the sweat and sensed the excitement of performing.

What would it be like to go back? To experience it again? Anticipation stirred. She could handle it. She was a different person now. She knew what was important.

No. The rational part of her brain shoved the fantasies aside.

She couldn't go back. She'd spent the last three years learning hard lessons. If she became Chantal again, even for a day, she'd fall into the same traps, the same trouble she'd spent so much effort escaping. She would have wasted all the hard work that got her here.

She was Delaney Spencer. Chantal was dead and buried. Slowly she straightened, feeling steadier now. "I'm sure. Sorry, Mr. McCabe. There are no bootleg tapes, and there won't be any publicity or reunion tours."

"Leo and Rennie need this to happen."

"Then you'll have to come up with the money some other way. I can't help them. Chantal is dead."

His voice was hard. "Not as dead as Diesel."

She flinched, but his words also brought a welcome surge of anger. "I'm not the only one who'd profit from this project. Since you're so eager to set this up, you must stand to make a lot of money from it."

"The money is for Leo and Rennie."

"But you'd get your cut, wouldn't you? Have you made yourself their business manager? Set yourself up as their advisor?"

"I'm their guardian," he said through clenched teeth.

"Why? What happened to Heather?" The mother of Diesel's children had been unstable, but she'd held on to those kids with a desperate grip. They'd been her money machine. Her little ATMs, she'd called them.

"Heather is in rehab. Will be for a while."

Delaney drew in a sharp breath as the pieces fell together. "Those kids in the car. They're not yours, are they? You've got Leo and Rennie."

"Yes. I had to drag them up here to Nowheresville because there was no one else to take care of them. I tried to hire someone, but couldn't find anyone suitable."

"Pickings must be really slim, then. You left them with a complete stranger tonight, and you were going to leave them with Myrtle Sanders tomorrow. You've set a very low bar for suitable."

"I didn't plan on bringing them with me," he said. "I had to improvise."

"Those poor kids haven't had any chance at a normal life."

"If you want to make things better for them, let me have the tapes. That's their best chance for any kind of normalcy."

"You think a private school is the answer? What about

a stable home and a loving parent?" It had taken her years of therapy to understand why she'd become a reckless, attention-starved thrill-seeker. Neglectful, indifferent parents were a quick ticket to the kind of destructive life she'd led. It sounded as if Diesel's kids were headed down the same path.

"There is no stable home with Heather. And 'loving parent'? I guess she loves them, but she sure doesn't show it."

"What about you? You said you're their guardian. Can't you give that kind of stability to Leo and Rennie?"

"You think I should take advice from the woman who destroyed their dad?"

She sucked in a breath and closed her eyes. It shouldn't hurt so much. "I didn't destroy Diesel."

"You're the one who got him hooked on drugs—the ones that killed him."

She gripped the desk harder. "Diesel was taking drugs long before I joined the Redheads."

A splinter pierced her palm, and she flinched.

Sam watched Delaney jerk and raise one hand. A bead of blood formed on the fleshy part of her palm, and she brought it to her mouth.

His gaze dropped to her hand, cupped to her mouth. Damn it.

"I don't believe you," he said. "Diesel was straight until you joined the band." Sam had no problem using guilt to get her to turn over the tapes.

"And you know this because you spent so much time with your brother. Right?"

Her barb hit its target with perfect accuracy. "My relationship with my brother is not part of this discussion."

"Since you have no idea what your brother was like, I think it is." She fumbled in her bag and pulled out a dark blue bandanna, which she wrapped around her bleeding hand. "I didn't even know your name until tonight. I barely knew Diesel had a brother. So don't try to tell me what he was like, or when he started doing drugs. You know *nothing* about his life."

Control of the conversation was slipping away from Sam, and he struggled to contain his anger. "I know that his kids need help. Help that you could give them. And you're refusing." He looked at her tousled hair and baggy jeans. "You're living a different life now. I get it. But no one's asking you to give that up."

"You're kidding me, right?" Anger flared in her eyes, and she took a step closer to him. "You think I could keep this life if people found out who I used to be? You're delusional."

"They're going to find out, one way or another," he said.

"What is that supposed to mean?"

He pulled the contract out of his pocket, the one his lawyer had drawn up. "If you sign this, agree to turn over the CDs and participate in the publicity for their release, no one has to know about Delaney Spencer. You can be Chantal for a couple of months, then come back here and forget about her."

Sam stepped closer, and was reluctantly impressed when she lifted her chin instead of backing up. "If you don't..." He shrugged. "Everyone in the music world wants to know what happened to Chantal. I'll write an article for *Rolling Stone* and I'll tell them all about you and your bootlegs of unreleased Redheads' songs. New Diesel Adams music."

"*Rolling Stone?*" She shook her head, but he saw fear in her eyes. "Good luck. You think they publish articles based on hearsay?"

She had guts. He'd give her that. "They'll take articles from writers who know how to back up a story with facts.

That's how I make my living. Trust me, they'd buy my piece."

She threw open the door, and the howling wind bounced it against the wall. "Get out."

He set the paper on the desk behind her. Her scent seemed to fill the room, and he hated the way it made his gut constrict. "I'll leave this here. Think about it before you make any rash decisions."

The paper fluttered to the floor, but she ignored it. "Threats won't work with me, you bastard."

"Maybe they should. Consider what you might lose, Delaney. If you change your mind, I'll be at the motel for the next couple of days."

DELANEY LISTENED TO THE sound of his Jeep as it retreated down the driveway.

Wrapping her arms around herself, she slid to the ground, trembling. The desk she'd been using to support herself was hard and unyielding. The knobs on the drawers poked her back and the floor of the barn was icy cold. The numbness that had descended while Sam was here vanished, replaced by panic.

Would he really tell the world where she was? Expose her to every morbidly curious Redheads fan who wanted to see what remained of the wreck she'd been? Every collector who wanted the CDs?

A story about her in *Rolling Stone* would be chum in the water to the tabloids. Reporters would park at the end of her driveway and wait for her to appear.

They'd sneak onto her property, follow her around Otter Tail, pack the Harp when she performed with the band.

She couldn't let that happen.

But she could not become Chantal again, either.

She'd have to destroy the CDs.

She stood up and walked over to the large cabinet in the far corner of the showroom. It was hidden behind her sample furniture, pieces she showed potential customers.

The simple maple storage unit was one of the first things she'd made when she set up her woodworking shop. She'd filled it with boxes from her previous life, then locked the door.

The key was still on top of the cabinet, covered with a fine layer of sawdust. She wiped it on her jeans, then inserted it into the lock.

CHAPTER SIX

"SHH, REN. He'll get angry if we wake him up." Paper rustled. "Read your book for a while."

"I can't read, Leo. You read it to me."

Sam opened one eye and saw Leo and Rennie huddled on the other bed, their heads together. He felt as if he'd hardly slept, and the darkness outside confirmed his suspicion that it was really early.

He rolled over, and the kids were instantly still. It made him feel guilty and ashamed. Heather's volatile moods had turned them into frightened rabbits.

Just another reason to get them into that school as soon as possible.

"Hey, guys," he said, sitting up. "You interested in some breakfast?"

"Yes," Rennie said cautiously. Leo shrugged and didn't answer.

"I'll take a shower, then we'll figure out if there's a good restaurant in town."

"In this hick place?" Leo's ten-year-old voice was scornful. "They probably don't even have a McDonald's."

"As a matter of fact, they do." He'd stopped there last night. "You want to go there for breakfast? I think they have one of those gym things." He could let the kids play and he'd have a few minutes of peace.

"Whatever." Leo showed no enthusiasm for anything Sam suggested.

"Okay, then we'll see if there's another restaurant."

The boy glowered at him. "McDonald's is fine."

"You two get dressed while I'm in the shower, then we'll leave."

AN HOUR LATER, Sam sat at a table in the restaurant and watched Leo and Rennie climbing up ladders and sliding down chutes. He couldn't take much more of this. If he had to stay in that motel room for another night, he'd lose his mind.

Clearing the remains of their pancakes and sausage, he found a local newspaper and opened the want ads. Maybe he could find a vacation house to rent for a few days. Being cooped up in a small room with him was probably making the kids just as nuts. Having some space to spread out would be good for all of them.

DELANEY STOOD AT HER kitchen window, watching the sun's watery light wash over her barn as her coffeemaker gurgled. Anticipation of that first soothing swallow warmed her as the rich scent filled the room. The bright yellow walls of the kitchen glowed in the soft light, and the blue accents—the towels on the stove, the cookie jar and stand mixer on the counter—soothed her. She was safe here, in her kitchen. In her house.

Or rather, she *used* to be. This morning, safety was an illusion. Sam McCabe had made sure of that.

The coffeemaker gradually quieted, and she poured the strong brew into a mug. Steam tickled her nose. What was she going to do about McCabe?

She'd been *attracted* to him last night, for God's sake. Not a real attraction, just the adrenaline of performing, but still. For a few minutes in his car, she'd welcomed that flare of lust. It had been a long time since she'd reacted to a man.

She'd almost wondered if that part of her had dried up when she'd dried out. That she'd only wanted sex when she was drunk or high.

Apparently not.

Shame scalded hotter than the coffee she swallowed. He hadn't been interested in her. He'd wanted her CDs. That was all.

Beneath her fear, anger stirred. He still thought his brother was perfect, that she'd led Diesel astray, and somehow that gave him the right to bully her and make demands.

She set her mug sharply on the table. Last night she'd been a coward. Instead of destroying the CDs, she'd fled back to her house without even opening the cabinet.

She'd do it this morning. The next time he asked for those recordings, she'd give him a box of charred and twisted pieces of plastic. Tell him he could have the damn demos.

She didn't bother with a jacket as she hurried outside. The cold of the barn enveloped her as she stepped inside, and she quickly started a fire in the wood-burning stove. But instead of opening the cabinet, she wandered through the showroom, cataloging the pieces and visualizing her schedule for their completion. And every time she caught a glimpse of that maple cabinet tucked in the corner, it loomed larger.

When it was the only thing she could see in the showroom, she walked over and stood before it. Putting a painful task off never made it easier.

The key was still in the door. She turned it and pulled the cabinet open.

The scents of rosin and stale cigarette smoke drifted out, reminders of her former life. She was careful not to look at the old guitar case on the bottom shelf. She couldn't face that. Not now.

As she hauled out the boxes and set them on the floor, emotion pinched at her heart. Grief for Diesel. Shame at the spectacle she'd let Chantal become. Regret for the mess she'd made of her life.

But as she rummaged through the cartons, the memories seduced, as well.

The set lists, photos, concert playbills, the news stories, all fueled the old longing. Instead of living in Otter Tail, making furniture, playing the drums and singing one night a week, she could be touring again. Listening to the screams and cheers of the audience. If she agreed to what Sam wanted, maybe she'd even be recording again.

She stood up and kicked the boxes to the side. That's why she never looked at this stuff. It was too tempting. Whispering in her ear, telling her she could be Chantal again, that she'd be smarter this time. That she wouldn't make the same mistakes.

Toxic murmurs. Dangerous ideas.

Quickly she dug out the carton of demo CDs and set it on the concrete floor. Then she shoved everything else back in the cabinet.

If she was smart, she wouldn't open this box. She'd put it into the stove and incinerate it.

But she'd never been smart. She lifted off the cover and stared at the neat stack of plastic cases, each holding a CD. She'd hoped these songs would help her and Diesel straighten out. Become musicians again, rather than a sideshow.

Instead, they'd helped kill him.

When he'd told Heather he and Chantal were going to take a break from the Redheads and try something new, his longtime girlfriend had freaked out. Afraid the money train would stop, she'd given him an ultimatum. End his affair with Chantal, throw her out of the band, or Heather was leaving and taking the kids. She'd make sure he never saw them again.

Slowly, as if it would burn her fingers, Delaney reached

for the plastic case on top. There was no liner, no notes, only the number 4 written on the disk with a Sharpie.

She didn't need notes. She knew exactly what each CD held.

Moving slowly, as if her whole body hurt, she walked over to her boom box and slid the disc into the slot. She sank to the floor as the first notes poured out of the speakers.

She and Diesel were both good vocalists, but their voices together had been magic. The hard rock of the Redheaded Stepsisters had disguised their power, but on these tapes, backed only by his guitar and her drums, their voices soared.

Sam was right. These CDs were gold. If the recordings were released, they'd bring in a flood of money. There would be enough to put Leo and Rennie in private schools ten times over. Money to give them whatever they wanted in life.

Except their father.

She sat with her forehead on her knees, her arms curled around her head, and listened to one song after another. One CD after another.

Her music. Diesel's lyrics. Songs about forgiveness. Family. Connections.

Love.

How could she destroy this last window into Diesel's soul?

How could she not? If she released them, she'd be destroying herself.

"You sound amazing."

She jerked her head up to see Sam, standing a few feet away. Scrambling to her feet, swiping furtively at her cheeks, she kept her back to him and turned off the CD player.

"What are you doing here? Get out. Now."

"That's one of them, isn't it?" He'd moved closer. "Jeremy was right. They're brilliant."

"No one was meant to hear them." The weight of her sorrow was crushing her heart. "Go away."

"My brother was an incredible musician. So are you."

"I'm going to burn them all."

"Don't do that." He was right behind her now. She sensed his hands hovering over her shoulders. "Please."

His fingers felt warm through her sweater. Almost comforting. She jerked away.

"Don't you have any decency?" Her voice was scratchy, and she tried to clear her throat. "Leave me alone."

"Decency? No. I'm not a decent man. But I'm not going to leave you here crying."

She whirled to face him. "You think you caught me in a weak moment? That you can take advantage of that weakness?" She forced the tears back. "You're out of luck. I don't have weak moments anymore."

"Trust me, Delaney. *Weak* is the last word I would use to describe you."

His hair was untidy, as if a woman had dragged her fingers through it. His leather jacket hung open, and he wore an ivory fisherman's sweater, the collar of a blue shirt poking out at the neck. His jeans were old and faded, the cuffs unraveling above his boots.

She walked to the CD player and pulled out the disc, snapped it back into the jewel case. Replaced it in the carton.

She picked up the box and hugged it to her chest. "Did you come back to threaten me again? Don't bother. I'm not changing my mind. Write your article for *Rolling Stone*." She shrugged, hoping it concealed her dread. "I'll deal with it."

"I didn't come back to torment you."

She rolled her eyes and headed toward the maple cabinet in the corner of the room. "Right. You're here because you enjoyed our scintillating conversation so much last night, you wanted to do it again, right?" She slid the box onto a shelf, locked the door and put the key into her pocket. "So if you didn't come here to fight, what do you want?"

"I wanted to see if you'd thought about the music, and I see that you have." His gaze lingered on her cheek, and she rubbed it, horrified to find it wet.

"You wouldn't really destroy them, would you? That would be…it would be a sacrilege."

She slapped the door of the cabinet hard enough to make her palm sting. "If I *could* have destroyed them, they'd be gone by now."

His shoulders relaxed, and he closed his eyes for a moment. When he opened them, she saw new resolve there. "Then we have room to negotiate. Not right now—the kids are at a story hour at the library, and I have to pick them up. But we'll talk soon."

"Just because I can't destroy them doesn't mean I'm going to turn them over to you."

"I'll introduce you to Leo and Rennie. You'll see how much they need them."

"It sounds as if Leo and Rennie need far more than a box of old CDs."

"I told you, they need the money. And maybe you need to reclaim your identity."

She shook her head. He had no idea who she was. "If that's what you think, you didn't listen to a word I said last night. Get out of here, Sam."

"I'll be busy for a couple of days. I found a house to rent—a good deal. You have some time to think about my offer."

"I've already done all the thinking I intend to do. So go ahead and write your article for *Rolling Stone*."

THAT NIGHT, she was the first band member to arrive at the Harp. After opening the cabinet and listening to the demos, she'd wanted to call Paul and cancel. To stay at home and sort through the complicated stew of fear and longing that Sam had whipped up.

Instead she'd packed her drum kit and left early. She wasn't going to let memories and grief make her a coward.

After assembling her drums, she glanced up at the top shelf of the bar and the bottle of Grey Goose Quinn kept there. Lingered on it.

"Hey, Delaney," a raspy voice said.

It was Myrtle Sanders, the owner of the local motel.

"Hi, Myrtle."

"I heard you were playing tonight."

"It's usually only Fridays. Do you come here on Saturday nights?"

"Haven't up until now." Myrtle reached into her pocket, then scowled as she yanked her hand out without the Marlboros. "I came to hear you sing. Patrick—" she tilted her chin toward a table in the center of the room "—told me it would be worth it."

Patrick O'Connor, a retired teacher, raised his drink in their direction.

"Good," Delaney managed to say. "I hope you enjoy it. Do you have a favorite song we could play for you?"

"How about something from Tony Bennett?"

Yikes. "We'll give it a try." Delaney usually sang the ballads. She'd planned to do fewer vocals tonight, to keep temptation at bay, but as she watched Myrtle sit down and order a drink, anger began to burn.

Singing less would be as spineless as not coming at all. She wasn't going to let Sam turn her into a coward. Forcing her to rummage through her memories had awakened her need to perform, to stand before a crowd and hear the roar of applause.

Myrtle had come to hear her sing. So, by God, she'd sing.

Delaney headed for the bar and slid onto a stool. Her foot bounced on the ledge, and she fingered the AA token in her pocket.

Quinn walked over. "Hey, Delaney. The usual?"

She wanted to ask him for two fingers of the Goose, neat. Liquid courage. But she managed a nod and a smile. "Thanks, Q."

By God, she would sing the way she wanted to sing. Maybe it was her last chance. Once Sam wrote his article, once the news broke, she wouldn't be able to play with Paul and Hank and Stu. It would bring chaos down on her friends and the pub.

So she'd go all out tonight. She'd sing as if her voice would disappear tomorrow, drum like it was the last time she'd hold the sticks. She'd put herself out there for everyone to see. And hear.

If she was going down, she would do it her way.

Twenty minutes later, as she and the guys huddled together to discuss the playlist, she said, "Paul, I want to sing tonight. Put in some songs that'll let me really crank."

He stared at her. "Seriously?"

Her heart thumped, but she nodded. "Yeah."

"It's about time, Del." He grinned and slapped Hank's hand. "We've been waiting for this." He erased the list he'd started and began a new one. "Man, we're going to rock tonight."

Before she took her seat behind the drums, she added, "And Myrtle Sanders wants to hear some Tony Bennett."

"She's got it."

No one left after the first set. Or the second. In fact, it seemed as if the pub got more crowded as the night went on. By the time the band finished playing, Delaney was drenched in sweat and her throat was raw. But she was floating as she disassembled her drums.

She'd sounded good. Better than good. And the four of them together had been juiced. Energy had jumped from the band to the crowd and back again.

Her skin felt too small for her body and blood raced through her veins. The adrenaline was flowing and she knew it would be a long time before she got to sleep tonight.

She'd done it. Without any Grey Goose, without any drugs.

Without sex.

Sam's image appeared in her head, and she pushed it away.

Before she could leave, people crowded around the band.

"You guys were incredible tonight."

"Awesome."

"When are you playing again?"

As Delaney waited for the crowd to thin, Myrtle came over. "You did a very nice job on 'Smile.'"

"Thanks, Myrtle." Damn straight she had. And she'd do it again next week, and for as long as she could.

CHAPTER SEVEN

SAM HAD SAID HE'D GIVE her some time to think, and he had. After harassing her about the CDs twice in less than twenty-four hours, he'd dropped out of sight.

He would get the same answer no matter when he showed up again. But Delaney was on edge, waiting for him to return.

Sunday and Monday, she'd jumped at any sound outside the barn or house, expecting him to appear and demand a decision. She blamed him for ruining several pieces of wood and disrupting her schedule.

On Tuesday, she'd begun to think he wasn't coming back. She congratulated herself on defeating him, then tried to focus on work.

Finally, this morning, she'd started on a new piece. A spindle bed. The sawdust dancing in the sunlight, the tangy aroma of freshly cut cherry wood, the hum and roar of her tools, all of it settled her. Reminded her that Sam and the world he'd held out to her, the world of recording and touring, were an illusion. Her workshop, her tools, the wood—that was reality.

The motor of the saw vibrated beneath her hands as she guided the length of cherry across the table. When it cleared the blade with a final shriek, she switched off the machine and removed her earphones. A Tony Bennett and k.d. lang duet played on the stereo in the background.

Placing the length of wood with the others she'd cut, she

turned to the two-by-two lengths she'd selected for the spindles. After arranging them in the order they would fit into the headboard, she prepared to form them with the lathe.

Before she could begin, she heard the faint sound of a dog barking. Switching off the stereo, she listened again, and the barking grew louder. Coming closer.

It was Fluffy, the dog she'd hit with her truck last Friday. She'd been setting food out in the garage for him, and it had disappeared, but she hadn't seen him since that night. She'd hoped he was the one eating it, that he wasn't lying injured in the woods somewhere.

She hadn't put the dog food out yet this morning.

Wiping sawdust from her face with a bandanna, she shut down the lathe and hurried to the front of the barn. She scooped a cupful of kibble from the bucket she kept beside the door, and stepped outside into the chilly air.

The thermometer had crept above freezing, and melting snow ran in twisting rivulets across her driveway. Fluffy was barking in the woods as she stepped over a puddle and punched the keypad numbers to open the garage door.

She'd barely gotten the food into his dish when the short black dog limped into the garage. Fluffy lifted his head into her hand, and as she petted him, she examined his leg. He stuck his nose in the food, ignoring her.

A jagged, dirty-looking scab ran along the outside of his thigh, but she didn't see any other injuries. She wondered if she could get him into her truck and take him to the vet.

"You doing okay, big guy?" she murmured as she slid her hand along his leg. She nudged the bowl closer to the truck with her foot, and the dog followed. Encouraged, she pushed it again.

She'd reached the truck door when she heard a high-pitched voice call, "Doggy. Where are you?"

It sounded like a child. Frowning, Delaney left the dog

to eat and headed toward the woods. There were no young children living close by. The neighbors on either side of her had teenagers.

"Hello?" she called. "Who's there?"

The sound of branches breaking and snow crunching stopped. "I want to see the dog," a voice called.

"He's here. Would you like to pet him?"

"Yes!"

A flash of yellow-and-blue burst through the bushes that bordered her property. The little girl wore a long-sleeved, blue-and-yellow-striped shirt and a pink polka-dotted skirt. Her skirt and legs were muddy, and as she got closer, Delaney saw red scratches crisscrossing her shins.

A tangled mop of red hair curled wildly around her face. She had no gloves, and her shoes looked like ballet slippers.

She must be freezing.

"Hey." Delaney crouched on the ground to equal the child's height.

"Where's the dog?" The girl's mouth trembled as she looked over Delaney's shoulder.

Delaney waited for her to come closer. "He's in the garage. What's your name?"

The child shied away like a spooked horse, and Delaney's heart contracted. "The dog is eating his lunch," she added quickly. "Would you like to see him?"

The girl slowly nodded.

"We have to go around the corner." Delaney stood up and held out her hand. "I'll show you, okay?"

The child came closer, but wouldn't take her outstretched hand. Instead, she watched Delaney carefully as they headed around the garage.

Fluffy appeared suddenly and barked at the girl. She lunged toward him, and Fluffy allowed himself to be caught.

He sat patiently while the child wrapped her arms around his belly and hugged him.

Delaney positioned herself between the dog's head and the girl, in case he tried to snap. His former owners, the Ryersons, had children, and Fluffy had always been a friendly, sweet animal, but the little girl was squeezing him hard. "His name is Fluffy," Delaney said, petting his head. "What's your name?" she asked for the second time.

"Rennie."

Her voice was muffled by the dog's fur, and Delaney thought she'd misheard. "Rennie? Is that your name?"

The child stared up at Delaney with Diesel's eyes.

Oh, my God. That was Diesel's flaming red hair, too. "Are you Rennie Adams?" she whispered.

The girl nodded. "I found him."

Diesel's daughter, running through the woods behind Delaney's house. Sam had said he was renting a place. It must be the Ryersons'. It was the only vacant one in the area.

She cleared her throat. "It's good you found Fluffy…." She paused. "He was lost for a while."

Rennie's arms wrapped tighter around the dog's belly. "How did he get lost? Did his mother go away?"

Oh, God. This poor baby. "Yes," Delaney said, trying to keep her voice steady. "His family went away. He's been looking for them ever since." She reached out a shaking hand, hesitated, then brushed the child's hair away from her face. "You look as if you're lost, too."

The girl glanced around, as if realizing she was with a stranger. "I have to find Uncle Sam."

"Was he with you?"

She shook her head. "He's working, and Leo's watching TV."

"So you ran after Fluffy by yourself?"

"I had to save him."

Blinking furiously, Delaney said, "My name is Delaney." She stood up and pretended to shiver. "I'm a little cold. How about you, Rennie?"

"Fluffy's cold, too."

"He probably is. How about we go into my house? I'll make us some hot chocolate and Fluffy can get warm."

"All right." Rennie stood, staggering as she tried to lift the dog.

"Why don't you let me carry him?" Delaney said. "You can open the door for us."

Delaney hoisted the dog into her arms, trying to avoid his injured leg. Rennie held the dog's front paw in her hand and didn't let go as they walked toward the back of the house.

"Can you open that door?" Delaney asked, struggling to hold the squirming animal.

"Fluffy is scared," Rennie said.

"That's probably because he's never been inside my house before. He might want to run away again. Maybe you can tell him he's safe."

She lowered the dog to Rennie's level, and the girl whispered something against the flap of his ear. Fluffy stopped squirming and his pink tongue swiped Rennie's cheek.

"Is he good now?" Delaney asked.

"He says he wants some hot chocolate."

"Then let's go make him some."

Rennie opened the door, watching over her shoulder as if afraid the dog would vanish. Once inside, Delaney set Fluffy down. She kept one hand on his back, worried that he might freak out at being indoors. But he flopped onto the floor next to Rennie and allowed the girl to pull him into her lap.

"Wow." Delaney stared at the pair, stunned. This was the dog who'd outsmarted every animal control officer in the county. "Rennie, are you cold? Would you like one of my sweatshirts?"

"Fluffy needs a sweatshirt, too."

"Then I'll get him one. Do you think he'd like that?"

The girl's hair had fallen forward to cover her face, and she didn't look up. But she nodded.

"I'll be right back." Delaney raced into her bedroom and tossed sweatshirts out of the dresser drawer until she found the two smallest. One said Hot Stuff. A gift from Emma, her friend in rehab. The sweatshirt was too small now, but Delaney refused to get rid of it.

The other one was sleeveless—she'd chopped the sleeves off and wore it for work. Half afraid the dog and the girl would be gone, she hurried back to the kitchen.

They were still on the floor, Fluffy lying in Rennie's lap. Asleep.

"Here you go." She crouched down and slid the Hot Stuff shirt over Rennie's head. The sleeves hung past her wrists, and the hem would probably be at her knees when she stood up. But it would keep her warm.

"We'll just lay this one over Fluffy. He looks like he's tired."

"Okay."

Delaney poured some milk into a pan, squirted in chocolate syrup and began heating it on the stove. "We need to call your uncle Sam and tell him where you are. He'll be worried about you."

"I don't like Uncle Sam."

Delaney's hand faltered, then she began stirring again. "How come, honey?"

"He's mean."

Her heart constricted. "How is he mean?"

"He made us come here and it's cold. And he makes us eat

stuff we don't like. Broccoli and carrots. He says it's good for us."

"Yeah?" Delaney's grip on the wooden spoon loosened a little. "What else does he do?"

"He doesn't read to us at night. One of Mommy's friends always reads to us. Uncle Sam just tells us to go to bed." Rennie's lip quivered. "He doesn't play with us." Her voice dropped to almost a whisper. "And he has mean eyes."

Delaney wanted to scoop the child into her arms and hold her tight. "Mean eyes?"

"He looks like our next-door neighbor when we play on his grass."

"He definitely should read to you at night," Delaney said. "And we'll talk to him about those mean eyes." She tested the milk to make sure it wasn't too hot, then poured some into a mug. "Here you go." She handed it to Rennie, steadying it until she let go of the dog and held on with both hands. Her fingernails were chewed off and ragged.

"Where's Fluffy's drink?"

"We'll give him a treat when he wakes up. Hot chocolate isn't good for dogs."

"Okay." Rennie drank from the mug, then looked up at Delaney with a brown milk mustache. "Uncle Sam doesn't make hot chocolate."

"We'll have to straighten him out about that." Delaney sat down on the floor next to Rennie, hesitated for a moment, then slowly pulled the girl against her side. The child tensed, then her small body relaxed against Delaney. She smelled like chocolate and baby shampoo.

"Do you know your uncle Sam's phone number?" Delaney asked softly.

Rennie shook her head. "Leo does."

They sat quietly as Rennie finished her drink. After a

while, Delaney felt the girl slump against her. When she eased away, she saw that Rennie had fallen asleep.

She lowered her to the floor, slipped a pillow under her head and tucked an afghan around her. Then she reached for her phone and headed into the living room.

Myrtle answered on the second ring. "Bide-a-Wee Motel."

"Myrtle, it's Delaney. Do you still have Sam McCabe's phone number?"

"I should. Let me find it." Pages turned. "Yeah, here it is." She read off the number, and Delaney wrote it down.

"He's a fine looking man," the motel owner said.

"Maybe. But that's not why I need his number. I found... something that belongs to him."

"Good luck," Myrtle said. "He checked out last weekend."

He hadn't gone far. "Thanks for the number, Myrtle."

"You playing at the Harp this Friday? I'll see you then."

"Sounds good."

Delaney glanced in the kitchen and saw that Rennie was still asleep. Then she dialed Sam's number.

He answered after two rings. "What?" He sounded out of breath.

"Sam? This is Delaney. Rennie is asleep on my kitchen floor. Where the hell are you?"

CHAPTER EIGHT

SAM STAGGERED TO A STOP and leaned against a tree, gasping for air. "We're in the woods, about a hundred yards behind a pole barn and a garage. Hold on."

He put his hand over the phone. "Leo," he yelled. "I've found her."

Sam bent over to ease the pain in his side. "Is she all right?"

"She's cold and she's muddy, but seems fine otherwise." Delaney's voice was as icy as the snow beneath his feet. "That's my pole barn you're looking at. I'll see you in a few minutes." The line went dead.

Leo crashed through the bushes on his left, his long blond hair whipping around his face as he looked for his sister. "Where is she? You said you found her."

"A…neighbor has her. She's fine. Let's go get her."

Sam reached for Leo's hand, but the boy ignored him and ran ahead, his jacket flapping open. Sam curled his fingers into his palm and followed.

By the time he reached the house, Leo was pounding on the front door. Delaney opened it.

She wore baggy overalls with a tank top beneath. The overalls were dusty, and her hair was tousled, as if she'd been wearing a hat. She stared at the boy hopping from one foot to another on the porch.

"You must be Leo," she said, her face pale.

How did Delaney feel, looking at Diesel's kids? Knowing she'd contributed to their father's death?

"Where's my sister?" the boy demanded.

Delaney stepped aside, then put a hand out as he charged in. "She's in the kitchen, but she's sleeping, so let's be quiet. She had hot chocolate. Would you like some?"

The boy studied her suspiciously. "Maybe. Are you sure she's okay?"

"I'll show you."

They disappeared into the house, and Sam stepped through the door, feeling like an outsider. He stared around Delaney's living room as he slipped out of his muddy boots.

The bookcases and tables were stunning, but the upholstered furniture was worn and a little shabby. The couch was blue denim, faded along the back cushions, with a coffee table in front. There was a red plaid chair flanked by end tables, and a small television on a wooden stand. Bookshelves lined one wall, and watercolors of trees and lakes were spaced haphazardly on another, along with a few framed photographs of furniture.

There were no pictures of people, no mementos. Nothing remotely personal, except for the books. The wooden pieces of furniture were beautiful, but everything else was unmemorable. It didn't look like a home. It was a place to stay. Nothing more.

He heard Leo's voice in the next room, then Delaney's, and he hurried toward them. He should have sent Leo home as soon as he knew Rennie was safe. He'd never intended for either of the kids to meet Delaney.

Who was he kidding about sending Leo home? The kid wouldn't have listened to him. His nephew tolerated him, at best.

Delaney appeared in the doorway. "What the hell is wrong

with you?" Her voice was a harsh whisper as she glanced over her shoulder.

Time to be polite and grateful and get the kids out of her house. "Delaney," he began, but she put her hand on his chest and shoved him backward. Then again.

"Keep your voice down. She's sleeping." She herded him toward the corner of the living room farthest from the kitchen. "She's *five years old,* Sam. She was running through the woods without a jacket, a hat or gloves. Without *shoes,* for God's sake. What were you thinking?" Delaney's hand curled into a fist. "And didn't anyone ever tell her about stranger danger? She walked right into the house with me."

"I didn't know she'd run away." He stopped, realizing what he'd just admitted. "I mean, she sneaked out of the house. I went after her as soon as I realized she was gone."

"It took you a hell of a long time." Delaney glared at him, hands on her hips. "Why weren't you watching her?"

"I was working. I thought she was in front of the television."

"You were working. Writing that article for *Rolling Stone?*"

"No, damn it. I have a book due in a month. I was…" He shoved his hand through his hair. She made him feel like a complete failure. Someone who shouldn't be trusted with kids. Which was exactly what he'd been trying to tell her. "Fine. You're right. I screwed up. Now can I have my niece back?"

"She says you're mean to her."

"What?" He reached for the bookcase to steady himself. "Mean? How am I mean?"

"You don't read to her or play with her. You have mean eyes, like her neighbor when she plays on his grass."

"Mean eyes?" Did the kids know he didn't want them? His stomach churned with shame.

"It's none of my business how you raise those kids," she began.

"Damn right, it isn't," he muttered.

Delaney paid no attention to him. "Do you have any idea what to do with them? What they need?"

"Of course I do. They need a safe place to live, some structure in their lives. Healthy food."

"That's it?" She stared at him, and he wished she'd rip into him again. Her silent perusal brought every one of his inadequacies roaring to life. Every one of his failures.

"When did *you* become an expert on raising kids?" he asked.

"My parents were just like you, Sam. They thought that if they threw enough money at me, they were doing their job. I had a beautiful place to live, plenty of food and all the toys I could ever want. Beyond that, they couldn't be bothered. So I know exactly how *not* to raise a kid."

"I'm doing the best I can. I've never spent any time with them, but there's no one else to take care of them while Heather is in rehab." Fear and frustration boiled over, and he shoved past her to stare blindly out the window. "I don't know the first thing about kids. I don't want to."

More silence. Then Delaney asked, "Are they seeing a therapist?"

"They were. Child protective services mandated it."

"Are you going to be in Otter Tail for a while?"

"Until I get what I came for."

"Then you're going to be here a long time. You'd better get a therapist up here."

"My God, stop jabbing at me. This isn't my proudest moment."

He wanted to snatch back the words. They'd just slipped out, along with the anxiety roiling inside him. He turned toward the kitchen, intending to take the kids and go.

She put her hand on his arm. "Wait."

He froze, and her hand dropped away. The instant flare of heat made him close his eyes. This was about the kids. That's all.

"I know a social worker who would be good for them." Her voice was softer. There was even a hint of sympathy. "She has experience with substance abuse issues and how they affect families. Emma Sloane. She's in Green Bay, a half hour away."

"Fine. Good." He needed help from someone. He had no idea how to comfort the kids. Leo refused to acknowledge his authority. And Sam didn't have a clue what Rennie was thinking. She mostly let Leo speak for her.

Some of the tension drained from Delaney's body. She'd been practically quivering with anger. "Do you know why Rennie ran away?" she asked quietly.

"Yeah, you told me. I have mean eyes."

She stiffened again. "You can joke about this? Are you that much of an asshole?"

"I'm not joking, damn it. I have no idea what I'm doing." He hated that she was seeing him like this. Unsure. Lost. Bumbling.

Delaney stared at him for an uncomfortable moment. "She was chasing a dog. She thought it was lost, and she wanted to rescue him."

"Did she tell you I wouldn't let her have a dog?"

"You weren't part of the equation. She thought the dog was lost because his mother left him."

"My God." Sam scraped his hands over his face. Even he could figure that one out. "How can she miss Heather? The woman is a disaster as a mother. When she wasn't neglecting them or screaming at them, she was clinging to them."

"She's still their mom. Kids love their mothers, no matter what." For a moment, Delaney's eyes looked bruised.

"Fine. If she wants a dog, I'll get her a dog."

Delaney smiled. "You've already got one, pal. He's in the kitchen, sleeping with Rennie."

DELANEY TRAILED BEHIND Sam as he strode into the kitchen. He stopped in the middle of the room and stared at the dog and child cuddled together on the floor. Delaney slipped past him to lean against the counter and watch. She was getting a really bad feeling about these kids and Sam. He was completely clueless.

He shouldn't be taking care of them. They needed a lot more than he was willing to give them.

These were Diesel's kids. Delaney had loved their father, but she couldn't save him. Maybe she could save Leo and Rennie.

She'd never spent any time around children. But at least she understood what these two had gone through. Clearly, their lives had been chaotic for a long time.

Would things have been different if Diesel hadn't died?

She picked up her morning cup of coffee from the counter and swallowed a cold, bitter gulp.

Sam knelt on the floor in front of Leo. "Hey, buddy, let me take a look at that dog in your sister's lap."

Leo had positioned himself on the floor in front of Rennie. Was he protecting her from Sam? From Delaney? Either way, it was a brave thing to do. And incredibly sad. A ten-year-old shouldn't have to feel responsible for his sister.

Leo didn't move for a moment. The two males stared at each other, neither of them blinking. They might as well be pawing the floor.

Clearly, Leo had been taking care of his sister for a long time and didn't want to accept Sam's authority. Finally, the boy moved. Slowly. To Rennie's side.

Sam stared at the snoring dog. The sweatshirt had slipped

onto the floor, and there was nothing to camouflage the animal's appearance. "What the hell is that?"

"That's Fluffy," she said. Looking at the dog objectively, she had to admit he was pretty ugly. Round body, short legs, rough black coat full of burrs and mud.

"*Fluffy?* He looks like a cross between a dachshund and a bowling ball."

"He's got a good personality, though." She smiled into her coffee cup at the horror on Sam's face.

"*This* is the dog she wants?"

"They chose each other," Delaney said. "Trust me, it's a done deal."

Leo shifted so he was in front of Rennie and the dog again. "I think he's pretty cool looking. I'll help Ren give him a bath." The expression in his eyes was far too adult.

Sam glared at her, as if she'd set this whole situation up. She shrugged. "His jerk owners, the Ryersons, moved out and left him behind. No one's been able to catch him. He trotted right up to Rennie."

"I'm renting the Ryersons' house." Sam's mouth tightened as he looked at the dog and his niece. "How could someone just abandon a dog?"

"How can someone abandon a child?" She kept her gaze steady on him, and he flushed.

"I didn't abandon them," he muttered. But he'd wanted to.

"Has the dog been hanging around the property?" Delaney finally asked.

"I have no idea."

"He has," Leo said with a satisfied sneer at Sam. "Me and Rennie saw him a few times." The boy clearly relished knowing more than his uncle.

Delaney moved closer to Leo. "Your sister's going to need some help with him. Fluffy's been wild since his owners left.

You'll have to make sure he's calmed down enough for her to handle him."

Leo nodded and put his hand on his sleeping sister. "Yeah, I'll make sure he doesn't hurt her."

Delaney ignored Sam's irritated frown and spoke to Leo again. "He wouldn't hurt her on purpose. But he's pretty strong." She squatted next to the dog and pointed to the dirty scab on his leg. "He should see a vet, too. He's hurt."

Rennie stirred and sat up. The hot pink sweatshirt pooled in her lap, and the sleeves covered her hands as she reached for the dog.

Sam raised an eyebrow at Delaney. "'Hot stuff'?"

She felt a flush sweep over her. "It was the smallest one I had." Too small for her now. She'd been rail thin and pasty, with buzz-cut hair and hollow eyes, when Emma had given her that sweatshirt. "I don't wear it anymore."

He glanced at her again, and this time his gaze lingered for a moment.

Then he turned to Rennie. "Delaney said you found him in the woods. Do you want a dog?"

"Fluffy." She curled her arms around the animal's belly again, as if attaching herself to him.

"I think he has owners." Sam crouched next to Fluffy and tentatively petted him.

"They're long gone," Delaney said.

He shot her an irritated look, and she shrugged. "It's the truth."

"Then I guess we better get home and give this guy a bath. You, too, Rennie."

"We'll take a bath together."

When Sam didn't nip that plan in the bud, Delaney said, "I think that might make Fluffy nervous, Rennie."

The girl looked at her uncle. "Are you going to give me a bath?"

"Sure, I'll help you."

Delaney could see his discomfort. "Do you want me to do it?"

"No. I can take care of my niece and nephew myself."

"Come into the other room for a moment," she said, walking out of the kitchen without waiting to see if he'd follow.

In the living room, out of earshot of the kids, she said, "Leave them here, Sam. I'll take care of them. You clearly don't want to be burdened."

"Leave my niece and nephew with a stranger?" He looked shocked at the suggestion.

"That's what you wanted to do, isn't it? You tried to find a woman to take care of them."

"That was different. You're…" He stopped, as if he'd just realized what he was going to say.

"Yes, I was their father's lover. Maybe that's inappropriate. But I'm willing to try and figure out what they need." She saw Diesel in each of his children, and the memories were bittersweet. "I loved Diesel."

"I'm not leaving them with you. The only thing we need from you are those CDs."

"And you're not getting them."

He stared at her for a long moment, and she couldn't read his expression. Was he actually thinking about her offer? Part of her was terrified of the responsibility. What would she do with two kids? Even temporarily. The other part wanted to give Diesel's kids what their father could no longer give them.

Sam headed into the kitchen. "Let's go, guys. We've taken up too much of Ms. Spencer's day."

"You can call me Delaney," she said to Leo and Rennie.

Sam clenched his jaw as he bent to help Rennie pick up the dog. "I'll carry him, Ren."

"Why don't I give you a ride home?" Delaney said as she

watched the silent tug-of-war between the girl and her uncle. "It'll be warmer for Rennie."

"Thanks, but we'll manage."

"Right." Just like he was managing everything else with the kids.

He must have read her mind, because he put the dog on the floor and picked Rennie up. She squirmed in his arms, trying to reach Fluffy.

"He'll come with us, Ren," Sam said. "I need to carry you so you don't get cold."

"I want Fluffy."

Delaney opened the kitchen door and followed them down the stairs. Sam was trying to get a firm grip on the wriggling child as they headed away from her house. Leo was trying to carry Fluffy, and was staggering under the dog's weight.

As they disappeared past the bushes, Delaney heard Rennie sobbing.

CHAPTER NINE

RENNIE'S SOBS FOLLOWED Delaney into the house. They echoed painfully in her head as she washed the pan she'd used for the hot chocolate and swept the dirt off the kitchen floor. Finally, restless and edgy, she headed into the barn. Work would take her mind off Diesel's children.

By the time she'd ruined two of the spindles in the lathe and hit her thumb twice with a hammer, she gave up. There would be no more work done today.

Leo and Rennie's faces lingered in her mind. She wanted to get to know them. Help them.

Sam wanted no part of that. He'd all but told her to butt out.

But those kids needed her.

And she needed them.

Sam seemed like an intelligent man. How could he be so clueless when it came to his niece and nephew? He'd all but told Delaney he was marking time until he could get them back to Miami and hire someone to take care of them.

Diesel would have wanted more than that for his children. He'd loved Leo and Rennie with a fierce, all-consuming passion. It was their mother's threat to take them away from him permanently that had pushed him over the edge.

As she finished cleaning the lathe, Delaney felt her phone vibrate in her pocket. She didn't recognize the number.

"Hello?"

"Delaney? It's Sam."

His voice was strained. Raw.

"What's wrong?"

Wails sounded in the background, mixed with frantic barking. "Rennie won't take a bath. She says she wants you. I tried reasoning with her, but now she and Leo have locked themselves in her room. If I go to open the door, she starts screaming." He sounded like a man at the end of his rope.

Delaney didn't feel any sense of satisfaction. Or validation. She only felt sad. "What do you want?"

"I—I know...I know I was rude this afternoon."

"Yeah, you were." The words hung between them as she tightened her grip on the phone and waited for him to speak. She needed to be clear about what he was asking her.

He blew out a breath. "Will you come over here and help Rennie take a bath? See if you can calm her down?"

Delaney could picture Rennie's lost eyes. Leo's, too. "Why are you asking *me?*"

"Because I don't know anyone else up here."

That was brutally honest. She wouldn't do this for Sam. She would do it for Leo and Rennie. "Fine. I'll be over as soon as I change my clothes."

"What's wrong with what you're wearing?" Desperation filled his voice.

"They're my work clothes."

"Hell, I don't care. Rennie won't care, either. Just get over here." He started to say something, then hesitated. "I can't take much more of this screaming.

"I'll be right there."

She swept the sawdust off her overalls as well as she could, and brushed it out of her hair. Not bothering with a coat, she grabbed her keys and her purse.

Her truck started on the first try. Thank God she'd gotten the new battery. Right now, it was worth eating peanut butter and jelly for a week.

It took ten minutes to drive around to the Ryersons'. She heard Rennie crying as soon as she got out of the truck.

The white house with black shutters was a single story, similar to a lot of the houses in the area. This one, though, had a neglected feel to it, as if the Ryersons had stopped caring about it long before they'd moved. The shutters sagged and the paint on the front door was chipped. Even the bushes at the front of the house were drooping.

She hadn't gotten all the way up the steps when Sam threw the door open. "Thank God," he said. He'd taken off the sweater he'd had on earlier, and now wore only a blue work shirt, sleeves rolled up and tails hanging out. A damp stain spread over the right side of his chest. When he noticed her looking at it, he said, "Grape jelly."

They stopped at a closed door down the hall. Delaney heard Leo's voice, but couldn't make out what he was saying.

She tentatively knocked, and Leo went quiet. "Rennie? It's Delaney. May I come in?"

Sam leaned closer, as if trying to hear what was going on. His head was near enough for her to see the stubble of his beard and the tiny lines around his eyes. They looked like laugh lines, but she hadn't seen him smile since she'd met him. The subtle scent of pine clung to him, along with the fainter aroma of grape jelly.

"Come in," Leo said.

Sam stepped back so fast she felt a breeze. She gave him a questioning look.

"Better if they don't see me right now," he said.

"Why?"

"Because Rennie will start screaming."

"Maybe she should see you. She asked for me, and you got me to come here. You *listened* to her."

He stared at her for a moment, his dark gray eyes

unreadable. But he didn't move away when she opened the door.

The bedroom was small, and held a twin mattress on a frame and a dresser that leaned to one side. The walls were white, and the dark green rug in the middle of the floor and matching quilt on the bed were the only bits of color in the room.

Rennie, still wearing the hot pink sweatshirt, was curled up in the far corner, sniffling. Her eyes were swollen, her nose was red and mucous smeared her cheeks. Leo was plastered to her side, his arm around her. Fluffy lay on the rug, panting.

"Hey, Rennie." Delaney eased to the floor to sit cross-legged near the children. She felt Sam watching them.

"You came." The girl reached for Fluffy.

"Your uncle Sam called me and said you wanted me to come."

Rennie gave a tiny nod, and Sam moved away from the door. Was he ashamed he'd given in to his niece's demands? Or was he afraid that she'd be grateful? See him in another light?

Delaney would think about that later. Right now, she needed to focus on Rennie. "Would you like me to give you a bath?"

"Don't like baths."

"How come?"

"They make my hair hurt." She swiped the back of her hand across her nose.

It looked as if her hair hadn't been combed for days. "You have very pretty hair." Delaney slowly reached out and touched the tangled mass of curls. "Who brushes it for you?"

"I do."

How long had it been since anyone had *looked* at these

children? "Can I help you comb it before you take a bath? Then it won't hurt afterward."

Rennie hooked an arm around the dog. "Fluffy doesn't like baths, either."

There were no burrs or mud in the dog's coat, and his hair looked a little shinier. "Did you give him a bath this afternoon?"

She nodded. "He tried to jump out of the bathtub."

"That must have been funny." Delaney stroked Rennie's head.

The child nodded again.

"Let's go sit in the living room. Maybe Uncle Sam will read you a story while I do your hair."

Rennie glanced at her brother, who nodded once. Delaney stood up and held out her hand. "What's your favorite book?"

The girl took a picture book out of a small suitcase on the floor and held it up. *"Cloudy with a Chance of Meatballs."*

"I don't know that one. I'd like to hear it, too."

When they walked into the living room, Sam was in the kitchen. Cooking, it seemed. The aroma of tomato sauce drifted through the house. Leo sprawled on the floor and picked up a cell phone. Delaney left Rennie on the couch, then went into the kitchen.

"Rennie needs to be distracted while I comb her hair," she said in a quiet voice. "Can you read her a book?"

"I should stay away from her. I couldn't bear it if she started screaming again." Steam from the pan of boiling water swirled around his face, but it couldn't hide his misery. He didn't look at her as he prepared to pour pasta into the pot.

Delaney caught his hand, stopping him. The hair on his

wrist tickled her fingers, and his muscles tightened beneath her grip.

She let him go and took a step back. "She's already picked out the book. I can't read to her and comb at the same time."

He turned off the stove and finally looked at Delaney. "How do you know so much about taking care of kids? Did Diesel...?"

"No." Her throat closed and she shoved her hands into the pockets of her overalls. "No, I never met them."

"All Rennie wanted this afternoon was you."

His words made her feel worse. She was nobody's idea of a savior. "Because I caught the dog for her. Let me take them, Sam. You clearly don't want them." She spoke in a whisper, knowing the children were probably listening. "How long has it been since someone paid attention to them?"

"Probably quite a while." Guilt and sadness swirled in his gray eyes. "Heather was... There's a reason she's going to be in rehab for a while. They were basically raising themselves."

"Then you took them and brought them up here, away from their home and their friends."

He picked up a wooden spoon and started stirring the sauce. "They need money and this is where the money is."

"No, it's not. You're not going to get those CDs."

"Look at them." He gestured toward the living room with the spoon, dripping sauce on the stove. "They need stability in their lives. The income from those CDs will provide it."

"They need someone to love them. No amount of money is going to do that."

"I'm doing the best I can, Delaney."

"Really? You can't love two kids?"

"No." He tossed the wooden spoon into the sink, and splatters of red streaked the white porcelain. "I'll just..."

He slammed the lid onto the pan with the sauce. "Let's go read the damn book."

Delaney sat on the couch and guided Rennie to the floor at her feet. Leo made a show of playing with his cell phone, but he was watching them closely.

Sam sat on the couch, as well, a safe distance away. But the worn cushion tilted beneath his weight, and his thigh settled against Delaney's as he opened the book.

He hadn't done it on purpose, she knew. The couch was old, and the cushions sagged. The Ryersons had left their oldest, shabbiest furniture, in hope of getting a vacation rental. Sam had slid against her and hadn't even noticed. That's why he didn't move away.

But the pressure of his thigh against hers, the heat from the hard muscles in his leg, reminded her how long it had been since she'd touched a man. Since a man had touched her. It made her yearn for more.

She forced herself to concentrate on combing the tangles out of Rennie's hair, but her breath caught as Sam's arm brushed hers.

There was no sign he had noticed her reaction to him. He didn't try to get closer to her. He just kept reading, his voice steady, rolling over all of them. Soothing them.

He stopped reading, but she barely noticed, her awareness of him fading as her fingers moved gently through Rennie's red curls. She remembered a song Diesel had written: "Red-headed Baby." A lullaby for his daughter.

Had he ever sung it to Rennie? Had she ever heard the love in that song?

Delaney untangled the last knot of hair, but still she continued to stroke the child's head. Slowly. Gently.

Diesel would have wanted her to help his children.

"That's a pretty song," Rennie said, twisting around to look at her.

"What?"

"You're humming a pretty song."

Delaney had thought the lullaby was only in her head. Sam shifted away from her, but after a moment, he touched her cheek and wiped away a tear.

His gray eyes were dark and there was a faint flush on his face. "Shall I read another book?" he asked the kids. But he was looking at Delaney.

She held his gaze for a long moment as her heart thumped in her chest. Then she said, "I think it's time for a bath." She was annoyed that her voice sounded hoarse.

Rennie's shoulders tensed, and Delaney helped pull her upright. "C'mon, hot stuff," she said. "Time to get clean."

"I'll finish making dinner," Sam said, surging to his feet. For a moment he stood too close to her, then he spun away and walked into the kitchen.

Leo picked up his phone again. "Leo," Delaney said, "why don't you set the table for your uncle?"

He looked surprised, as if no one had ever asked him to do a chore. Then he shrugged. "Okay."

Twenty minutes later, Delaney was soaked, but Rennie was clean. There had been a lot of splashing and even some giggles. Rennie put on a brand-new pair of footed pajamas, and insisted on the tear-dampened sweatshirt, as well.

Sam and Leo were sitting silently at the kitchen table. Delaney had heard their voices as she'd helped Rennie get dressed. Apparently, they'd run out of things to say.

Rennie scrambled into a chair, and Delaney stood awkwardly in the door as all three of them watched her. "Have a good night, everyone."

"You're not staying for dinner?" Sam asked.

There were four places set at the table, and she backed up a step. "Um, thanks, but I don't want to intrude." Sam needed to interact with the kids on his own.

"No, stay. Please." He half stood, then sank back into his chair. "We'd like you to stay. Right, guys?" He looked from Leo to Rennie.

Leo shrugged, as if he didn't care. But he watched her from beneath his too-long bangs. Rennie nodded, her wet curls bouncing on her back.

Delaney's place was next to Sam, and she scooted the chair a little farther away from him before sitting down. One corner of his mouth curled up. He'd obviously noticed.

She struggled to make conversation as she ate bottled spaghetti sauce and overcooked pasta. Leo gave one-word answers to her questions. Rennie kept her head down and shoveled food in. Sam was mostly silent, although whenever she glanced at him, their eyes met and held.

The meal was almost over when Rennie slowly tilted forward. Sam pushed her plate out of the way just before her forehead touched the table. They all stared at the mass of red curls hiding her face.

"What's wrong with her?" Sam asked, leaning over the table toward her.

Leo lifted up his sister's hair to see her face. "She's sleeping," he announced. "Awesome."

"Do you think she's all right?" Sam sounded worried.

"She's exhausted," Delaney said. "Maybe you should just put her in bed."

She and Leo followed Sam down the hall to the dreary bedroom. Leo pulled back the covers, and Sam laid Rennie carefully on the bed. She seemed lost, just a tiny lump beneath the ugly comforter.

After they'd shut the door, the three of them stood in the living room, avoiding looking at each other. Finally, Leo said, "I'm going to check on Rennie." He disappeared back down the hall.

That was Delaney's cue to go. "Good night, Sam."

"Wait a minute," he said, catching her hand. "You can't leave like that."

Sam gripped Delaney's palm, his thumb resting on the back of her hand. The contrast was fascinating—her palm was calloused, but the rest of her skin felt soft and silky smooth.

Her hand trembled against his for a moment before she drew it away. "What do you mean, I can't leave like this?"

"Rennie splashed you. You're soaked." The top of her overalls gaped away from her body, revealing a damp red tank top covering her breasts. Her braless breasts, he was pretty sure.

She must have noticed his attention, because she adjusted the buckles on the overalls to pull the bib taut against her chest. Tiny bumps from her hard nipples poked through the worn denim.

"...worry about it."

"What?" He had no idea what she'd been saying.

"I said it's not a big deal." Her cheeks were pink. "I'll be in my truck the whole way."

He edged a little closer and was fascinated when her color deepened. "That very reliable truck of yours?"

"I got a new battery. It's fine."

Her hair was a spiky mess, as if it had dried standing straight up. He wanted to run his fingers over it, smooth it down. She'd rubbed any evidence of tears from her face, but a trace of sadness lingered. He wanted to brush that away.

The truth was, he didn't want her to go.

It had nothing to do with the grief in her blue eyes or the vulnerability he saw there. Or the loneliness she wore like an old cloak, familiar and comforting. Protecting.

"You sure you don't want to dry off for a while?"

"No, I'm good."

Reluctantly, he stood away from the door. "Thanks for everything. I was...desperate."

"I know. You wouldn't have called me otherwise." She plucked her keys from the bookshelf by the door, where she'd dropped them on her way in, and turned to go.

"I didn't mean that the way you think." He put a hand on her shoulder, felt the cold dampness of wet clothes beneath his palm, the warm, solid muscle of her arm. "I meant..."

She turned, forcing him to drop his hand. The weary understanding in her eyes was a surprise. He'd expected anger.

"I know what you meant, Sam. You don't want Diesel's lover around his kids. I get that. You don't have to apologize."

"What?" He didn't want to acknowledge the flare of jealousy he felt at the words *Diesel's lover*. "This has nothing to do with Diesel."

Her eyes were pools of sorrow. "This has everything to do with your brother. Getting me involved is your last resort, isn't it? I'm sure you want to keep me as far away as possible from your family. But you can't do that, because I have something you want."

"You have something I *need*." He banished the mental picture of Delaney and his brother. "I meant I didn't want to admit my life was out of control. That I couldn't handle the kids. That you were right."

"Believe me, Sam, I don't enjoy being right."

He slid behind her, blocking the exit. He couldn't let her leave until she understood. "No, you wouldn't, would you?"

Some of his assumptions about Delaney had been wrong.

"You could have rubbed my nose in the mess here when you showed up, but you didn't. You just calmed Rennie down." She'd calmed him down, too. And she'd made Leo feel involved. Sam had had no idea how to connect with his aloof, hostile nephew. "I'm...I had no clue what it was like, taking care of kids. I've never felt so unprepared in my life. So completely ignorant." He touched her arm. "I didn't want to look like a fool in front of you."

She stared down at his fingers on her wrist, then drew away slowly. "You would have figured it out eventually."

"Maybe." Maybe not. "But for now, no one's upset. No one's crying. Rennie's in bed, sleeping. This afternoon was horrible. It tore me apart."

"Then figure out how to make it better. Damn it, Sam. It's not rocket science. People learn to be parents every day."

"You can make it better for them. Let me have the demos. Release the songs."

"That's not going to help them," she said. She waved at the house. "*This* will help them. Living with you. Getting to know you. Finding out they can count on you. If you don't want to put any effort into doing that, let them stay with me."

But they *couldn't* count on him. And he didn't want them around long enough to figure that out. "I rented this house for a week. They're only going to be here until..."

"Until I give in?" Delaney stood rigidly, as if she had a steel rod for a spine. "I hope you're not holding your breath."

"I can't give Leo and Rennie what they need," he said desperately. "But you can."

"What do you think they need, Sam?"

He'd already told her that. "Stability. Security."

"You don't need a box of CDs for that." The way she stood staring at him made him want to squirm.

"Sending them to a good school is the best thing I can do for them."

Delaney shook her head, as if she felt sorry for him. "What a load of crap. A fancy school isn't going to solve their problems. I went to one, and look how I ended up."

Memories darkened the blue of her eyes, and he watched her shake them off. "Rennie wants her uncle Sam to love her and read her bedtime stories. She wants you to pick her up and hold her when she's scared. That's what Rennie wants.

"Leo? I was the same way when I was ten. Resentful, sullen, disrespectful. He's heading down the same path I took. The same road as Diesel."

Her words quivered in his heart like an arrow, but he couldn't allow himself to feel sorry for the child she'd been. "Leo is ten years old, for God's sake. And you're turning him into a drug addict?" Panic made him add, "Just like you did to Diesel."

She flinched as if he'd struck her. After a long moment, she said, "You can't seriously believe the drugs were my fault."

"Why wouldn't I?" She was backing him into a corner, and he couldn't let her do that. "I never saw him using until you joined the band."

"Do you think I had that much power over him? That I took a happy, well-adjusted guy and turned him into an alcoholic drug user?"

Delaney could make a man do just about anything, Sam thought. The poor sap would fall into those eyes of hers and never get out. "I know what I saw."

"You saw what you wanted to see. Diesel was using long before I joined the Redheads, as I told you. He just hid it better then." There was anger in her expression now, and grief. "I have pictures…." She closed her eyes. "Never mind. You'll believe what you want to believe, and I can't change the past."

"No, tell me. I want to hear what you have to say."

"Do you really, Sam?" She wrenched the door open. "I think you're holding on to your grudge as tightly as you can. It absolves you of any blame, doesn't it?"

"What?" He stared at her, stunned, but her eyes were sad and knowing.

"No one was able to help him. Not me, not you, not Heather. I know what I tried to do. How about you?"

As she stared at him, shame poured over him like acid, and he looked away. Couldn't she see that was why he was no good for Leo and Rennie?

"Is that what you want for your brother's children?"

"No, damn it. I want them to have some self-respect. To know who they are."

"Then you have to show them the way."

She was halfway out the door when she turned and nailed him with her gaze. "You should ask yourself—is this what Diesel would have wanted for his kids? Would he have wanted his brother to hand them off?"

"They'll be better without me," he said desperately.

"Really? Better off with strangers than a loving uncle?" She stood there, daring him to say she was wrong. "Are you going to do the right thing for those kids, Sam?"

He was still silent as he watched her drive away.

Leaving him alone with his brother's children.

CHAPTER TEN

SAM SMELLED SOMETHING BURNING as he cut up an apple for the kids' lunch the next day. When he turned around, blue smoke curled above the frying pan. Damn it! The grilled cheese sandwiches.

He pushed the pan to a back burner and lifted out one of the sandwiches, then reached over to dump the blackened bread in the garbage. It slid off the spatula and hit the floor. As it skidded across the linoleum, Fluffy bolted into the kitchen and grabbed the burned mess.

Sam lunged, but the dog managed to avoid him and run into the living room.

By the time Sam pulled him out from under the couch, half the sandwich was gone. As he tried to pry the remainder out of the dog's mouth, Rennie began wailing.

"You're hurting him. Stop it!"

"He's not supposed to eat cheese, Rennie. Remember what the vet said this morning?" Between making sure Leo and Rennie didn't touch the instruments in the exam room, and trying to calm Rennie when the vet gave Fluffy a shot, Sam didn't remember many of the woman's instructions. But as part of her "new dog owner" speech, she'd definitely said not to let Fluffy eat table food.

"He wants it." His niece threw her arms around the dog's neck, squeezing tightly. As Sam tried to loosen her arms, Fluffy gagged and vomited the partially digested sandwich onto the rug.

"That's gross," Rennie cried. "You made him do it."

Sam plucked her away from the dog and the mess. She kicked at his legs, landing a blow to his knee that hurt like hell. "Rennie! Settle down! Let me clean that up."

"You're mean, Uncle Sam." She flailed in his arms. "I want my mommy."

Yeah, like Heather was such a great mother. "Your mommy is sick," he said, trying to calm her. "But she's going to get better, and then you can live with her again."

If he had anything to do with it, neither Leo nor Rennie would go back to Heather. They'd be sheltered in boarding school, safe from both their mother and the paparazzi. But that was a discussion for another day.

"Leo," he said desperately. "Tell her to settle down, will you?"

Leo held out his arms for his sister, triumph in his too-old eyes. As far as he was concerned, Sam was admitting defeat.

Delaney had asked if he was going to do the right thing for the kids. Was this what they needed?

Hell, no. He'd made Rennie cry more than once. Everything was a power struggle with Leo. Sam had burned their lunch. What was Delaney thinking? These kids needed better care than he could give them.

As they ate a new batch of untoasted sandwiches, Leo said, "I want to go back to Miami. I texted Spike. He said we could live with him."

"Who's Spike?"

"My friend."

"And he invited you and Rennie to live with his family?"

Leo drew circles in the ketchup on his plate. "Yeah."

The kid actually thought Sam would buy that? "Sorry, Leo. You're staying here."

"I want to go back to school." He shoved his plate away. "I'm missing a lot of stuff."

Based on the grades he'd seen, Leo hadn't cared much about school until now. Unbidden, Delaney's words from the night before echoed in Sam's head. *He'll go down the same road as Diesel.*

God, what was he doing with these kids? He pushed away from the table and threw his plate in the sink. How was he supposed to do the right thing for them when he had no idea what that was?

"We can go back to Miami when I finish up my business here. Until then, you're staying in Wisconsin with me."

Leo shoved away from the table. Moments later, his bedroom door slammed.

Sam and Rennie finished the meal in silence. She stared at her food as she ate, responding to his questions with a shrug. What the hell was he supposed to do?

After lunch, he herded them outside to take Fluffy for a walk. Fresh air was supposed to be good for kids. Then Rennie let go of the leash and Fluffy scrambled for the woods.

"Fluffy!" She ran after him, followed by Leo. By the time Sam caught up, she was sitting on the ground with the dog, mud smeared on her jacket and in her hair. Fluffy was in worse shape. Leo crouched beside them.

"You're all wet, Rennie." Sam squatted next to her and picked up the end of the leash, which was covered with mud. "We need to get you home." The dog was lying on the ground, panting. It looked as if he'd rolled in the mud. "Fluffy needs another bath."

Sam wanted to wind the clock ahead to eight-thirty, when both of the kids would be in bed. He wanted peace and quiet and no crying. No messes to clean up. No more laundry to do.

Instead, he waited for Rennie to stand up, and held out his hand. She took Leo's instead.

After they'd bathed Fluffy, Sam cleaned the tub and filled it with warm water again. "You want a bubble bath, Rennie?" he asked.

"I want Delaney."

He wasn't going to call her. She'd calmed the kids yesterday, but she'd also pointed out every one of his failings. He didn't need anyone to do that—he knew all too well why he shouldn't be taking care of Leo and Rennie.

The memory of her scent washed over him. It could make him forget the smell of burning toast and wet dog. He'd rather look at her than two kids who made him feel helpless and inept.

"Just take your bath, Rennie."

She shook her head. Bits of mud from her hair splattered the bathroom walls. "I want Delaney."

"We don't need Delaney. We can take care of ourselves."

As DELANEY WALKED from the barn to her house that evening, twilight purpled the sky and turned the tall pines at the side of the house to black. A breeze was blowing, but it was warmer. The air almost smelled like spring.

She'd managed to keep Sam and Leo and Rennie out of her head while she worked by focusing completely on the bed she was building. But now, stepping into the dusk, she wondered how their day had gone.

Not her problem, she reminded herself. Sam had made that very clear. He'd only called her because there was no one else.

But that didn't stop her from wondering about the kids. Had they had a good day? Had Sam paid attention to them?

The lullaby she'd hummed the night before drifted through

her head as she unlocked the kitchen door. Leo and Rennie had lost so much. They were adrift—she recognized the sadness and confusion in their eyes.

She wanted to reach out and kiss it away. Make them giggle and laugh. Act like goofy kids instead of lost souls. Maybe then some of the guilt she felt over their father's death would ease.

She couldn't do anything tonight, though. Leo and Rennie would be in bed and asleep soon, and she had to concentrate on herself. She needed to get ready to go to the Harp. To sing.

Excitement swirled inside her, along with anticipation.

Silly. She'd been performing there on Fridays for the past two years.

Last week had been different, though.

Last Saturday, she hadn't held back. Hadn't tried to disappear into the woodwork. She'd been herself again. Not Chantal.

Delaney.

And she'd done it without Grey Goose. Without drugs. Without sex.

She'd thought about sex, though. She'd thought about Sam while she was drumming.

She was deciding what to wear when her phone buzzed in the kitchen. She ignored it as she held up an aqua blue tank top. It was one of her favorites. She'd always worn baggy T-shirts when she played at the Harp. But she was done hiding. She slipped on the tank, then covered it with a thin gray sweater. When she got too hot, she could take off the sweater.

As she tugged on her jeans, the phone buzzed again. This time she picked it up. Sam.

She glanced at the clock. Bathtime.

Her hand tightened around the phone. She wanted to

answer it. It would be another opportunity to connect with Leo and Rennie.

She could stop by their place on her way to the Harp, then grab something to eat once she got to the pub. It wouldn't take long.

She forced herself to set the phone on the kitchen table. It vibrated in a circle, but she wouldn't let herself pick it up.

Not tonight. She had a job to do. And she was helping no one if she charged to the rescue every time Sam had a problem.

A tiny voice whispered that she was being selfish. If Sam had enough problems, he'd be more willing to let her get involved with Leo and Rennie.

She ignored the voice. She'd never claimed to be a saint.

Once Sam figured out that money couldn't help what troubled Leo and Rennie, maybe he'd stop asking for the CDs.

Selfish.

She ignored the voice again. The publicity storm those CDs would produce would change her life forever. She'd paid enough for her sins as Chantal. She couldn't afford any more.

BY THE TIME DELANEY reached the Harp, excitement swirled with terror, just like it did every Friday. As soon as she walked in the door, her gaze went to the bottle of Grey Goose on the shelf above the bar.

No. She didn't need it. She'd performed last week without it, and she could do it again.

Some of the anxiety faded as she set up her drums, and her confidence grew. She felt as if she were floating. A burden had shifted, become a little lighter. The craving for alcohol hadn't gone away, but she could control it. She was in charge, not the bottle.

It felt damn good.

She slid onto her stool, anticipation thrumming through her blood. Hank leaned over. "You're going to sing tonight, aren't you?"

"Damn right I am."

He raised his hand and she gave him a soft high five. "Yeah, baby," he said.

They were halfway through the second song when the door opened again, letting in the pine-scented breeze.

Along with Sam, Leo and Rennie.

CHAPTER ELEVEN

THEY LOOKED TERRIBLE.

One of the sticks began to slip out of her hand, but Delaney caught herself and kept playing. Thank goodness she wasn't the featured singer right now.

Sam's shoulders were hunched, his hair disheveled and his coat hanging open. The lines on his face were deeper and more prominent than yesterday, and he seemed desperate. When their eyes met, he didn't turn away. It was as if he was drowning and she was his life preserver.

The kids looked worse than Sam. Rennie's hair was a tangled mess and her dress was inside out. She wore one boot and one house slipper. Her jacket was unzipped, too, and she had a neon-orange mustache, as if she'd been drinking orange soda. Her eyes drooped, but when she saw Delaney, she tried to run up to her.

Leo caught her hand and dragged her back. His face was sullen. Sam led them over to a table, and Leo slouched in the chair as if he would rather be anyplace else.

What had happened today?

Maddie came over to take Sam's order. When she returned with the drinks, Delaney was surprised to see he'd ordered soda. If ever a man looked as if he needed a drink, it was Sam.

Something softened inside her. He had the kids with him. He was driving.

She joined in the chorus of the song, and by the time she

looked back at Sam's table, Rennie had laid her head down. Her eyes were closed.

The little girl should be home in bed. Why had Sam brought them to the pub?

Leo was playing with his straw, swirling the ice in his glass. Some of the stiffness in Sam's shoulders eased as he took a drink and watched her.

It was hard to miss the plea in his eyes, even from twenty feet away. His day must have been hellish. He'd come here tonight because he needed her.

She hadn't been needed in a long time. For the past three years, she'd kept herself carefully separate from everyone in her life. If there were no expectations, there could be no disappointment.

Tonight, she wanted to help Diesel's kids.

As Sam continued to watch her, a different kind of need built. It beat heavily in her blood, drummed through her body, until all she saw was Sam.

Tonight, she wasn't craving a drink. She had a different demon to battle.

This wasn't unfocused lust that she could easily dismiss.

She wanted Sam. She could blame it on the adrenaline of performing, but there was nothing impersonal about it.

He was Diesel's brother. The man threatening to tell the world who she was.

She finally understood the true meaning of irony.

Sam slumped in his chair, and she yearned to kiss the weariness from his eyes, make them darken with desire instead of worry.

She watched him as she played, her muscles flexing and releasing, sweat pouring down her back. When she sang, she was singing to him. All the lyrics about love and tenderness, heartache and heartbreak, were for him.

His laserlike gaze was focused only on her. It was like kindling to the fire building inside her, and she shifted restlessly on her stool. Sam gripped the plastic soda glass but didn't drink. Maddie went to the table and said something to him, and he answered without looking at her.

Maddie glanced at Delaney, back at Sam, and smiled.

Paul hit the first chord of "Learning to Fly," and Delaney pounded out the drum combination in time with the beat of her heart. Then Paul nodded at her to take the lead.

As she sang about loss and learning to live again, she thought about the long road she'd taken as she struggled to fly without wings. Sam wanted to tear it all down, make her relive her past.

It didn't matter. She still wanted him. Maybe she hadn't evolved as far from Chantal as she'd thought.

When she finished the song, the room was silent for a heartbeat. Then it exploded in applause.

THE FINAL NOTES of "Learning to Fly" washed over Sam, then the pub came alive with yelling and clapping. He barely noticed the noise. Nothing existed but Delaney and her heartbreaking cover of that song.

She'd been singing about loneliness and need. His heartache. His pain. He'd never hear that song again without thinking of her.

The words still seemed to quiver in the air around him. His skin tingled, as if she'd been touching him. His heart raced as he watched her.

She'd been watching him all night.

The pregnant waitress came to the table with another soda for Leo.

"So you're a friend of Delaney," she said as she set it down.

It was an effort to turn away from Delaney. "She's a neighbor."

"Is that right? She hasn't mentioned any new neighbors." The redhead rested her order pad on her enormous stomach.

"We just moved in."

"Didn't take you long, did it?"

"It's a long story," he muttered. This was why he didn't live in a small town.

The band began another song, and he glanced at Delaney. She smiled a little, a tiny upturn of her lips. He wanted to taste that smile.

"Your kids look kind of tired." The waitress nodded at the sleeping Rennie.

"We're not his kids." Leo's straw made a hollow sound as he slurped the last drops of soda from his first glass.

There was pity in the waitress's gaze as she glanced from Sam to Leo. "God, Delaney," she muttered as she turned away. "What have you gotten yourself into?"

Sam was pretty sure he wasn't supposed to hear that. Delaney hadn't gotten herself into anything. He'd dragged her into his mess.

Tonight, he wanted to drag her into his bed. For one night, he wanted to forget about his niece and nephew, forget about the horrible day he'd had, forget about everything but her. He wanted to drown his uncertainty, his turmoil, in Delaney, and let her wash it all away.

Tomorrow, they'd be on opposite sides again. But for one night, he wanted to forget the wall that stood between them.

She hadn't sung this way last week. She'd been subdued, as if she didn't want anyone to notice her. Tonight, everyone in the pub was riveted. They all watched the band, but it was impossible to see anyone but Delaney.

Sam wished the pub was empty. She was singing for him, and the connection was too intimate, too personal to share.

He shook his head. Everyone in the pub probably felt the same way.

The band finally took a break, and the audience began moving around. Rennie still slept, oblivious to the commotion. Leo lounged in his chair, trying to project an air of world-weariness. Instead, he just looked lost.

Delaney picked her way through the tangle of equipment at the front of the room, and her footsteps slowed as she neared the table. When she reached them, her face was flushed. Sweat pearled on her temples and the sweater she wore was plastered to her chest. She peeled it off and slung it over her shoulder, revealing a blue tank top that was the exact color of her eyes.

Forcing himself to look at her face, Sam said, "Hey, Delaney. You sounded amazing."

"Thanks." She held his gaze for a beat too long, then glanced at Rennie and Leo. "The guys are really good."

"I was talking about you."

The blue of her eyes was the color of a stormy sea. "It takes four of us to make music."

"You were okay," Leo said with a sneer. "My dad was better."

Sam opened his mouth to tell him not to be rude, but Delaney put her hand on the boy's arm. "Yeah, he was. You should be very proud of your dad."

Leo shrugged one shoulder, using his straw to stir the ice in his glass. "He's dead."

"But he left a lot behind. You and your sister and some wonderful music."

"I guess."

Sam nodded at the remaining chair. "Can you sit with us for a minute?"

"Sorry. I have to...I have to get something to eat." She looked at Rennie again. "And you need to get going."

Their waitress appeared and handed Delaney a drink, which she gulped down. "So, Del," she said when Delaney set the empty glass on the table. "How's it going?"

"Good, Maddie."

"We'll get together soon," the waitress said. It sounded almost like a threat, and Delaney laughed.

"You can try."

She turned back to Sam. "Take these kids home, Sam," she said. "They need to be in bed."

Before she could escape, several people stopped to compliment her.

When the last person left, Sam said quietly, "No one could take their eyes off you. You were good last week, but not like this. What changed?"

Delaney shrugged. "There was no reason to hold back. This might be my last chance to sing with the guys."

"Why's that?"

She stared at him for a long moment. "I won't drag the band or the pub into my messes. Do you know what it would be like here if I played and sang after…?"

She picked up her glass, saw it was empty and put it down again. "Anyway. I decided that if I was going down, I might as well enjoy it."

"Going down?" Then he realized what she was talking about—his threat to write the article about her. It made him feel small and cheap.

"Thanks for coming, Leo." Her gaze touched Rennie, then lingered on him. "Sam."

He watched the sway of her hips in snug jeans as she walked away.

"Leo, I need to talk to Delaney for a moment. Can you wake your sister up and help her get her coat on?"

"Duh," the boy said sarcastically. "What do you think, dude?"

Leo's eyes were bruised and forlorn. Sam put his hand on the boy's shoulder. Leo let it rest there for a moment before he jerked away.

"I think you do a great job of looking after your sister, Leo."

When he turned, Delaney had disappeared into the crowd. He craned his neck and saw the tips of her blonde hair headed toward the back of the pub.

She was almost at the kitchen door when he caught up with her. "Delaney, hold on."

She glanced over her shoulder. "What were you thinking, Sam, bringing those kids here so late?"

He was thinking he needed her. "We had an awful day. Rennie was crying because she wanted you. This was the only thing I could think of."

Delaney shook her head. "I'm sorry to hear that." Her gaze softened. "You seem like a smart guy, Sam. You'll work it out."

Another person congratulated her, and she deflected the praise as usual. She was far from the selfish, self-centered woman he'd assumed her to be.

Shame burned in the pit of his stomach. If he'd been wrong about that, maybe he'd been wrong about other things, too.

"I'd like to see you tonight. There are some things I have to discuss with you." He wanted more than talk, but they could start with that. Suddenly, he had a lot of questions. "Could you stop over after you're finished here?"

Her face was still flushed and her eyes dark. Her gaze dropped slowly to his mouth. Lingered. "That wouldn't be a good idea, Sam. For either of us."

Lust arrowed through him. "Why not? I just want to talk."

She studied him closely. "Really?"

"Are you afraid you wouldn't be safe?" he asked.

Her mouth sent his simmering desire to a boil. "I'm more worried about you."

"What?" He reached for her, but she stepped through a swinging door and disappeared. He wanted to follow her. To find out what she meant. He glanced over his shoulder at Leo and Rennie. Leo's blond head was bent close to his sister's red one. Was he telling her that Sam would be right back? That he hadn't abandoned them?

Delaney would have to wait. With a quick, fruitless glance through the small circular window in the door, he turned away.

Had she really implied *he* wouldn't be safe with *her?* Desire throbbed with a heavy beat as he hesitated, torn between what he wanted and what he needed to do. Finally, he headed toward Leo and Rennie.

Want would have to wait.

But not for long.

BY THE TIME HE REACHED the dark house, both the kids were asleep. Leo's head lolled against the door, his mouth open, his hair hanging over his face. Rennie had slid down to lean on her brother's shoulder, suspended there by her seat belt.

It took only minutes to carry them into the house, pull off their shoes and put them into bed. Sam brushed Rennie's hair out of her face and tucked the blanket under her chin. There must be something he could do with all those curls to keep them from getting so tangled. He'd ask Delaney. Hair was one of those mysterious female things that men never understood.

Delaney's hair had been damp when she finished playing. She put everything into her drumming—he'd seen the sweat-darkened spots on her tank top, the perspiration sliding down her temples.

Did she throw herself into everything she did the same way?

He closed his eyes and took a steadying breath. He couldn't think about Delaney. He needed to get some work done tonight.

He left Rennie's door open a crack and went into Leo's room. The boy had burrowed under his covers and curled into himself. Sam brushed the blond strands of hair out of his face. How long had it been since either of these kids had a haircut?

He watched his nephew breathing for a moment, then left his room, too.

As he opened his laptop at the kitchen table, Sam glanced out the window. There was nothing but darkness.

A couple of hours later, he'd written two pages of his book, a crucial action scene where the hero flees to Switzerland from Austria. He glanced out the window again. Had he hoped she would see his light on and maybe think about coming by, as he'd asked her to?

The house was quiet, except for the occasional creak of wood settling, the click of the furnace turning off and on. He imagined he could hear the kids breathing in their rooms, slowly and steadily, filling the house with life.

He'd always been alone when he worked. But he liked having the kids close by. Liked knowing they were here.

As he was struggling with a sentence, he heard a groan from one of their rooms. Then a whimper. Leo.

He hurried into the boy's room. He was thrashing on the bed, kicking the covers away. "No! No! I want my daddy." His voice rose in a howl of anguish. "Where's my daddy?"

Sam dropped onto the mattress and tried to wake him. Leo clutched at him. "Daddy, come back. Don't leave."

His heart breaking, Sam scooped him into his arms, holding him tight and rocking him back and forth. "It's okay,

Leo," he murmured. "It's okay. I have you. It's going to be okay."

"Daddy," Leo sobbed.

He shouldn't have taken the kids to the pub. It must have triggered memories of Diesel.

Sam smoothed the damp hair from his nephew's face and wiped away the silvery tracks of tears. He remembered waking Diesel from a bad dream when he was about Leo's age. Sam had had the same scared, helpless feeling then. He hadn't known what to do for Diesel, either.

Leo shifted, wrapping his arms around Sam's neck as his sobs subsided. It took a long time for the boy to relax and go limp.

Even after Sam was certain Leo was sleeping peacefully again, he cradled him against his shoulder. Finally, when he laid the boy back on the bed, he whispered, "It's all right, Leo. I'm here. We'll fix this. We'll make it right."

When Leo sighed in his sleep and hugged a pillow to his chest, Sam went into his own room and grabbed his blankets and pillows. Then he returned to Leo's room and made a bed on the floor in case Leo had another nightmare.

CHAPTER TWELVE

SAM KNOCKED ON DELANEY'S door late the next morning, but there were no sounds coming from the house. He leaned over the railing to peer into the window, but there was no movement.

He'd found her in the barn once before. Listening to the demos and crying. Maybe she was there today.

As he got closer, he heard the beat of heavy rock. When he leaned close to the window to peer inside, he felt it vibrate. Even as he knocked on the door, he knew it was futile. No way could she hear over that much noise.

The door was unlocked, so he stepped inside, inhaling the scents of freshly cut wood and sawdust. He didn't recognize the female voice singing about heartache, but it was loud and energetic. At a momentary lull in the music, he heard the whine of a machine. A saw, maybe, in a room at the back.

He wove through a maze of furniture. Desks, dressers, tables and chairs. He'd noticed it earlier, but only in the periphery.

The pieces were beautiful. Works of art. The stains were rich and complex, the varnished surfaces smooth as glass. The designs varied from simple to ornate, but all the wood glowed in the sunlight streaming through the windows.

When he reached the back room, he found Delaney dressed in overalls and a green tank top, safety goggles on and a yellow bandanna wrapped around her head. She pushed a piece of wood through a band saw, then set it in a pile with others like it. She positioned another plank on the table, adjusted a couple of knobs on the saw, and began to guide it through.

A bag hung in front of the blade, collecting sawdust, but a fine stream of particles escaped its suction and rose into the air. They drifted onto her overalls and clung to the fine hairs on her smoothly muscled arms. The overalls tightened across her rear end as she leaned over the saw.

She'd made all the furniture in the outer room, he realized. That's what she did in this barn. He hadn't made the connection before today.

He hadn't really paid any attention to *her*. He'd never asked what she did. Never showed any interest in who she really was.

She'd been one-dimensional in his mind—the woman who had what he wanted. The woman who'd gotten Diesel tangled up in the drugs that killed him.

She'd denied that. Maybe she wasn't lying.

DELANEY STARED AT THE stack of maple planks in her workshop, but she didn't see the wood. She saw Rennie, sleeping on the table at the Harp the night before. She saw Leo's bravado and his desperate attempt to appear older than ten.

She saw Sam, too. Loneliness had been a shadow enveloping him last night. Separating him from the brightness and warmth of the Harp, from any connection with the other patrons.

She longed to draw him into the light, sweep away the isolation she sensed in him.

The memory of his gaze last night, locked with hers, made her quiver. Even from twenty feet away, she'd felt the punch of his desire. Responded to it.

She wanted to give Sam a lot more than help with the kids.

Just as Sam didn't have talking in mind when he'd asked her to stop by his house.

That was lust. She'd experienced it before. Ignored it before. But this time, it felt like something more. For the first time in years, she wanted a connection with another person. And she wanted to be herself.

The thought terrified her. She'd shielded herself for so long, she wasn't sure where to begin.

She selected another length of maple and laid it next to the saw. Better to concentrate on helping Leo and Rennie. She could do that without baring her soul.

Maybe she should give Sam the demos and prove that money wasn't going to give those children the peace they needed.

She let the initial panic subside and considered the idea. Pictured the reporters who would arrive in town, the sidelong glances from people she knew.

The exposure would be painful. But she was strong now. She'd gotten clean, found work she loved, made a home for herself.

Maybe she could do this without destroying herself.

And maybe baring herself in public would make no difference for Leo and Rennie. By the time the CDs were released, Sam and the kids would be back in Miami. Leo and Rennie would be enrolled in some fancy school before Sam recognized that their problems went deeper, and she'd be too far away to do anything for Diesel's children.

She threw the switch to turn on the table saw. Maybe she needed to focus on making this bookcase and stop listening to her crazy conscience.

She hooked her iPod up to her stereo and picked a loud playlist. She wanted upbeat songs that would get her heart pumping, and lift her spirits.

The music helped. After cutting enough lengths, Delaney

turned off the saw and listened to the whine of the blade slow, then stop. A bouncy pop song about feelings blared from the boom box as she danced her way to the pile of wood on the floor.

As she bent to pick up the top slat for sanding, the back of her neck prickled and she spun around. Sam leaned against a wall, dressed in his uniform of worn jeans and leather jacket. It hung open to reveal a dark green sweater.

"Sam. What are you doing here?" She looked behind him. "Where are Leo and Rennie?"

"The neighbors across the road came over and introduced themselves this morning. They'd heard we were renting the place, and they invited Leo and Rennie to a birthday party at some cheesy place." He smiled, his eyes heavy-lidded. "I'm watching you dance. Don't stop on account of me."

She slapped the button on the stereo and the music stopped. She yanked the goggles off her forehead and wiped the sawdust from her face with the bandanna in her pocket. When she felt the one covering her hair, she pulled it off, too. She began to comb her fingers through her hair, then stopped. This sudden wish that she wasn't so scruffy-looking pissed her off.

"I don't dance in front of strangers."

"Strangers?" He pushed away from the wall, a disturbing light in his eyes. "I thought we were a little more than that."

"Acquaintances, then. I don't dance for them, either." Her heart thundered, and that irritated her, too. It was okay for this to happen when she was playing. She expected that.

It wasn't supposed to happen because Sam smiled at her in her workshop.

He was walking toward her, but before he could corner her, she stepped into the showroom and put a dresser between them. "What can I do for you?"

"I tried to call you early this morning, but you didn't pick up."

"I was busy." She'd heard the phone vibrating while she was doing yoga.

He paused, as if expecting her to tell him what she'd been doing. She watched him steadily, waiting.

His mouth lifted slightly. "I decided to come by, instead."

She swallowed. "How were...how were the kids this morning?"

"They were tired." His smile vanished. "We were worn out after yesterday."

"You looked exhausted last night." She wanted to ask him what had happened, but that wouldn't be smart.

"It was the mother of all bad days."

"I'm sorry." Now was the time to get brisk. "So what brings you here today?"

Instead of answering, he looked around the showroom. "I didn't know you made furniture."

She shrugged. "I'm a carpenter."

"More than a carpenter." He crouched down and ran his fingers over the elaborate edge of a coffee table. Smoothed his hand over the surface of a desk. "These are beautiful."

"I got a job as a carpenter after I got...after Diesel died. I was good at it, and went to work for someone who made furniture. Now I have my own business."

As he wandered closer to her, he let his fingers trail over each piece he passed. When he reached a Shaker-style dresser, he paused and curled one finger around the drawer pull.

God! Why did he have to be a toucher? She'd always had a weakness for men who knew how to use their hands.

"I like this. A lot."

The pleasure that bloomed inside her was all out of

proportion to the simple compliment. What did she care what he thought of her furniture? His opinion didn't matter in the least.

She was an idiot. "Thank you."

He moved closer, and she resisted the impulse to back up. On Friday night, she'd been revved after the first set. Keyed up. Energy had been humming through her, and she'd wanted Sam. Badly enough that she'd stayed in the pub's kitchen until the last possible minute.

So badly that she'd been crushed to find out he was gone.

That was Friday. This was Saturday. She was back to normal. Cautious. Wary.

It didn't matter how close he got.

He stopped a few feet away, disappointing her. "The other day, you said you had some photographs. Pictures of my brother that would prove he was doing drugs before he got involved with you. I'd like to see them."

All of the fantasies she'd enjoyed since last night vanished.

Ignoring the disappointment, she said, "That's in the past. Looking at a bunch of pictures isn't going to change anything."

"It'll tell me the truth."

"Why do you want to do this, Sam? It's not going to bring Diesel back. I shouldn't have said anything, but I was…" She'd been hurt that he'd blamed her for Diesel's death. "I was angry."

"So get your revenge. Show me the pictures."

"I'm not angry anymore."

He leaned over the dresser between them, his eyes almost silver in the sunlight. "You're protecting me, aren't you, Delaney? Trying to keep me from being hurt."

She shouldn't feel cornered. She had the whole showroom

at her back. "Why would I protect you? You're a big boy, Sam. You can take care of yourself."

"Then show me the pictures."

He'd maneuvered her neatly into a trap and slammed the door. "Fine." She pushed away from the dresser and headed over to the maple cabinet in the corner. She reached up and grabbed the key. There was no dust to wipe off this time.

She swallowed as she stared at the door. *You've already listened to the demos. Nothing in there can hurt you more than that.*

Chantal was in that cabinet.

Finally, she pushed the key into the lock.

She pulled out the box that held most of her photos, and set it on a desk, thumbing through them without allowing herself to really look. To think. As she found the ones she needed, she laid them on the desk.

Sam picked up the first one. It was a picture of Diesel at a club with the rest of the band. There was powder on the table, and Diesel had a small white mustache as he grinned at the camera.

"That's Bogeyman," Sam said, pointing to the guy at Diesel's left shoulder.

"Yes." Bogeyman had been the drummer before her. Diesel had hired her when Bogeyman went to rehab.

The next photo was from a concert. Diesel was drinking from a bottle of Goose on the stage. Again, Bogeyman was the drummer.

The next one was taken in a dressing room. There was a small bag of white powder on the dressing table, and the band members were posing with rolled up money in their noses.

"Lovely," Sam said.

"I warned you."

Finally he looked up. "I had to know. I made a lot of

assumptions about you, based on your public persona back then. I wondered if I'd made assumptions about your relationship with Diesel, too."

"Our relationship is off the table. I'm not discussing it with you." She snatched up the pictures, stuffed them into the envelopes and slammed the container back into the cabinet.

"You don't have to." He looked away from her for a moment. "I wanted to talk to you the other night because I've made a decision, and these pictures just confirm that I'm making the right one. I still want the demos, but I'll figure out a way to keep your identity secret. You won't have to do publicity, or interviews, or join the rest of the band for a tour." He shrugged. "I heard Bogeyman was out of rehab and straight. He can be the drummer."

"What?"

"I'll respect your right to privacy. I don't want to out you."

"But you'll still write the article for *Rolling Stone* if I don't give you the CDs."

"The kids need that money."

She could stay here in Otter Tail. Continue to build up her business.

Continue to play at the Harp with Paul and Hank and Stu.

"Thank you." She studied Sam for a moment. He seemed uncomfortable. "Why did you change your mind?"

"Because I developed a conscience? Hell if I know. But I don't want to hurt you, just help Diesel's kids."

"I'll think about the CDs." She put her hand on his arm. "It would take a few months to put together something that can be released. Where are you and Leo and Rennie going to live until then?"

"If I know the money will be coming in, I can take out a loan for their tuition. Then they could live at the school."

"At the school? You're sending them to a *boarding* school?" She snatched her hand away.

"I thought I made that clear. It's the best place for them. They'll be sheltered from the negative publicity Heather gets. It's as close to normal as I can make it for them."

"A boarding school is close to normal? You're out of your mind. They're already lost souls. How is living with a bunch of strangers going to help them? Rennie's only five years old, for God's sake."

"What's the alternative? Heather? I don't think so."

"What about you? Why can't you take care of them?"

"It's better for them if I don't. But I'll stay a part of their lives."

"What does that mean? You'll stop in and see them on visiting day?"

"You're making it sound as if I'm sending them to some kind of prison. This is one of the most exclusive schools in the country."

"And Leo and Rennie would be just a couple of ATMs for the school." Just like they'd been for Heather.

"It's not as if I'd dump them there and forget about them. I'll be around." He shoved his hands into his pockets. "That's the best I can do."

"Really? You can't bring yourself to love two children?"

"I couldn't save my own brother. How am I supposed to save his kids?"

"You blame yourself for Diesel's death?" She shook her head. "No one could have saved him." God knows she'd tried. The new songs on the demos had been her last, desperate hope.

Fear made her hands tremble, but she knew what she had to do. Sam had left her with no choice. "All right, Sam,

I'll make you a deal. You stick around here, with Leo and Rennie. Promise not to put them in that boarding school, and I'll release the demos."

CHAPTER THIRTEEN

"*WHAT?*" SAM TOOK A STEP back from her. "You want me to stay up here? With the kids?" He shook his head. "I can't do that."

"Why not?"

He paced through her showroom, and she knew he was trying to think of a reason. "I don't even know if I can extend the lease on that house," he finally said. "And there weren't any other houses available for rent in this area."

"Come on, Sam. You're a writer. You can come up with a better excuse than that."

"Leo and Rennie belong in Miami."

"With Heather? I thought you said she'd be in rehab for a while. And you can work anywhere."

Sam stared at her with panicked eyes. "Why are you so determined to keep Leo and Rennie up here?"

"For selfish reasons. I want to get to know them." She wanted Sam to get to know them, too. He'd be a part of their lives much longer than she would.

"Heather won't be happy about that. About the kids spending time with you."

She shrugged. "Not my problem. If you want those CDs, you have to stay here. I'll have my agent contact the Red-heads' recording company and tell them I have some demos that Diesel and I did. I'm sure they'll be interested. It'll take a while to decide which ones to use, longer to get them ready for release."

"You're doing this because you think you can make Leo, Rennie and me into a happy little family," he said, his voice flat.

She wasn't going to admit that to Sam.

"I'm doing it for myself." That was also true. She wanted to do it for herself and Diesel.

"You're full of crap." Sam kicked at one of the poles in the center of the barn. "You're trying to force me to be part of their lives."

"I'm giving you what you want. The demos will mean lots of money for Leo and Rennie."

"I can't take care of them." Desperation tinged Sam's voice.

"Why not? You rearranged your whole life to come up here. You already have a house, and I'm sure the Ryersons will be thrilled to extend the lease. You can enroll Leo and Rennie in school in Otter Tail." Better to quarrel with Sam than to think about the implications of what she was about to do. The chance she was about to take. She would have to trust Sam to keep his word about not exposing her. Would he? "I'm caving, and you're getting cold feet?"

"You're asking too much of me, Delaney."

"You're not asking enough of yourself."

He shoved his hand through his hair. "Okay, forget about Leo and Rennie for a moment. You told me releasing those demos would destroy you."

"If I had to do publicity. If I don't have to give interviews or appearances, it shouldn't be a problem." People had been looking for her ever since she'd disappeared into rehab. Every once in a while, there was a story about someone who claimed they'd seen Chantal. Sam was the only one who'd succeeded in finding her. "Your choice, Sam. You can get what you want. But you have to pay a price."

She'd pay a price, too, if she got to know Diesel's kids,

fell in love with them, and then they left. Maybe that would be her penance.

She picked up the broom and began sweeping the floor, pretending to ignore him. Hoping he'd take the hint and leave.

He didn't, of course. He simply moved out of her way.

Finally, when she dumped the dust and sawdust into a garbage can, he took the broom out of her hand.

"There must be something else you want. Something I can give you for the demos."

"There isn't."

"I can't give you what you're asking for," he said. "I'm just not that man."

She took the broom away from him and snapped it into the bracket on the wall. "Why are you afraid of them?"

"I'm not…" He shook his head. "I'm afraid *for* them. I'm not a reliable person, Delaney. You saw what happened the other day. I got involved in my work and Rennie ran away. I didn't even notice. I don't have room in my life for kids."

"You're telling me you can't change? I think that's bull, too."

She watched him steadily, and his cheeks darkened. "What about you?" he said, a thread of desperation in his voice. "What if someone slips and the press finds out where you are? Aren't you afraid that might happen?"

"I'll take my chances."

"Your stubbornness isn't going to change anything," he said. "I can't give Leo and Rennie what you think they need."

She stared out the window. Dust motes dancing in the sunlight blurred and wavered in front of her. She remembered her childhood, being shuffled from one nanny to another, savoring every tiny scrap of attention her parents gave her. Acting out just to get their attention. "Leo and Rennie need someone who loves them." She wrapped her arms around her waist. "Kids need someone to hold on to."

"It sounds as if you're speaking from experience."

His voice was too understanding.

She moved away. "We're not discussing me."

"You're trying to force me to do something I don't want to do." He stepped in front of her. "You're trying to blackmail me into living with them. Taking responsibility for them. Loving them."

"I can't force you to love anyone. Emotional blackmail never works, and resentment doesn't make a good parent." She tried to back away. "I just want you to give it a chance."

"What if I hurt them?" he whispered. "Made it worse."

"You're protecting them from yourself?" She finally got it. Pain for all three of them swept over her, and she cupped his face in her hands. "That's insane, Sam."

"I'm not good for them."

"You can be. You're trying to protect Leo and Rennie. That's a start." The rough stubble on his cheeks scraped her fingers. "You're even trying to protect me."

"Why do you sound so surprised?"

"I can fight my own battles." She dropped her hands from his face, but he grabbed them and pressed their palms together. Without thinking, she twined her fingers with his.

He smiled.

"Why do you want to protect me, Sam?"

His fingers tightened on hers. "Last night, I asked you to stop by my house on your way home. Why wouldn't you do that?"

"I didn't think you wanted to talk." She hadn't, either. And she'd known what would happen if she went to him after she performed.

The same thing that would happen now, in her barn, if she didn't move. Heat from his body poured through hers, warming her. Softening her. His gray eyes gleamed like silver, hot and molten.

"I did, actually." His lips curved, and she wanted to touch the vulnerable corner of his mouth. To feel his tongue against her finger. She gripped his hands more tightly. "I wanted to tell you I wasn't writing the article. But it sounded as if you were protecting me. From you."

Desire had been a drumbeat in her blood last night. She'd wanted to push him against the wall, cover his mouth with hers and taste him. Touch him. Lose herself in him.

She'd thought it was performance adrenaline. That she'd be sane in the light of day.

Apparently, she'd been wrong.

"It would have been late," she said. There would have been no talking if she'd shown up at his house that night. Only hands and bodies, mouths and tongues.

"I thought about you after we got home. Waited for you." He leaned closer, until his breath feathered against her mouth. "Wanted you."

He let her hands go, one finger at a time, and cupped her face in his palms. "Did you want me last night, Delaney? Were you thinking about me as you sang?"

She struggled for sanity. For control. "I think about a lot of things when I'm playing."

"Did you think about this?" He slid one finger slowly across her mouth, as if he was memorizing every dip and swell of her lips, gauging every tiny shiver she made. Her lips parted and the pad of his finger grazed the sensitive inner surface. She couldn't suppress the hitch in her breath.

"How about this?" He slid his hands into her hair, tracing the contours of her skull, letting the short strands slip through his fingers like water.

One palm drifted to her nape, drawing her closer. "I

wanted to know what you tasted like. How your body would feel against mine."

His mouth followed the path his finger had traced, then he bit lightly on her lower lip. When she shuddered, he smiled against her mouth.

"Tell me I'm not the only one who wanted last night, Delaney. Tell me you felt it, too."

Surrender weakened her knees. "I did. I do." She wrapped her arms around his neck and pulled him closer. But instead of deepening the kiss, he tasted his way across her cheek and nibbled on her neck, just below her ear.

His fingers danced over her back, touching the bumps of her spine, shaping her hips. When he cupped her rear in his hands and squeezed gently, she heard herself moan.

If she didn't kiss him, she would die. She rose onto her toes and fused her mouth to his. Not satisfied, wanting so much more, she shifted against him, trying to get closer. She needed to feel every inch of his long body, every hard muscle, every sharp angle. Desire throbbed in a frantic rhythm through her blood, obliterating everything else. It had been far too long since she'd kissed a man. Far too long since she'd tasted a man's passion, allowed herself to *want*.

When his tongue teased her lips, she didn't even try to stifle her moan. He tasted of coffee and chocolate and sin, and she was beyond thinking.

His arms tightened around her, and she felt a vague sense of movement. She realized her back was against the wall, and he'd lifted her up so his erection was exactly where she wanted it.

He took his mouth from hers and she turned blindly, seeking it. Then he tugged on the buckles of her overalls and the front dropped away. Cool air puckered her nipples beneath the thin tank top.

"I've wanted to do that since the night you gave Rennie a

bath." He put his hand over one breast. "You weren't wearing a bra, were you?"

"No bras when I'm working." Delaney kissed him again, tangled her tongue with his as she pressed her breast into his palm.

"No?" His hand tightened, then he stroked his thumb over her nipple. She arched back, silently begging him to do it again. As his finger circled, she pushed his jacket down his arms. It slid to the floor and she burrowed beneath his sweater.

His abdomen was hard with muscle, and he tensed when she touched him. She shoved the sweater out of the way and pressed her mouth to his chest, swirling her tongue around his flat male nipple. He tasted salty, like sweat and musk and man.

He pulled her away from the wall and laid her on one of the desks. Then he yanked up the flimsy tank and looked at her.

"Perfect," he said, cupping her breasts. "Beautiful." He bent and took one nipple in his mouth, and she whimpered helplessly.

He tried to tug the overalls down, but she was lying on them. Frustrated, he lifted her off the desk.

"Your house," he managed to say, tasting her again. "Bed."

Her house. If he kept kissing her, touching her, in a few moments they'd be having sex.

Delaney grabbed his hands and held them. "Sam. Stop."

"Why?" He stared at her pebbled nipples. "You want me." He swallowed. "I want you."

For one insane moment, she leaned closer and inhaled his scent. Wanted to run her hands down his ribs, over his flat belly. Lower.

She released him and stumbled backward. "Sam, we can't do this. I'm…Chantal. Your brother's lover."

His eyes were heavy-lidded with desire. "I know who you are."

CHAPTER FOURTEEN

THE SUN-DRENCHED BARN WAS a cocoon of intimacy, and Delaney's hands shook as she pulled down her tank top and rebuckled her overalls. Sam had stripped away far more than a thin cotton shirt. She'd been emotionally naked in front of him, completely exposed.

"I wasn't kissing Chantal." He skimmed his fingers down her cheek, and she wanted to press against his hand. "I want to make love with *you*, Delaney. The woman who plays a table saw like a virtuoso. Who breaks hearts when she sings. Leo and Rennie's champion."

"You don't know me," she whispered. She was afraid she'd let him see far too much.

"Then let me in. You hide behind thick walls, but they cracked a little last night. A little more this morning." He took her hand and drew her closer. "Enough to catch a glimpse of a dazzling woman."

His heat warmed the cold places inside her. She wanted to rest her head on his shoulder and let that warmth fill her. She wanted to surround herself with Sam.

The impulse terrified her. She hadn't let anyone get close to her since Diesel. She wasn't sure she could anymore. Grief and guilt had encircled her heart with a thicket of thorns. Nothing got in. Or out.

"It was the music last night." She freed her hand from his. "It's emotional. Sensual. It's supposed to draw you in, make you feel." She tried to smile. "I guess it worked. For both of us."

"You think it's only music in my head?" He touched his fingers to her mouth, stirring the embers back into a flame. "Not the music. You. But maybe this is the wrong place and time." He glanced at the maple cabinet in the corner. "There'll be a better one."

"Sam, that happens when I'm playing." She sounded desperate. "It's the adrenaline. I want…I need to have…"

"Drumming turns you on? Is that what you're trying to say?" He didn't look offended. He didn't look like a man who'd just been told he was being used. He looked amused. "Good to know. I'll make sure I'm around whenever you're playing. To help you out with that."

"That's not what I meant," she started to say, but he pressed a finger to her mouth.

"I know what you were trying to say—that you would have wanted anyone last night." He shook his head, still smiling. "Nice try, but there was no one else in the pub last night for you. Or for me. And this morning?" He brushed his hand over the desk behind her. "You weren't playing the drums when I came in."

He knew her too well. After a week. Bone-deep scared, she said, "Sam, I…"

"I have to go, Delaney. The kids will be home soon." He looked around for his jacket, and she saw it spread out on the floor where she'd let it drop. The sleeves were flung wide, as if welcoming her in.

She snatched it up and brushed off the sawdust, then handed it to him. He shrugged it on without taking his gaze off her.

"Are you…are you staying in Otter Tail?" That sounded too needy. "I have to know if I should call the record company," she added hastily.

"I'm staying." He bent close and kissed her again, and God help her, she sank into him for a moment. Then she caught herself and pulled away.

When she stepped back, he began to follow her, then stopped.

"We'll talk about the demos later," he said.

"Nothing to talk about." This was more solid ground. Fewer dangerous places. "We made a deal. If you stay here with Leo and Rennie, I'll release the demos."

"I'm staying."

"All right." Her throat felt as if she'd inhaled sawdust. "Good."

"Don't do anything with them yet. Not until we figure out a plan to keep you hidden."

"Goodbye, Sam." She herded him toward the door, afraid that if he stayed longer, she'd lose her tenuous control.

He glanced at his watch. "Yeah. I have to go." He kissed her again and lingered for a moment, a promise of more. Then he walked out of the barn. His car door opened, and moments later, his Jeep disappeared around the bend in her driveway.

She leaned her head against the window, staring at the opening in the trees. She heard the engine hesitate, then it accelerated and faded away.

Thank God she'd had enough presence of mind to stop herself. She'd almost led him into her house, into her bedroom.

She couldn't do that. She wanted something from Sam, too. She wanted Leo and Rennie. And she wouldn't use her body to get them.

Taking a deep breath, she began to weave through the furniture in the showroom, her legs still wobbly. Sam's scent clung to her, and she wanted to wrap her arms around herself to hold it close. Instead, she grabbed a dust rag and wiped off the desk. But it was impossible to get rid of the memories.

He thought she wasn't Chantal anymore, but he was wrong. Chantal still lurked inside her, waiting for a chance to come out of hiding. Delaney fought with Chantal every single day. Sometimes, when she played, she was afraid Chantal was winning.

She stood in front of the maple cabinet, her hands clammy, her heart racing. Every time she opened this cabinet, Chantal stirred. When she showed Sam the pictures, the bitch had hovered over her shoulder, reminding her what it was like to feel that rush from the drugs. The burn in her blood from the vodka.

Her hand shook as she reached for the key, and the sound of it turning in the lock shuddered through her like a crack of thunder.

She swung the door open and saw the guitar on the bottom shelf. Waiting.

She picked up the box of CDs. Touched each jewel case as the songs played in her head. She remembered writing and recording them with Diesel. Finally, she dug her phone out of her pocket and opened it.

SAM WAS HALFWAY DOWN Delaney's driveway when he hesitated. He didn't want to leave. Delaney was running scared. He'd seen the shock in her eyes when she realized what she'd done, what she'd revealed. She'd scrambled to cover herself, but it had been too late.

This wasn't the time to press her. He touched the gas pedal again.

It hadn't been performance adrenaline. It wasn't random. What had happened between them was damn personal. It was Sam and Delaney, not rocker and groupie. She could deny it all she wanted, but it didn't matter.

He knew.

And so did she. That's why she was so scared.

Although he had to admit, playing the Diesel card had been brilliant, reminding him that she was the woman he'd blamed for his brother's death. She'd probably expected him to recoil from her in horror.

He turned onto the road that led to his house. She didn't know him very well.

He'd never been interested in Chantal. Even when most of the rock world had been panting over her—brash, sexy, outrageous Chantal—he'd felt nothing but distaste.

Delaney was no longer that woman. He'd had glimpses of the rocker—the incandescent performer who'd held every eye in the pub. Poured out her heart when she sang.

But Delaney was the woman he knew, the one who'd emerged after all of Chantal's excesses had been stripped away, leaving only the best of the rocker.

As he walked into the house and absently petted Fluffy, he glanced at the clock on the kitchen wall. He had twenty minutes until Leo and Rennie were due home from the party. He should try to get a little work done on his current thriller.

But as he stared at the computer screen, he saw only Delaney.

It was almost a half hour before he heard Leo and Rennie on the front porch. He hurried to open the door, Fluffy at his heels.

"Hey, guys," he said as they walked in. "How was the party?"

Rennie held a slightly tattered looking pink bag, and clutched Leo's hand. "I got candy," she said, holding up the sack. But her mouth quivered.

Sam squatted in front of them. "What's wrong, Rennie?"

"There was a clown." Leo set his blue bag on the bookshelf and took off his sister's jacket.

"A clown?" Sam peered at Rennie. Tears were welling in her eyes. Fluffy nudged her hand, but Rennie hardly noticed.

"She's scared of clowns," Leo said in a low voice.

Scared of clowns? Sam looked at Rennie, who nodded and threw her arms around his neck. She squeezed tightly, and he felt her shaking. She was crying.

Without thinking, he stood up and held her close. "It's okay, Rennie."

She sobbed more loudly and burrowed into his shoulder. He patted her back awkwardly.

Leo rolled his eyes and held out his arms, offering to take her. This was what Delaney had been talking about, Sam realized. Rennie needed someone to hold her.

Rennie needed him.

He shook his head slightly and walked backward until his legs hit the couch, then he sat down. Rennie sniffled into his shoulder.

What was he supposed to do? He knew how to tell stories, not comfort frightened children.

"I know a story," he heard himself say, his voice tinged with desperation. "About a little girl and boy and a bad clown. Do you want to hear it?"

Rennie lifted a tearstained face from his shoulder. "Do they kill the bad clown?"

"You're awfully bloodthirsty, aren't you?" He grabbed a tissue from the box on the end table and wiped her runny nose. "They don't kill him. They make him into a good clown."

Was that the right answer? Should he have said they killed the clown? He studied Rennie's face, watching for a reaction.

Finally she nodded. "Where did they live?"

He tried to set her on the couch next to him, but she clutched his sweater in her small fist, so he let her stay. "They lived in a little town called Otter Tail. The clown thought Otter Tail was a stupid name for a town. He made fun of it all the time."

Leo leaned against the bookcase, watching them. "You want to sit here with us, Leo?" Sam asked.

"Whatever," he said. When Sam slid over, Leo dropped onto the couch and crossed his arms. He eyed Sam warily, as if wondering what he was up to.

"The boy was afraid of clowns," Sam said.

Rennie gave her brother a superior look, and he stuck out his tongue at her. But she wasn't crying anymore.

"What's the boy's name?" Rennie demanded.

"Joe," Sam said. "The girl's name is Jenny. They have a dog named Buster."

By the time he finished the story, Joe and Jenny and Buster had saved the bad clown from drowning because he couldn't swim. His clown outfit had disappeared, and he wore a pair of jeans and a sweater. "And the clown went to live with Joe and Jenny, and they all lived happily ever after."

"That's a good story, Uncle Sam." Rennie bounced on his lap, apparently recovered. "Tell us another story about them."

"Why don't you tell me about the party?"

"Mike liked our present," she said.

"Yeah?" Rennie had made a card, and Sam put some money into it. He'd had no idea what else to do.

He glanced at Leo, who shrugged. "He said he wanted this new video game."

As Rennie chattered about cake and punch and ice cream and games, Sam got the impression that the party had been filled with chaos and noise. And sugar. Lots of sugar.

"Do you guys want some lunch?" Sam asked.

"We had pizza." Leo rolled his eyes again. "Cheesy Pete's is a *pizza* place."

Rennie stilled. "I don't feel good, Uncle Sam," she said. Her face was ashen.

"What's wrong?"

"My tummy hurts."

Oh, God. What did he do now? "Do you want a glass of water?"

She gagged once, and he scooped her up and raced into the bathroom just in time.

THAT EVENING, when he was sure Leo and Rennie were asleep, Sam opened his laptop and collapsed onto an uncomfortable kitchen chair. How did people with kids do it? It felt as if he'd been running from one fire to the next all day. Just as he put one out, another flared.

Maybe he was stuck in Otter Tail for a while, but at least it was temporary. Eventually, they'd all go back to Miami and he could enroll Leo and Rennie in the boarding school. He'd have his life back.

But did he want his old life back? Did he want to be alone in that quiet house, where the only sounds were the birds calling in the distance and the clicking of his keyboard as he typed?

There wasn't a lot of color in that life.

Since he'd come to Otter Tail, he'd been surrounded by color. Delaney. Leo. Rennie.

Was he capable of being the person Leo and Rennie needed? Delaney seemed to think so. But she didn't really know him.

What if he screwed up, the way he had with Diesel?

What would that do to Leo and Rennie?

He remembered the way Rennie had clung to him that afternoon.

And Leo had acted all tough and indifferent.

What if he failed them?

The phone in his pocket rang, and he pulled it out. Maybe it was Delaney, calling to see how his day had gone.

It was a Miami area code. He didn't recognize the number, but his heart started a slow, heavy beat. "Hello?"

"Hey, Sam, it's Heather."

"Heather." His hand tightened on the phone. "This is a surprise. How are you doing?"

"I'm doing good. I got phone privileges today. Can I talk to my babies?"

"They're asleep, Heather. It's almost nine o'clock."

"Asleep?" She sounded confused. "What did you do to them? They never go to bed before midnight."

Even *he* knew kids should go to bed earlier than that. "They were busy today. Tell me how rehab is going."

"It's good. They told me I might get out in a few weeks. I can't wait to see Leo and Rennie. Does my little man miss me?"

Leo wasn't a little man. He was a child. Sam shoved away from the table and made sure the kids' bedroom doors were closed. "Of course he misses his mom. Rennie does, too."

"I can have visitors now. Maybe you could bring them to see me."

Thank God he didn't have to make that decision. "We're not in Miami. We're in Wisconsin. Remember I told you I was looking for Chantal and some demos she had?"

"Chantal?" Heather's voice rose. "You're with Chantal?"

"I've talked to her. I'm trying to convince her to release those demos."

"Keep Leo and Rennie away from her." Her voice held an

edge of hysteria. "She stole Diesel from me. She's not going to steal my kids."

"Calm down, Heather. No one's stealing your kids." Delaney had said she wanted to get to know Leo and Rennie. That wasn't stealing. But he probably shouldn't tell that to Heather. He tried to make his tone reassuring. "All I want from Chantal are the demos." Nothing could be further from the truth.

"Really?" There was a beat of silence. "When you get the demos, you're coming back to Miami, right?" She sounded like the old Heather. Calculating.

"That's the plan." Could he turn Leo and Rennie over to their mother again? Would Heather be capable of raising her children after she got out of the hospital?

He wouldn't have to make that choice. They'd be in boarding school. Safe.

"So you'll be back here with Leo and Rennie by the time I get out of this place?"

"I'll do my best, Heather."

Another silence. Finally, she said, "I'll be waiting." He heard her hang up and disconnected.

He scrolled through his list of contacts, stopping at Delaney's name. He pushed Send, putting a call through to her.

It went directly to voice mail.

He slowly closed the phone. Foolish to feel so bereft.

Even more foolish to wish Delaney was here, with him.

CHAPTER FIFTEEN

"I'LL SEE YOU LATER, Sam," Leo said as he strolled into the fourth-grade classroom at Otter Tail Elementary School. But he spoiled the nonchalance when he glanced back at Sam with a worried expression.

"After school," Sam promised. "I'll be waiting for you."

"Whatever."

Rennie's arms tightened around his neck as she watched her brother walk away. The teacher nodded at them and smiled reassuringly as she led Leo to a desk near the front of the room. Sam had been dismissed. With one last look at his nephew, he followed the principal to the kindergarten classroom.

Rennie clutched his sweater in a viselike grip as they stood in the doorway. Colorful pictures decorated the wall, and books and games sat on bookshelves. Small desks stood in groups of four, and there was a large rug at the front of the room.

"Welcome to kindergarten, Reading," said the teacher, using Rennie's formal name, one Sam hated as much as Rennie did. Diesel had clearly been high when he'd named his children after trains. He'd thought he was clever and trendy. He'd just been pathetic.

The teacher was a young woman with brown hair pulled into a ponytail. She barely looked old enough to be in college, let alone teaching, Sam decided. "We were just going to do some puzzles. Do you like puzzles?"

"Her name is Rennie." He felt his niece tense as he set her on the ground. "I'll be back for you after school, Rennie. I'll make sure I find you, and your teacher won't leave you until I do. Okay?"

She nodded slowly.

"Why don't I help you pick out a puzzle?" The teacher held out her hand, and Rennie finally let go of Sam.

"You're going to have fun," he promised as the teacher eased the door closed. His chest was tight as he stood there, watching through the window.

"Many parents have a hard time leaving their children for the first day in a new school," the principal said. It felt as though she was patting him on the back. "The children will adjust quickly."

"I'm not their parent," he said.

"But you're acting as one until their mother is well." Sam had told her that Leo and Rennie's mother was ill and they'd be staying with him in Otter Tail for a while. She urged him toward the front door. "I'll make sure the teachers know about Lionel and Reading's situation. Now…" She smiled and opened the door.

"Their names are Leo and Rennie."

"I'm sorry." She colored. "I'll make sure their teachers know, too." She smiled. "We'll all keep a close eye on them."

She was smooth. She'd herded him out of the building before he could have second thoughts.

Not that he would. But both Leo and Rennie had looked so lost. Sam felt as if he was abandoning them.

He was almost home, with ideas for the next chapter of his novel swirling in his head, when a chirpy voice on the radio related the latest celebrity gossip. "An unidentified source has reported that Chantal, the notorious drummer from the Redheaded Stepsisters, has surfaced three years after lead singer Diesel's overdose death and the dissolution of the band. In the wake of stories about a torrid affair between Chantal and Diesel, the drummer vanished from the music scene. We'll bring you more details as we learn them."

"Heather. Goddamn you."

He slammed on the brakes, did a U-turn and headed for Delaney's.

Ten minutes later, he rolled to a stop in front of the barn. Grabbing the keys from the ignition, he jumped out and ran to her house. He rang the bell several times, then pounded on the door.

She wasn't there. He ran down the steps and hurried to the barn. As he got closer, he heard music. Not the hard rock from last time, but something exotic. Sitar music, maybe.

He was heading for the door when a movement from the window caught his eye. He stepped closer, then caught his breath.

Delaney stood on a blue mat with her back to him. She was dressed in short black pants and a multicolored, full-length sports bra. The pants hugged a perfect rear end that bunched and released as she moved.

She raised her arms, swept them down to the floor, then dropped to her hands and feet and did what looked like a push-up. Then she raised her rear end until her body formed an inverted V. She stayed that way for a moment, then repeated the moves.

It had to be yoga. He had no idea it was so graceful.

So *sexy*.

She looked steady. Calm. He was about to throw her completely off balance.

Maybe he shouldn't tell her. Heather didn't know where they were. He hadn't said anything about Wisconsin, had he? Stories about Chantal sightings surfaced periodically, so maybe it wasn't Heather. Maybe it was just another rumor floating around the internet.

He wouldn't worry Delaney about what could be nothing.

He opened the door and stepped inside.

She looked at him from another of those inverted Vs. Her hair brushed the mat, and her shirt crept up her back, exposing two smooth bumps of spine.

Their eyes met and held for a long moment, then she stood up. Her face was pink and her hair was damp with sweat. The front of her sports bra was damp, too. His gaze flickered over her breasts, and he remembered their creamy whiteness and the pale rose of her nipples.

Her flush deepened and she grabbed a sweatshirt lying on a chair. It was worn and shabby and hung halfway to her knees—a very effective cover-up. "Sam. What are you doing here?"

"I enrolled Leo and Rennie in school this morning. I wanted to let you know. There are only a couple of months left, but we'll be here until school is over, at least."

She'd been rubbing her face and head with a towel, and she tossed it over a chair. "That's good," she said. "They'll meet other kids. Have a routine."

"I hope so." He had to tell her about Heather—at least the part about getting out of rehab soon. "Heather called Saturday night."

Delaney hesitated. "What does that mean?"

"It means that she's progressing in rehab. She got phone privileges."

"So she's close to getting out."

"She thinks so. I don't. Heather can put up a good front for a while, but she can't sustain it. She may have fooled the counselors, but it won't last."

"Did she talk to Leo and Rennie?" Her fingers tightened on the dark green towel.

"No. They were asleep."

Delaney frowned. "You didn't wake them up?"

"Hell, no." There was no way he'd wake them up after the day they'd had. Especially to talk to their mother, which would probably upset them all over again.

"How do Leo and Rennie feel about missing her call?"

"I didn't tell them about it. They'll only be disappointed if she doesn't call back."

"Poor kids." She raised her eyebrows. "So why did you come over today, Sam? I'm glad the kids are enrolled in school, but you didn't have to make a special trip to tell me."

"Maybe I wanted to see you, and this was a good excuse." When her cheeks grew a little more pink, he smiled. "I also talked to the Realtor and extended my lease for two months. We can start working on ways to keep you safe once the demos are released."

"My agent understands she has to keep me out of the equation. She'll be very careful with the record company."

"Wait. You've already talked to your agent?"

"Yes. I told her what was going on."

"We agreed you were going to wait."

"You told me to wait. I didn't agree to anything." She walked over to a coffeemaker sitting next to the stereo, and he watched the sway of her hips beneath the sweatshirt. She turned off the music and picked up a pot of coffee. "Would you like a cup?"

"No, damn it. I don't want any coffee."

She poured some for herself, then took a sip as she studied him over the rim of the mug. "Once I decided to do it, there was no point in waiting."

Delaney watched Sam pace, frustration and a hint of anger

on his face. He stabbed his fingers through his hair. The memory of how his hands had felt, touching her, had lingered all weekend.

She took another gulp of the too-hot coffee.

He sighed. "We could have figured out some safeguards. Ways to make sure you weren't exposed."

"No, we couldn't have." She began to tremble, and she gripped the cup more tightly. Anger would be a lot easier to deal with than his concern. "Don't you think I took every possible precaution? Even my agent doesn't know where I live. She sends my royalty checks to an address on the other side of the country, to a fictitious name. They forward it here. No one knows where I am."

He pried the coffee cup away from her, then took her hands. "You could have waited for a day or two until we came up with a strategy."

We. She looked at their linked hands. She hadn't been part of a "we" in a very long time. She drew away. They were business partners. She was releasing her demos for a chance to spend some time with Leo and Rennie. A chance to get to know them. It was a simple trade.

That was all.

"I didn't need a strategy. My safeguards are already in place. If I had waited, you might have changed your mind. I had to call before you lost your nerve. It's a done deal."

"You wanted to make sure I couldn't back out. That if things got bad, I couldn't panic and head back to Miami with the kids."

She shrugged. "Yes, I want that time with Leo and Rennie. I told you I was selfish."

She'd expected him to be angry. But the expression on his face was closer to fear. "You can't control everything. What if reporters find you, in spite of all your precautions?"

A jolt of panic made her heart race. "I can't do anything about that."

"How can you be so calm about this?" he demanded.

She was far from calm. She'd been jittery and on edge since she'd made that call to her agent. But she didn't want to let him see how the thought of being exposed unnerved her. That would really be stripping herself bare. "I'll be okay unless you lead the press to me. Are you going to do that, Sam?"

Instead of the instant denial she expected, he drew her close and wrapped his arms around her. "Not if I can help it."

She pushed him away. "*Not if I can help it?* What's that supposed to mean? Of course you can help it. If you don't tell anyone, nothing will happen."

"What about Leo and Rennie? They're smart kids. If you're spending time with them and working on the music, they might figure it out."

"I hadn't thought about the kids." Sam was right. Leo, she suspected, would be very good at picking up clues. He had to be, in order to survive with an unpredictable mother. And Rennie was just a baby. She wouldn't think twice about telling anyone about her father's new music.

"You shouldn't have made that call." Sam's face was bleak as he wrapped his arms around her again. "I'm going to kick your ass," he murmured into her hair. "Any minute now."

She put her arms around him and inhaled his scent, and some of the tension in his body eased. She'd wanted to talk to him Saturday night, when she'd tossed and turned in bed, edgy and scared.

She'd wanted to see him yesterday, while she paced the barn, unable to work.

Last night, she'd just wanted him.

They stood holding each other in the silence of the barn.

Outside, a robin sang, and the sun poured in through the window. His heart beat against her chest, steady and comforting. Reassuring.

When she finally stepped away, he slid his hand down her arm and clung to her for a moment. "So." She cleared her throat and stepped back. "How did the kids make out this morning?"

"Leo acted the way he usually does—like he's cool and it's no big deal. But he looked a little anxious. Rennie was clingy. The teachers and the principal were experts at dividing the herd and sending me into the 'out of the building' chute."

He didn't realize he'd identified the three of them as a herd. "New situations are always hard, but they've had to adapt to a lot of changes already. I'm sure they'll be fine." Delaney smiled brightly. "Now you probably want to get home so you can do some work."

She tried to lead him to the door, but he shook his head. "Forget it. I've already been handled once today." His voice became serious. "Any idea how to work the Chantal thing with Leo and Rennie?"

Delaney wanted a relationship with them. Could she have one if they knew who she was? "I suppose 'ignore it' isn't an option."

"Sure it is. We'll just have to be careful what we say around them."

She didn't want her relationship with Leo and Rennie to be based on a lie. "No, we need to tell them. I don't want to be another adult who lied to them."

"You want to be the anti-Heather?"

The Heather she remembered didn't deserve those kids. Was that what she wanted? To push Heather out of their lives? "I can't take their mother's place, but I can be an adult who is honest with them."

He leaned against the door frame. "Okay, but it doesn't have to happen yet. You can get to know them a little better before you drop that bomb."

She wanted to put it off as long as she could. But that was only cowardice on her part. "No, we should do it right away. Get it over with."

"Not yet."

"Why not?"

He shoved his hand through his hair again. "Heather might have talked about you. I have no idea how the kids will react."

"Badly, probably." She tried to sound matter-of-fact as her stomach twisted into a knot. Heather wouldn't have said anything positive about her. "It will hurt if they reject me. But it would be worse if I got close to them, and then they found out. They'd feel betrayed."

His jaw worked. "Damn it! How am I supposed to make that choice?"

"It's not up to you. It's my choice."

"I'm their uncle. I'm responsible for them. I should have some say in this."

Did he realize what he'd just said? Delaney had never heard him refer to himself as their uncle. "It will be really hard if they tell me they hate me. Or that they never want to see me again. But I can't spend any more time with them without telling them the truth." She knew what she had to do. "Bring them over here tonight. I'll make dinner for us, and we can tell them who I am."

"I shouldn't have brought them up here with me. I should have taken out a loan and put them in that school before I came looking for you."

"Unintended consequences are a bitch, aren't they?" She

knew all about them. She'd lived with the guilt for three years. "But I'm glad they're here. Glad I met them." Even if it ended up hurting in the long run.

CHAPTER SIXTEEN

"THIS IS GOOD, DELANEY," Rennie said as she chewed on a mouthful of pasta. "It doesn't taste anything like regular macadoodle."

Both kids had been astonished at the idea of macaroni and cheese that didn't come in a box. "Thanks, Rennie." Delaney pushed a pasta curl from one side of her plate to another and forced a smile. "I'm glad you could come over for dinner."

Telling the kids tonight was going to be so hard. But if she became a part of their lives, she didn't want it to be under false pretenses.

She felt Sam watching her, but instead of looking at him, she took a tiny bite of salad. He read her far too easily, and he'd use her reluctance to try and change her mind.

Rennie picked up the slice of cucumber from one of the little vegetable people Delaney had made, and announced, "I'm going to eat my person's head." She dunked it in the little dish of ranch dressing, then bit off a piece with delight.

"You don't eat the head first," Leo said scornfully. He grabbed a celery stick leg. "You have to torture them first."

Sam raised his eyebrows as the kids raced each other to eat the vegetables. He moved his arm a little so his hand was almost touching Delaney's, then brushed one finger over the back of hers. "You're a genius."

No, she wasn't. A genius would have kept Sam and the kids at a distance from the very beginning.

But Rennie had crept into her heart the moment she'd seen the girl, cold and wet and lost. Leo, with his tough shell and his bruised eyes, had broken her heart.

She wanted to be part of their lives, and this was the price she had to pay.

She moved her hand away from Sam's. "Why don't you all go into the living room while I clean up?" She forced a smile. "Anyone want some ice cream?"

Both Leo and Rennie were smiling as they carried bowls of chocolate chip ice cream into the living room. She watched until they disappeared, then began rinsing dishes and loading them into the dishwasher. Would they be smiling after she told them who she was? She doubted it.

As she was wiping the table, hoping to put off the painful revelation for as long as possible, Sam returned to the kitchen. He watched her for a moment, then took the dishrag out of her hand.

"Don't do this, Delaney. Don't tell them."

"I have to." She watched as he tossed the cloth into the sink.

"Why? Rennie adores you. Leo likes you, too, although he won't admit it." Sam took her hand. "I know you want to get to know them. Why jeopardize that before it's necessary? They may not figure out who you are right away—we might be back in Miami by then. You'll have hurt yourself for nothing."

A new wave of pain struck her. Regardless of whether or not she told Leo and Rennie who she was, they weren't going to be part of her life. She had a couple of months with them. That was all.

It was a good reminder that she shouldn't start to build dreams. That their time together would end, sooner rather than later.

"But when they do find out they'll feel betrayed. Hurt.

They'll hate me." A lot of people probably hated Chantal, but she didn't want to add Leo and Rennie to the list. If she told them now and they took it badly, she'd have time to help them past their anger.

She put her hand into her pocket and fingered the AA token. There was no reason to keep it a secret from Sam. He knew far worse about her. She pulled it out. "Do you know what this is?"

He read it, then put it back into her hand and closed her fist around it. "AA?"

"Yes. I have to apologize to the people I've hurt. I have to make it right. I hurt those kids when I had an affair with their father. Maybe saving them from more hurt is all I can do for them now. Maybe it won't make a difference, but I have to try." She slid the token back into her pocket.

"And when do you get to finish beating yourself up?"

His eyes were soft. Understanding. It was so tempting to allow herself to lean on him, to accept the easy way out he was offering. She took his hand. "I have to do this for me, too. Do I want to? Of course not. But I know...I know it has to be done."

He kissed her palm, then brushed his lips over the sensitive skin. "You're one of the bravest women I know. I want to spare you this."

Sam was still trying to protect her, and it made her heart yearn for him. "The other day in the barn, I...I let myself want you, Sam." She still wanted him. "I should tell all of you to stay away, but God help me, I can't." She twined her fingers with his and held on.

His eyes darkened as he watched her. "I want you, too, Delaney. And since I'm not going to keep the kids away from you, I guess I can't stop you from telling them."

"Smart man," she said, trying to smile.

He kissed her palm and sighed. "You win."

She clung to his hand as they walked into the living room, then let go as they sat on the couch. The warmth of his thigh and his shoulder, almost touching hers, eased some of the chill inside her.

"Hey, guys, turn off the television," Sam said. "We need to talk to you."

Leo complied, then turned to face them. The worry in his eyes made her hesitate. These kids had been through so much already.

As if sensing her hesitation, Sam raised an eyebrow.

No. She shook her head. It would be far worse if someone else told them who she was.

"Leo, Rennie, I have something to tell you." She drew in a shaky breath, and Sam squeezed her hand. She wasn't strong enough to let it go. "Leo, do you remember the people in your dad's band?"

Leo watched her warily. "Yeah, I know who was in the Redheads."

"Remember the drummer?"

"There were two—Bogeyman and Chantal." He furrowed his forehead, and it was easy to read his mind. Why was she asking him about the band? "Bogeyman was a cokehead. Chantal came on after he crashed."

It was heartbreaking that he knew those sad details. Worse, that he recited them so matter-of-factly. As if it was normal for people to crash and burn on drugs.

For him, she realized, it was. His mother had done it more than once. His father had died of an overdose. Delaney wanted to gather him close, to protect him from what she was about to say. But she knew that Leo wouldn't let her get that close.

"You're right, there were two drummers." She licked her lips. "I'm…I used to be Chantal." Her heart battered against her chest as she waited for their reaction.

Rennie only looked confused. She probably had no idea what Delaney was talking about.

Leo did. He scrambled to his feet, his face pale. His brown eyes, so like Diesel's, were wide. Accusing. "*You're* Chantal? You said your name was Delaney."

She clung to Sam's hand. "That's right. Delaney Spencer. Chantal was the name I used when I performed."

Leo looked at her closely. "Chantal had black-and-pink hair. She had a nose ring and lots of earrings. She had tattoos on her arms."

He knew all the details. Had he studied pictures of the band? Imagined his father alive again?

Sam edged closer. The reassuring pressure of his thigh against hers steadied her. "My hair was dyed." She touched her ears, her nose. "I took out the nose ring and the earrings. I had the tattoos removed."

Rennie scooted closer to her. "You knew my daddy?" Her eyes sparkled, as if she'd just been given a huge gift.

Delaney's throat swelled. "Yes, honey, I did. We were in his band together."

"Were you friends?"

She swallowed hard. "Yes, Rennie. We were good friends."

Leo tugged Rennie behind his back, and the message was clear—*stay away from her.* "My mom doesn't like you. She and my dad yelled about you a lot." Leo's mouth was tight and his eyes were angry.

Rennie probably didn't remember her father, but Leo did. He would have been around during Diesel and Heather's arguments.

So much pain Delaney had caused. So much anguish. "I'm sorry you had to hear that," she said. She wanted to hug Leo, but she forced herself to remain still. "That must have been scary."

"My mom wouldn't want us to be here." He looked around wildly, as if desperate to escape. "Why did you bring us here, Sam?"

"Because Delaney is afraid that everyone will find out that she was Chantal," he said evenly. Calmly. "There might be reporters hanging around town. You're going to hear stuff. Delaney wanted to tell you herself."

"Did she think we wouldn't *care?*" He pulled Rennie toward the door. "That we would be, like, so what?" When Rennie resisted, he let her go and fixed his grief-stricken gaze on Delaney. "You're a bitch, and we hate you!"

"Leo!" Sam jumped to his feet, but Delaney tugged him back onto the couch.

"Leo, I have some CDs that your father and I made. No one's ever heard them, but Sam is going to make sure they're released. People will be talking about your father. And me. I wanted you to know who I was."

"I don't care about any frickin' CDs," he shouted. "I want to go home. This is a stupid town. With stupid people." He swiped his arm across his eyes, then threw open the closet door. He yanked his coat so hard that the hanger clattered to the floor, then fled out the front door and disappeared into the evening darkness.

The three of them stared after him, frozen in silence. Then Sam jumped up. "I have to get him."

He glanced at Rennie, and Delaney nodded. "Leave her here."

After Sam left, Rennie came closer and looked up at Delaney. "I don't hate you, Delaney."

"I'm glad, Rennie."

The little girl put her small hands on Delaney's face and held it, as if she was studying her. "Why is Leo mad?"

"I think he misses your dad. And your mom." Delaney hesitantly put her hand over Rennie's for a moment. When the girl didn't flinch, she patted the cushion. "Want to sit with me?"

Rennie scrambled up, then snuggled next to her. "Leo wanted to live with Daddy, not Mommy. But Daddy died. Now we have to live with Uncle Sam." She leaned against Delaney's side, and Delaney put a tentative arm around her. The scents of baby shampoo and vanilla ice cream drifted over her.

And Diesel had wanted them, as well. No matter what else he'd done, he'd loved his children with a single-minded ferocity. "Do you remember your daddy, Rennie?"

She shook her head. "Leo showed me pictures. He had hair like me."

"He did. But I think yours is prettier." Her hand hovered over Rennie's head, then she tucked a curl behind the girl's ear. "Your daddy was a wonderful man," she said softly. "And he loved you very much."

"Can you tell me a story about him?"

CLOUDS SCUDDED ACROSS the moon, leaving the woods dark and mysterious. Quiet. There was no trace of Leo on the path ahead. Was he hiding behind a tree? Beneath a bush? He could be anywhere.

Fear spurred Sam into the rental house. "Leo? Are you here?"

Nothing. He must still be outside.

Sam searched frantically through a kitchen drawer for a flashlight. He'd yanked open the second drawer when he heard a sniffle. Thank God.

"Leo?" He hurried out of the kitchen. His nephew's door was closed. "Leo, may I come in?"

Silence.

"Please, Leo? I'd like to talk to you."

The door opened and Leo stood blocking the way. "Are you gonna tell me I have to be nice to Delaney?"

That's what he'd intended to say. "No."

"Okay. You can come in."

The boy threw himself onto his bed. Sam saw wet spots on the dark green comforter near the pillow. He'd been crying. Sam started to reach for him, then backed off when his nephew stiffened. He sat on the floor instead.

After more muffled sniffling, Leo said, "How can she be our friend? She did drugs with my dad." He lifted his face, red and blotchy and swollen, and Sam's heart ached. "That's how my dad died. From drugs."

Oh, God. He wasn't ready for this conversation. He had no idea what he was supposed to say, so he opted for the truth. "Yes, your dad did drugs. Delaney did, too. She and your dad both made big mistakes."

Leo's lip quivered. "*She* should have died. Not my dad."

Sam wanted to wrap him in his arms. "No one should have died."

The boy swiped the back of his hand across his nose. "Does Delaney still do coke?"

Oh, Leo. Sam edged closer to the bed. His nephew must have been reading about his father on the Web. Why had Heather allowed that? She was supposed to protect him from the ugliness that had surrounded Diesel, at least until he was old enough to understand.

"Delaney doesn't use drugs. Or drink alcohol. After your dad died, she changed herself. Made herself better."

"Like Mom's doing?"

"Yes. I think she went into a hospital, just like your mom." That was the only thing the two women had in common.

Besides Diesel.

No. Sam refused to think about Delaney and Diesel.

Leo curled into a ball on the bed and buried his face in his legs. "You like Delaney, don't you?"

"Yes, I do," he answered cautiously.

"The way my mom likes her boyfriends?"

In for a penny, in for a pound. "Yes, Leo. I like her that way, too."

He lifted his head and eyed Sam warily. "Is she gonna move in here with us?"

"No." Did Heather's boyfriends move in with them? "She has her own house."

His lip trembled again. "Mom's going to be mad at me. She's going to say I should have kept Rennie away from Delaney."

Sam's anger surged again. "It's not your job to take care of Rennie, Leo. That's my job. I promise your mother won't be mad at you."

He put his head down. "Are we going to stay with you after Mom gets out of the hospital?"

"I don't know, Leo. We'll figure that out later."

Leo picked at a thread on the comforter. "Mom's scary sometimes."

The boy's voice was muffled, but Sam had no trouble hearing the guilt and anguish. No ten-year-old should have to admit that.

"Your mom will be different when she gets out of the hospital." *You damn well better be, Heather, or I'm taking these kids away from you.*

"You think so?"

Sam sat on the bed and pulled Leo into his arms. "I promise you'll be safe, and so will Rennie. I'll make sure of it."

The boy was stiff as a rod. "How can you do that if you're up here?"

"I'll be in Miami with you."

"Is Delaney moving there, too?"

"No." There was a weight crushing his chest. "Delaney lives up here. Maybe she can visit, though."

"You said you liked her."

"I do, Leo. But you and Rennie are more important." Was that true? Would he be able to walk away from her?

"Yeah?"

"Yes," he said firmly. "You and Rennie are more important than anything." They had to be, right now. But maybe once he got them enrolled in the school, he could focus on Delaney.

Leo sighed and relaxed as the house creaked and the wind blew through the trees outside. After a long time, he slid off the bed and wiped the back of his hand across his face. "Can I watch TV? *The Simpsons* are gonna be on in a few minutes."

"Sure." Sam stood up. "I love *The Simpsons*," he said lightly. "I'll watch it with you tomorrow. Right now, I'm going back to Delaney's to get Rennie. Lock the door behind me, okay?"

"Duh." Leo rolled his eyes.

Ten minutes later, Sam peered in the front door of Delaney's house. She was still on the couch, Rennie in her lap, blonde head resting against the red one. He wanted to scoop both of them into his arms.

When he eased the door open, Delaney sat up. "Sam."

One word. Amazing how just the sound of his name could get his pulse racing and his heart pounding. He brushed his fingers over her cheek, then lifted Rennie off her lap and settled the sleeping child on the couch. He tucked an afghan over her, then led Delaney into the kitchen.

"How are you doing?" he asked.

She smiled, but her mouth trembled a little. "Rennie said she doesn't hate me."

"Leo doesn't, either. He was just shocked."

"Of course he was." She looked out the window. "I caused so much pain."

"Delaney…" he began, but she interrupted.

"How is he?"

"He's upset. He told me Heather scared him." Anger flared.

Delaney took his hand in hers and pried open the fist he hadn't realized he'd made. "What did you tell him?"

"I said I had no idea what was going to happen, but I said I'd keep him safe. And I will."

"I know you will," she whispered. She wound her arms around his neck. "You're very good at keeping your promises."

No, he wasn't. He'd failed Diesel when his brother had needed him most. "I have no idea what to do."

"You'll figure it out." She nuzzled his neck. "You're good at that, too."

The scent of fresh cut wood and Delaney's hair swirled around him. Her breath ruffled the hair on his neck, and her hands played with his hair. Her body was stretched against his, her breasts pressing into his chest, thighs against thighs. He forgot all about Leo and Rennie. "There are other things I'm good at," he murmured as he tightened his hold on her.

She moved her head away from his neck. Her incredible eyes were languorous. Heavy-lidded with desire. "I'll bet there are." She unwound her arms from him and eased back. "I'll be thinking about them."

"God, Delaney." He wanted to snatch her back. "What's that supposed to mean?"

"Give it some thought," she said as she headed toward the living room. "Right now, let's get Rennie into my truck so I can drive you home."

CHAPTER SEVENTEEN

WEAK EARLY MORNING sunshine poured into her kitchen window as Delaney leaned against the counter in her pajamas and waited for her coffee to brew. She'd barely managed to brush her teeth before stumbling to the coffeemaker. Her mind was foggy and her body was restless and edgy.

She'd lain away for hours, wondering if she'd done the right thing by telling the kids. Leo had been so upset. *I hate you, bitch.*

She understood his reaction. But how much worse would it have been if she hadn't told them? How much worse if he found out later that she was Chantal? She couldn't let him be blindsided like that.

She'd done the right thing. But it had been hard.

Leo wasn't the only thing she'd thought about last night.

Remembering what else she'd done, she closed her eyes. When Sam had returned for Rennie, he'd woken her up. Caught her off guard, and she'd been honest with him. Implied that she wanted to sleep with him.

Heck, there had been no implying. She'd told him flat out.

Was it smart? No.

But he'd reminded her that he and the kids would be leaving soon. He'd go back to Florida, and she wouldn't see him again.

So she'd thrown caution to the winds.

It was time to take a chance. Time to reach out to someone.

To Sam.

Last night, she'd imagined him in the bed with her. Kissing her. Touching her.

Groaning with frustration, she poured the first cup of coffee and opened her laptop to find out what had happened in the world overnight. It was easier than wondering what was happening in the house on the other side of the woods.

As she read about a presidential summit, she heard car tires crunching on the gravel driveway. When she looked out the window, Sam was halfway to her front door. All her yearning from the night before came rushing back. Her heart pounded as she raced into her bedroom to dress.

Before she could get the pajama top over her head, he was knocking at the door. Struggling back into it, she threw on her robe and ran to let him in.

"Sam." She was ridiculously out of breath for someone who'd run only a few yards. "What are you doing here so early?"

He shut the door, closing out the world. "The kids are in school. And you expected me."

Yes.

He moved closer. "I wondered all night—did you think about it, Delaney?"

"About what?" Her body quivered, and she took a step toward him. She knew exactly what he was asking her.

"About what I might be good at." He kept his gaze on her. "Besides keeping promises."

She gripped the tie on her robe, not sure if she was going to pull it tighter or tug it open. "I had a few thoughts. How about you?"

"I came up with a couple ideas. Maybe we should compare notes."

His eyes were dark silver, lit by an inner flame. His jaw was tight. His whole body hummed with tension, mirroring her own.

Her fingers fumbled as she tugged at the knotted belt on her robe. "Mine didn't involve my pajamas and bathrobe."

"God, I hope not." He gripped her upper arms and pulled her close. She wondered if he could feel her trembling. "Are you going to let me see what's under that robe?"

"You're going to be disappointed." Why hadn't she worn something sexy? Or nothing at all. She'd known he wouldn't be able to resist her challenge.

"I doubt that." He turned her around so her back was against the door. The tile on the floor was cold on her bare feet, but she barely noticed as he pulled the belt off. Her robe fell open, and she struggled not to wrap it around herself again. The first man she'd wanted in years, and she was wearing flannel pajamas.

"Ducks, Delaney?" He smiled, but his hand wasn't quite steady as he traced one of the cartoon animals above her heart. "Sexy, wild Chantal wears flannel pajamas with ducks? I think I'm in love."

Her breath caught in her throat at the *l* word. He was teasing. It didn't mean anything. But she closed her eyes and wanted it to be true.

His hand drifted lower, and she looked at his long fingers on the light blue fabric. He had big hands, but they moved over her gently, as if she was fragile. Breakable. "I didn't mean for you to see them. I didn't want to spoil your fantasies."

"Fantasies?" His fingers tightened on her hips. "Not a problem. Trust me, honey. In my fantasies, you're not wearing anything."

His hands gentled, then cupped her rear end as he brushed his mouth over hers. Lightly, as if they had all day. When he lifted his head, she made a little noise in the back of her throat and leaned into him. "Kiss me, Sam. Please."

He groaned and threaded his fingers through her hair, holding her in place. His kiss was that of a man pushed to the limits. Tasting. Sucking. Demanding a response.

She opened her mouth, needing more. When his tongue caressed hers, she curled one leg around his and tried to get closer. The flannel of her pajamas, the cotton of his sweater, the denim of his jeans were all too thick. She wanted her skin against his, wanted to feel the heat and the hardness and the need.

One of his hands cupped her breast, and she arched into him. When he touched her nipple, she shuddered. "More," she whispered.

His fingers were clumsy as he undid her shirt. The last button skidded across the floor as he pulled it open. He swirled his tongue around one nipple, then took it into his mouth and suckled.

Her heart thudded in her chest, pounding so hard she knew he could feel it. Feel how much she wanted him. Desire rose like a tide, sweeping away everything else besides Sam. His scent, so familiar now, surrounded her. His body, which she'd longed to touch, was hers for the taking.

While he tasted her, she tried to pull off his shirt. But his jacket was in the way. Frustrated, she yanked the soft cotton out of his jeans and tunneled her hands beneath it. His chest was lean and hard, all ridges and planes. There was no softness to him, nothing easy. But as she explored him, he quivered.

Moving lower, she danced her fingers over the hard length of his erection, then cupped him in her palm. When his mouth stilled on her breast and he jerked against her, she reached for the button at the waist of his jeans.

She tugged on the zipper and freed him. But as her fingers

curled around him, he captured her hands and put her arms around his neck.

"No." He bit gently on her lip, then soothed it with his tongue. "Not this time. If you play, I'll embarrass myself."

He shoved the robe and pajama top to the floor. His eyes darkened even more as he looked at her, touched her. "You're beautiful. And I want you so badly, I'm shaking." He moved his hand to her belly.

"I want you, too, Sam." She stepped away from him and took his hand, leading him into her bedroom. She hadn't made the bed yet, her clothes from the night before were thrown over a chair, but she didn't care. Nothing mattered but Sam.

She pushed the jacket from his shoulders, and he yanked the T-shirt over his head. A sprinkling of dark hair dusted his chest and arrowed down his belly. Leaning in, she licked one of his flat nipples. It hardened beneath her tongue.

As she reached for his jeans, he tugged them off, leaving only midnight-blue boxers. But when she wanted to pull them down, he took her hands and eased her down onto the bed. "Not yet. You first."

He slid the pajamas down her legs, kissing the insides of her thighs, her knees, her calves. When he finally tossed the pj's onto the floor, she tried to pull him on top of her.

"I don't think so," he said. Stretched out next to her, he tangled his fingers in the dark blonde hair at the juncture of her thighs. She arched into his palm. "I've thought about this for too long. It's not going to be over that quickly."

He started at her feet and kissed his way up her legs, lingering at the crease of her thigh. Mindless with need, she squirmed against him, and she felt him smile. "Tell me what you want, Delaney," he murmured.

"You, Sam. I want you. Around me. Inside me. Part of me."

She tried to tug him up to her, but he resisted, pressing his mouth between her legs. She heard herself cry out as he licked and tasted. When he sucked gently, her climax exploded through her.

He held her hips as tremors shook her, one after another. Finally, he let her go, shucked his boxers and leaned over to grab a packet out of his jeans.

"Let me." She tried to take it from him.

"Not this time." He kissed her as he slid the condom on, then pushed into her. "Delaney," he whispered as he began to move.

She wrapped her legs around him, loving the weight of him, his sweat-slicked skin, the hardness of his muscles.

The scent of their lovemaking surrounded them, and she drank it in. He intoxicated her. His face was buried in her neck, and she found his mouth and kissed him as the tension built again.

Her climax rushed through her, and she sobbed his name as she came. He followed her there, shuddering above her. Finally the tremors slowed, then stopped. After a few moments, Sam eased to the side and gathered her close. Arms and legs tangled together, they let their breathing return to normal. But he didn't let go of her.

And she didn't let go of him.

SOMEONE WAS STROKING HER back.

Slow caresses, neck to hip, then back again. She stirred, cuddling closer, and arms tightened around her.

Sam.

She opened her eyes to see him smiling down at her. "Welcome back."

Stretching, she let her nipples brush his chest. Saw his eyes darken. Felt his erection move against her belly.

Desire rushed through her again, as if they hadn't just

made love. "There was talk of next time," she murmured, pressing her mouth to his skin.

"And I always keep my promises," he answered, biting lightly on her earlobe.

"I'm counting on it."

He trailed his mouth over her cheek and nibbled at her lips. She let her mouth linger on his for a long moment, then she moved down to his chest. Then lower.

His hands tightened on her arms. "Delaney."

"Hmm?" She touched her tongue to him, smiled when he sucked in a breath. "It's my turn to play."

Hours later, she was sprawled, boneless, on top of him. Her head on his chest, she listened to the rhythmic thumping of his heart. Steady. Sure. Strong.

Sunlight poured in her window, splashing warmth on the bed. She barely noticed. Sam warmed her completely, from the inside out.

His hands tightened on her, then he opened his eyes and lifted his head. "You have to make some furniture, don't you?"

Back to the real world. "Yes." At dinner the night before, she'd mentioned she was falling behind on her orders. "And you have to write a book."

"I'm afraid so." He sat up and pulled her against his side. "Can we have dinner again with the kids tonight?"

Back to the real world with a vengeance. She eased away. "I'm not sure that's a good idea. Leo isn't going to want to see me."

Sam leaned his head against the spindles. "Yeah, I know. I just want to spend time with you."

She did, too, because they didn't have a lot of time. Sam would be gone soon. He'd gotten what he came for, and the kids belonged in Miami. With their mother.

They had days. A week or two at the most.

She didn't want to waste a minute.

He trailed his hand up and down her arm, absently caressing her. "I love your arms," he murmured. "So strong. Sleek. Sexy." He bent to kiss her biceps, then paused. His breath made her skin prickle.

"I can see a faint image on your arm." He traced the swirling drum set with one finger. "Like a ghost."

"They can't remove tattoos completely." Sam was the only one who'd gotten close enough to see the ghosts.

He pressed his mouth to the inside of her elbow, and she shivered. "I don't want to leave," he said.

She didn't want him to leave, either. She nuzzled his chest, then slid out of bed before she could kiss him again. Once her mouth touched his, neither of them would get any work done. "There's always tomorrow. And the next day. I'm up early in the morning," she said as she headed for the shower. "You are, too."

He'd followed her, and he nipped her shoulder. "Is that an invitation?"

She reached behind and squeezed him as she stepped into the hot water. "Damn right it is."

ON THURSDAY MORNING, Sam waved goodbye to Leo and Rennie, watched until they entered the school, then headed for Delaney's house. His heart was drumming in his chest before he spotted the entrance to her driveway. By the time he stopped the Jeep and got out, he was uncomfortably aroused. Delaney had the front door open as soon as he reached the porch, and when he saw her in the dark blue bathrobe, he could barely walk.

He couldn't wait to get to her house in the morning. This was the third day she'd met him at the door, in her robe. Yesterday, instead of her flannel pajamas, she'd worn nothing beneath it.

She drew him inside now and he kicked the door shut, enveloping her in his arms, desperate to taste her. She molded herself to him, hooking one leg behind his, as if she wanted to crawl inside of him.

Voices came from the kitchen. A radio, maybe. Ignoring it, he tried to tug her robe open. "I have to know."

She pulled the robe tighter with a wicked smile on her face. "What's it worth to you?"

"Anything." He tightened his hands on her waist, imagining what he would find. "Name your price."

"I think I like this game." She ran her foot up and down his leg, and his knees went weak. Her smoky, sensual voice made his heart flutter, and turned him to stone. He'd been astonished by the playful, sensuous, tender woman hiding beneath her tough exterior.

He was besotted. Crazed with need for her. The hours after he dropped Leo and Rennie off at school had become the focal point of his life.

"You can have whatever you want," he said, "but later." He eased the lapels apart and sucked in a breath. Red silk. A sheer, filmy teddy. Matching tap pants that fluttered around her thighs. "Much later."

Laughing, she dashed into her bedroom, the robe floating behind her. Like a sailor spellbound by a siren, he followed.

Later, he lay beside her, panting. Something soft fluttered onto his face. It held her scent, and he inhaled deeply.

Her giggle made him open his eyes. All he saw was red.

She drew the tap pants away from his face. "They must have landed on top of the headboard." She tossed them to the floor, then snuggled into his side. "Let's talk about my price."

He turned to face her. The radio was still on in the kitchen, and as he bent to kiss her, she stiffened. She grabbed his hand, and he felt her tremble.

"What?"

"Shhh. Listen."

As he focused on the radio, he heard, "…Chantal… Wisconsin."

Everything inside him turned to ice. They knew where she was. He held her more tightly and felt her slipping away.

CHAPTER EIGHTEEN

SHE JERKED UPRIGHT, clutching the sheet to her chest. "How did they find out? Who did you tell?"

"How do you know it was me?" He reached for her, but she scrambled out of the bed.

"Who else could it be? No one else knows. You must have told someone."

He stepped out of bed and pulled on his pants. "Maybe I did mention Wisconsin to Heather without realizing it."

"Heather." Delaney fumbled for her clothes, then threw them on. She needed a shield. "And Heather told the world."

"I'm sorry, Delaney." He started toward her, and she backed out of the bedroom.

"I agreed to give you the demos. All I wanted was my privacy. But you took that, too."

"Not on purpose."

"No?" She remembered their conversation in her barn the other day. "When you came over after you enrolled Leo and Rennie in school, you knew, didn't you? You knew Heather had told someone."

"I suspected. But I hoped it wouldn't go any further."

"You could have been honest with me. Let me prepare myself. But you didn't." His betrayal cut deep. "You wanted this to come out. It's going to boost the sales of the new CD."

He paled. "You can't believe I was that devious."

"You write thrillers, Sam. With convoluted plots. It sounds exactly like something a writer would come up with."

"It was a mistake, Delaney. A slip of the tongue. I didn't tell Heather where we were in Wisconsin."

Her hand trembled as she threw the door open. "The sex was great. Thanks for that. Now get out."

"Delaney…"

When he reached for her, she shoved him backward out the door. He stumbled on the first step, and she slammed and locked the door.

THEY DIDN'T KNOW ABOUT Otter Tail.

A few hours after hearing that story on the radio, Delaney set the piece of sandpaper on her workbench. They'd look for Chantal in the big cities first. Milwaukee. Madison.

Why would they think she'd be in a tiny place like Otter Tail?

But the voice on the radio announcing that Chantal's location had been narrowed down had crushed her illusion of safety.

Sam had been responsible for that. So much for the stupid fantasy she'd been living for the last few days. This hadn't been about some laughable dream of happily ever after for her and Sam and the kids.

It had been about the money, pure and simple. The money Sam needed to throw Leo and Rennie into a boarding school and forget about them.

Sam and the kids were in the past. Later, she'd focus on the pain of losing her last connections to Diesel. Of letting herself fall for Sam. Right now, she had to plan, because sooner or later, the reporters would find her. It was only a matter of time.

She had to tell Jen and Maddie. She pressed a hand to her churning stomach. She'd thought she could get away without saying anything to them. It would be months before the CD would be released. And why would anyone in Otter Tail connect it with her?

But everything had changed now.

Before she lost her nerve, she picked up the phone, dialed Jen and arranged to meet her and Maddie at the Harp. It wasn't open for lunch, but the three of them got together there once in a while, fixing themselves sandwiches and catching up.

She wouldn't be eating anything today.

As she was walking out the door, her phone rang.

Sam.

She turned the phone off and shoved it into her bag. Tried not to think about him as she got into her truck and headed toward town.

As she drove into Otter Tail, she watched carefully for a sign the press had tracked her down—vans with television cameras on top, RVs full of antennas, crowds of people on the sidewalks. There was nothing.

She saw Jen's and Maddie's cars in the parking lot as she pulled in. Thank goodness. Small talk would be impossible today.

The pub was dim and cool. Her friends were sitting at a table in the middle of the room, talking. Quinn was working on his laptop at a table next to the front window.

"Hey, guys," Delaney said, hesitating at the door. Why had she wanted to do this in person?

She was ashamed at her cowardice when Jen jumped up and hugged her. Maddie started to rise, as well, but Delaney pushed her back into the chair. "Pregnant women don't stand up," she said, bending to hug her friend.

She got herself a soda from behind the bar, then pulled out the chair between Jen and Maddie. She'd barely sat down when Maddie leaned forward. "Okay, Del, prepare to be grilled. We want all the details about the hunky guy with the two kids who was here last week."

Oh, God. Of course they'd want to know about Sam. "I don't—"

"Don't bother trying to say you don't know what she's talking about," Jen warned. "Maddie said the two of you watched each other all night."

If only this could be as simple as a hot guy at the pub. Delaney's hand tightened around the cold glass, and a little lemon-lime soda spilled when she picked it up.

"I'll tell you about him, but there's something else I need to tell you first." In spite of the soda, her mouth was dry. "There are going to be reporters in Otter Tail soon. Looking for me."

"Yeah?" Maddie's eyes twinkled. "How come? Did you win the lottery?"

"No!" She closed her eyes for a moment. "God, Maddie, this isn't a joke."

Her friend's smile disappeared, and she leaned forward. So did Jen. "What's wrong?" Maddie asked.

This was so hard. Delaney's heart thudded painfully, and her hand cramped on the glass. She set it down and tucked her fingers beneath her thighs to keep them from trembling. "I used to be…famous." Notorious, really. They'd realize that soon enough. "I was running away when I came to Otter Tail. But they're going to find me."

"Famous? Running away?" Jen stared at her as if she was looking at a stranger, and Delaney shriveled a little. "Who are you, Delaney?"

Delaney Spencer. Your friend. "I used to be in a band called the Redheaded Stepsisters. I was the drummer." She swallowed. "My name was Chantal."

Jen's eyes widened. "Oh, my God." She sucked in a breath. "I listened to your music. I loved Diesel. I…"

Her expression became more guarded. Clearly, she'd remembered the gossip.

"Yes. That Chantal. And just to get it all on the table, the gossip was true. I had an affair with Diesel. He died in my bed."

A horn blared in the distance, and close by, a car door slammed. No one in the pub spoke. Delaney felt Quinn watching, but he didn't say anything. Neither did Jen or Maddie. She had the sensation that all three were drawing away from her. Distancing themselves.

"Wow," Maddie finally said. "That's a pretty big secret." She leaned back in her chair and rubbed her huge belly.

Delaney's throat tightened. "I should have told you a long time ago. I just...I was ashamed. Afraid to let anyone find out."

No one rushed to assure her she had nothing to be ashamed about.

"There's more," she said, her foot jiggling on the floor. *Say something. Don't stare at me like I'm a freak show.* "The two kids who were here last week? Those are Diesel's kids. Leo and Rennie. And Sam? He's Diesel's brother."

"Holy Mother of God!" Jen stared at her, her expression horrified. "You're involved with Diesel's *family?*"

She had to get out of here. She shoved away from the table. "I'll tell you everything. Just not right now, okay?" Not while she felt like an exposed nerve. She grabbed her purse and headed for the door.

"Wait, Delaney," Maddie called after her, but she pushed the door open and fled into the sunshine.

Her hand shook as she tried to unlock her truck. The key slipped and gouged the paint, but she got it open. Eyes blurring, chest aching, she pulled into the street. She didn't look at Jen, who'd run into the parking lot.

It would be a long time before she forgot Jen's horrified

expression. Or the way Maddie had leaned away from her, as if Delaney had some contagious disease.

What had she expected? Her friends had shared the most intimate parts of their lives with her: Maddie had told her about her teen-aged humiliation, and Jen had confided what she'd done in high school—but Delaney had kept her own secret. She hadn't trusted them, the way friends trusted one another.

She had no right to expect their unquestioning support.

She was halfway through town when she saw the first van with a camera mounted on the roof. By the time she reached the highway, she'd seen another one.

No. Not yet. I need more time.

She gripped the steering wheel tightly as she watched them in the rearview mirror. It was too soon. They weren't supposed to be here yet.

Suddenly a horn blared and she jerked her attention back to the road. She'd begun to drift over the center line, and an RV was lumbering toward her.

Heart pounding, she wrenched the steering wheel to the right and rolled onto the shoulder as it passed her. What was she going to do? She hadn't even stocked up on groceries yet.

Make a plan. The Piggly Wiggly was just ahead. She'd stop there before she went home.

When she walked in, one of the clerks waved. "Hey, Delaney. How's it going?"

"Good, Shelley." She grabbed a cart and started down the aisles. Would Shelley be as friendly once she knew who Delaney really was? Feeling sick, she stared blindly at all the food, seeing only Jen's and Maddie's faces.

She had to get home. Where she'd be safe. She began throwing things into the basket. Bread. Coffee. Tea. Pasta.

Canned tomatoes. Frozen pizzas. Any fruit or vegetables that looked fresh.

As she passed the liquor section, she slowed. She dug her hand into the pocket of her jeans and fingered her token. *Move. Get out of here.*

Instead, she stopped in front of the vodka display. Her fingers touched the etched glass on a bottle of Grey Goose. Liquid courage.

She dropped the bottle into the cart. It fell on top of the bread, crushing it.

She made stilted small talk with Shelley as she paid for her groceries, then rushed out of the store. Throwing the bags into the front seat of the truck, she raced home.

Putting the groceries away gave her a job to focus on. Steadied her. But when that was done, she stared out the window, wondering how long it would take for the reporters to show up.

SHE WAS SANDING THE spindles for the headboard, the vodka bottle on her workbench, when she heard the rumbling of a large truck in the driveway. She peered out the window and saw an RV squatting in her driveway, the engine idling. The same RV that had passed her on the road. A woman jumped out of the passenger side and walked up to the house.

Delaney shrank back into the shadows. Her hands trembled as she made sure the door to the barn was locked. Then she reached into her pocket for her phone.

"Sheriff's office," a female voice said.

"I need to speak with one of the deputies." Delaney edged closer to the window. The RV was still there. The woman was walking down her front steps and heading toward the barn. Delaney darted into the workshop.

"This is Deputy Salerno," a male voice said. "How can I help you?"

"Deputy, this is Delaney Spencer." She tried to keep her voice low. "I live on County M. My RFD number is 806. There's an RV in my driveway. Trespassing. Could you send someone out here to get rid of them?"

"Did you ask them to leave?"

"No." She gripped the phone more tightly. "They're looking for me, and I don't want them to see me."

"I beg your pardon?"

"They're reporters," she whispered as the woman knocked on the barn door. "I don't want to talk to them."

"Tell them to leave, then." The deputy sounded impatient.

She closed her eyes to steady herself and keep from yelling at him. "That would defeat the purpose, since I don't want them to see me. Please. I need your help."

"Wait a minute," Salerno said. "You're Delaney Spencer? The woman who plays in the band at the Harp?"

"Yes, that's me."

"And you have reporters looking for you?" His voice sharpened.

"Yes." She knew what was coming next.

"Are you her? Chantal?" The tone of his voice changed. It went from bored bureaucrat to salacious male. If she could see the guy, she was sure he would be leering.

He was only the first. There would be more.

"Does that matter? I don't want to deal with these reporters."

"You used to like publicity."

"Not anymore." She closed her phone before he could answer.

Moments later, it rang. The sheriff's office. She pressed the button to disconnect the call. When she did, she saw that she'd missed several calls. She turned off the phone.

It took only ten minutes for a deputy to arrive. She heard

him talking to the people in the RV, his voice rising. Eventually, the huge vehicle backed down her driveway.

"Ms. Spencer?" He rapped on the barn door. "This is Deputy Salerno. Are you all right?"

"I'm fine, Deputy. Thank you."

"I need to see you to make sure."

No, he didn't. He just wanted to catch a glimpse of Chantal. "I'm fine," she repeated. "Please keep them off my property."

"You need to open the door, Ms. Spencer."

"I know damn well I don't have to open the door," she yelled. "Now get out of here."

There was silence for a moment, then he muttered something in a low voice that sounded like "bitch." Finally, she heard his footsteps walking away. She hurried to the window and saw his car disappearing down her driveway. When she was sure he hadn't turned around and come back, she grabbed the bottle of vodka from her workbench and headed toward her house.

She had no idea how long she'd been sitting at the kitchen table, staring at the vodka and her AA token, when someone knocked on the front door. "It's Sam. Let me in, Delaney."

She looked down the hall and saw him staring in the window. Something moved in the undergrowth in front of her house. The reporter who'd been outside her barn? She yanked open the door, dragged Sam inside, then slammed it behind him.

"What do you want?" she demanded.

"To apologize. See if there's anything I can do."

Reporters wouldn't have been staking out her house if Sam hadn't come to Otter Tail. "You've done more than enough."

You were only half-alive before he showed up. She pushed

the thought away. "You need to leave, Sam. Someone already saw you here."

"No, they haven't. I drove over, but kept going when I saw the circus out front. I went back home and cut through the woods."

The reporter who'd been in front of her house had seen him. Once Sam was identified, it would be a short step to Leo and Rennie.

The tabloids would have a field day with Diesel's lover, his children and his brother.

The vodka was on the kitchen table. Oblivion was beckoning, and it was hard to resist.

"Was it always like this?" He took a step toward her, stopping when she backed away.

"More or less." She'd always hated the invasion of privacy. But back then, alcohol had helped to blur her vision.

"How did you handle it?"

"I drank. And when they caught me, I'd give them their sound bites, their photo ops, and try to ignore them."

"Was it worth it?"

"I thought it was." She noted the regret in his expression, and felt it echo inside her. Sam could never be part of her life. Neither would Leo and Rennie. "I'll let you out the back door," she said. "There's more cover there."

He glanced out the window, then shoved his hands in his pockets. "I know you blame me for this. I want to make it better."

"How would you being caught here with me make it better, Sam? They'll find out you're Diesel's brother—Leo and Rennie's guardian. You all need to stay away."

"I'm responsible for this. And you want me to just walk away?"

"Yes. It would be easier for all of us if you did."

He shook his head and pushed himself from the wall. "It's dark in here. And cold. I'll make you some tea."

"I don't want any tea," she said, but it was too late. He'd stopped in the door to the kitchen. The vodka bottle was sitting on the table.

"Aw, hell, Delaney. What did you do?"

"Nothing. Not yet." She stepped past him, picked up the bottle and shoved it into a cupboard. She grabbed the AA token and replaced it in her pocket, but not before he'd seen that, too.

He dropped onto one of the chairs and pulled her into his lap. For a moment, she let herself savor his warmth, his strength, the now-familiar contours of his chest. Then she eased away from him.

"You need to go, Sam."

"And leave you alone with the bottle?"

"Yes. This is my deal. Not yours. I have to work it out myself."

"I can stay here and distract you."

"I don't want you here." She didn't want anyone to witness her struggle. Especially not Sam. She'd trusted him and he'd let her down.

He stared at the cabinet where she'd put the bottle, then shoved his hands into his pockets. "This is hard for me."

"Is it?"

"Delaney, I…"

"Go," she said, pushing him toward the door. Before she broke down and asked him to stay.

She watched until he disappeared from sight. Then she opened the cabinet door, removed the vodka and headed out to the barn.

CHAPTER NINETEEN

DELANEY TOOK A DEEP breath as she waited for her sponsor, Caroline, to answer her phone. Finally, she picked up and said, "Delaney? Are you okay?"

"No, I'm not." Delaney swallowed. "I bought a bottle of vodka today."

"Did you drink it?" Caroline's voice was steady. Nonaccusing.

"No." The bottle beckoned her from a desk in the showroom.

"Why did you buy it?" Caroline asked.

"Because everything's falling apart," she answered softly. "I told my friends who I am, and they looked at me like I was a stranger. Reporters showed up in my town." *I've gotten involved with a man I can't have.*

An hour later, Caroline asked, "Are you ready to put Diesel in the past, where he belongs?"

"He is in the past," Delaney answered.

"Is he?" Caroline's voice was gentle. Sympathetic. "You made music with Diesel. Evaded reporters with him. You drank and did drugs with him. Are you that surprised that when the music and the reporters resurfaced, the drinking did, as well?"

"I didn't think of it like that," Delaney said slowly.

"There's a new man in your life, and he's connected to Diesel. Do you want to go forward, Delaney? Or back?"

"Forward," she said, closing her eyes.

"Then do it. You're a strong woman. You can handle it." Her voice softened. "You've been clean for almost three years. Put Diesel where he belongs."

Delaney closed the phone, turned it off and set it on the desk, next to the bottle. After a few minutes, she put one of the demo CDs on the stereo, then took the guitar from the bottom shelf of the cabinet. She lowered herself to the floor, then settled the bulky leather case on her lap. There were a lot of memories inside, both good and bad.

Tears dripped down her face as she listened to Diesel's voice and stroked the pebbled leather. *I have to let you go, Diesel. I'm sorry I couldn't save you. Sorry the music wasn't enough.*

Swiping her sleeve over her face, she opened the case. She'd give the guitar to Leo. It had belonged to his father, and Diesel would have wanted his son to have it.

Other than the demos, it was her last link to her old lover. The final thing that connected them.

She was sending the demos out into the world. It was time for the guitar to go, too.

She fumbled her phone from her pocket and pressed the button to call Sam. When it went directly to his voice mail, she said, "I need to see you. And the kids, too."

She picked up the bottle of Grey Goose and stashed it in the cabinet, along with the memories. It would stay there to remind her that it, too, was a part of her past. Not her present.

Not her future.

DUSK WAS FADING TO NIGHT and one of the demos was playing on the stereo as she hand-sanded the trim for a table. Lost in the bittersweet memories, she didn't hear anyone coming until the door to the barn began to open.

In her distressed state of mind she'd forgotten to lock it.

Scrambling to her feet, she ran toward it, but the crack widened before she could get there.

"Don't you dare come in," she yelled.

"How come, Delaney?" Rennie stuck her head through the doorway. "It's us. Me and Uncle Sam and Leo."

Delaney slid to a stop on the sawdust-covered floor and saw Leo behind Rennie. Sam behind both of the kids. Worry faded to relief.

"Sorry, sweetie," she said. "I thought it was someone else."

Leo pointedly ignored her as he leaned against the wall, pulled out his cell phone and began to text.

"I drawed you a picture in school," Rennie said happily. "Uncle Sam said we could bring it to you. But we had to be very quiet." Her voice dropped to a whisper. "He said the trees were guarding your house, and we had to sneak past them. They might try to talk to me."

"That's right," she said, ignoring Leo's snort of derision as she crouched to put an arm around Rennie. "You don't want to talk to trees. They're very boring." Rennie had a piece of orange construction paper clutched in her hand. "Is that my picture?"

She handed it to Delaney. It showed a stick figure with curly red hair standing in an oval. Another stick figure with yellow hair stood outside the oval. A small drawing that looked vaguely like an animal was off to the side.

"I bet this is you." Delaney touched the smaller figure. "And this is me. And Fluffy. And we're...we're..." She glanced up at Sam.

"*Bath*," he mouthed.

"We're taking a bath."

"Yes," Rennie squealed. She gave Sam a disdainful look. "Uncle Sam didn't know what it was."

"That's because he doesn't appreciate art," Delaney said.

The picture was crumpled at the top, where Rennie had been holding it, and she smoothed it out. "He's a guy."

"Leo said it was a stupid picture." Rennie narrowed her eyes.

"There you go. Leo's a guy, too. What do you expect?"

"Guys." Rennie's voice was filled with such scorn that Delaney had to swallow a smile. She caught Sam's gaze. Held it. The gray of his eyes had warmed.

"Delaney?" Rennie put her hands on Delaney's cheeks to get her attention.

"Right," she said hastily. "May I keep this?"

"Yes. Uncle Sam puts my pictures on the 'frigerator."

"Then that's where I'll put mine. This is my first refrigerator picture, and that makes it very special. Thank you, Rennie."

"Let's go put it there now," she said.

"Okay. Let me turn off the music first."

"I like that music," Rennie said.

Delaney froze, then turned around slowly. "Do you, Rennie?" Without thinking, she picked the girl up. "That's your daddy singing."

Leo looked up from his phone. He shoved it into his pocket as he pushed away from the wall.

"Really?" Rennie rested against Delaney's arm as if it was the most natural thing in the world. "That's my daddy?"

"Yes."

"It's Delaney, too." Sam had circled around the furniture to come up next to them. "She and your dad are singing together."

"Can I hear more songs?"

"I'll tell you what, Rennie." Delaney set her on the floor and ejected the disc from the stereo. "I'll make you a copy so you can take it home with you. Okay?"

"Okay," she said happily.

"Would you like a copy, too, Leo?"

"Whatever." But he stared at the disc as Delaney snapped it into the jewel case.

Sam moved closer. "You don't have to do that," he said in a low voice.

"Of course I do. Diesel would love knowing his daughter liked this music." And maybe that was all the reason she needed to release these songs. "I'll burn two copies before you leave."

She glanced at the cabinet again, which stood open. "Leo, I have something I'd like to give you."

"Yeah?" He'd pulled out his phone again and was pressing buttons, as if he was texting. But it looked random to Delaney.

"Leo. Put that away." Sam moved next to him and dropped his hand on his shoulder. "Be civil."

The boy flushed, but he slipped the phone into his pocket. Delaney walked to the cabinet, hesitating before she pulled out the guitar. Diesel had entrusted it to her. It had brought her comfort in the days after his death.

It was right that Leo have it.

She pulled out the battered leather case, holding it at each end, afraid the worn handle might break. She laid it on a desk and opened the lid.

A well-used acoustic guitar rested inside on blue-green velvet. Three picks were lined up in the slots on the lid. The shine of the pick guard had been dulled from use, and the strings would probably break if they were tightened. Nicks and scratches marred the body.

"This was your dad's first guitar," she said to Leo. "He used it when we recorded those songs."

Leo reached out to touch it, then snatched his hand back. "How come you have it?"

Diesel had given it to her for safekeeping, because he'd

been afraid Heather would smash it. After his death, Delaney hadn't returned it to Heather. The instrument had meant too much to Diesel, and she refused to let a vengeful woman destroy it.

"Your dad made beautiful music with this guitar, and I loved it. Now it's your turn to have it." She'd loved Diesel, too, but it was time for her to move on, as well.

Leo plucked one string, then another. "Do you know how to play it?"

"A little." She kept her voice carefully neutral. "I can show you the basics, if you like."

He raised one shoulder but didn't answer as he stroked the golden wood.

Rennie tugged at Delaney's hand. "What about my picture?"

"Yes. Let's go put your artwork up on the refrigerator."

Sam stayed next to her as they made their way to the back of the house, where the reporters wouldn't see them. After discussing the best place for the picture, Delaney attached it to the fridge door with a magnet. They admired it for a moment, then Sam said, "Leo, take the guitar into the other room and have a look at it, okay? I need to talk to Delaney."

After the kids had gone into the living room, he tugged her into the corner farthest away. "What's going on? I thought you didn't want to see the kids."

"I didn't want Leo to get upset again. I didn't want to take a chance on the reporters seeing him. But I…I talked to my sponsor this afternoon and figured some things out. I needed to give Leo the guitar."

"How come?"

"Diesel would want him to have it." She laced her fingers behind her back. "It's part of the past. And I have to put the past behind me."

"I like the sound of that. I like that a lot."

"You're part of that past, Sam. So are Leo and Rennie. I was wrong to try and have a relationship with them." *With you.* "I need to move on."

"Hey, what's going on outside?" Leo called from the living room.

Sam closed his eyes in frustration. Why did his nephew have to interrupt now? Delaney was telling him something important, and he had to make sure he understood.

She pushed past him, and he followed her out of the kitchen. The living room was awash with light, and he peered out the window.

"What the hell?"

Several bright lights shone through the trees in front of her house. As Delaney and the kids joined him at the window, flashes went off. Photographers.

"Damn it." He pulled the kids back and Delaney closed the shades. But the damage had been done.

"Why are they taking our pictures?" Leo asked. He lifted the edge of the blind, and another flash went off.

"Don't, Leo," Delaney said quietly.

Sam was watching Leo, and noted that the boy was surprised, but not shocked. He'd seen photographers before, Sam realized. Heather's trips in and out of rehab were staples of the tabloids.

Rennie appeared confused.

Delaney looked resigned.

"Damn it. I'll get rid of them." Sam wrenched the front door open, and the flashes went off again. More of them this time. They'd been ready for him.

Delaney pushed the door closed, then grabbed the back of his shirt when he reached for it again. "That will make it worse," she said.

"Worse? How could it be worse?" He shook off her hands.

"They took pictures of all of us. Are Leo and Rennie going to be on the cover of some trashy tabloid?"

"I doubt it. The flashes probably reflected off the windows. They *want* you to go after them. They want you in the open."

"How can you sound so reasonable? Aren't you angry?" He shoved his hand through his hair, appalled at the invasion of their privacy. "What happened to the woman who was so shaken by the press she was ready to crawl into a vodka bottle this afternoon?"

"I talked to my sponsor and got my head on straight. The vodka was about more than the intrusive press. I was…upset before they showed up this afternoon, and they surprised me. Once I agreed to release the demos, I should have been prepared for this. This was always a possibility."

"Damn Heather."

Delaney pushed him into the kitchen. "You're the one who told her." Her voice was low and stung like a whip. "Once the word was out that I'd been found, that there was music Diesel and I hadn't released, of course the press was going to show up. I'm sorry they caught you and Leo and Rennie, but you brought this on yourself. I shouldn't have asked you to come over here, but I was thinking of what *I* needed."

Fear for Leo and Rennie roiled within Sam, mixed with anger at the photographers. Worse that it was his own fault. "I had no idea it would be like this."

She rolled her eyes. "Come on, Sam. Heather is on the cover of a tabloid at least once a month, and her spending, her affairs and her trips to rehab are boring compared to this. You're part of Diesel's family. How could you not know what it was like?"

She was right, and it fueled his anger at himself. He couldn't protect any of them. They would always be targets. "He died three years ago. When does it stop?"

She shook her head. "It doesn't. Not for a while. Those un-intended consequences again." She pulled the kitchen blinds, then went from room to room to close all the shades. "They'll leave in a while. They don't like to stand around in the cold. It's not good for their cameras."

This had been her life when she was part of the Redheads. Her life and his brother's. How had she endured it?

And this time Sam was the one to blame.

"We need to go home," he said abruptly.

"Go the same way you came. Out the back door and right into the woods. Unless the house is surrounded, they won't see you."

He needed to protect her, too. "Delaney, you should come with us. Unless you like sleeping in a house surrounded by photographers?"

"No," she said quietly. "But I'll be fine here."

The warm, loving woman was gone. She was self-contained and cool again, the way she'd been when he met her. His fault. He took her hand and tried to ignore his fear. "Please, Delaney. I need to know you're safe."

She looked down at their joined hands for a long moment. She nodded slowly. "All right, Sam. I'll stay at your place tonight."

CHAPTER TWENTY

DELANEY WAS GIVING an exhausted Rennie a bath when Sam's phone rang. Miami area code. He hesitated, then opened it. He'd have to speak with her sooner or later. And the kids might want to talk to her.

"Hello, Heather."

"Hey, Sam. How are things up in north Dullsville?" She sounded cheerful. Happy. He hoped it was only because she was feeling better.

"Did you call the reporters?" he demanded. "Are you the one who told that gossip site Chantal was up here?"

"What's the matter? Doesn't she like the publicity? Can't Diesel's little wh—"

"Heather. Stop right there." He wanted to reach through the phone and strangle her. "You put the kids at risk. They're going to be in the tabloids, too."

"Why would they?" Her voice hardened. "Unless they're spending time with her."

"*I'm* spending time with her." A vision of Delaney in her bathrobe and nothing else filled his head. "To work on the demos," he added hastily. "The kids are with me. Connect the dots."

"Leo knows what to do about the press," she said. As if it was perfectly normal for a ten-year-old to fend off photographers.

"He shouldn't have to know that." Sam gripped the phone tighter and his finger hovered over the off button.

Leo was watching him from the living room, his eyes carefully blank.

Damn it. She was still his mother. "Do you want to talk to the kids?"

She hesitated, then said, "Sure. Put Leo on."

"Leo," Sam called. "Your mom is on the phone."

He looked from the phone to Sam, but made no attempt to reach for it.

"She'd like to talk to you," Sam said softly. He put his hand over the microphone and handed it to Leo. "Give her a chance."

"Hi, Mom," Leo said. His voice sounded rusty. He listened for a while, glancing at Sam. "Good. We're going to school."

Sam heard Heather's voice rise, and Leo held the phone away from his ear. Finally he said defiantly, "I like it here. The kid across the road is cool."

He stared at Sam, the message clear. *Save me.* Sam reached for the phone.

"Heather, what did you say to Leo?"

"I told him he belongs in school down here. Why the hell did you put them in school?"

"It wasn't doing them any good to sit around the house all day." He lowered his voice. "They needed *normal.* Still do. I'm not going to let you talk to Rennie unless you promise you won't upset her."

"Who are you to tell me what to do with my kids?" she said.

He struggled to control his temper. "Yes, they're your kids. Do you want her to cry herself to sleep?" He paused, but Heather didn't answer. "And why are you pissed off about them being in school? You might not be out of the hospital for another couple of weeks. They'll get behind."

There was a longer pause. "I guess that's true," she said grudgingly. "Fine. Let me talk to her."

God, what if Rennie told her mom that Delaney had given her a bath? "Hold on."

Rennie was giggling in her bedroom when he opened the door. She and Delaney both turned. Delaney's smile faltered as she looked at him.

"Rennie, your mom is on the phone. Why don't you tell her about show-and-tell at school today? And about recess."

Delaney went white and backed out of the room. Rennie didn't seem to notice as she grabbed the phone. "Hi, Mommy. I brought Fluffy to school today for show and tell."

She chattered nonstop about school. When she said, "I just had my bath," Sam took the phone.

"I'm going to get her to bed," he said to Heather. "We'll talk again, all right?" He turned off the phone without waiting for an answer.

Rennie looked confused. "I didn't say goodbye to Mommy."

"She'll call again," Sam said, drawing her close. "She's in the hospital, remember? She shouldn't talk too long. We want her to get better, don't we?"

Rennie tilted her head. "Will Mommy give me a bath when she's better?"

He tightened his hold on his niece. "If you want her to, she will."

Leo stood in the door of the bedroom, clutching the guitar case in his arms. "Mom said she's getting out of the hospital next week." His fingers pressed into the leather. "She said she'd see us then."

"We're not going to make any plans before I talk to her doctor," Sam replied. "I don't know what's going to happen. But try not to worry about it, okay?"

Leo looked at him doubtfully. "She sounded pretty sure, Uncle Sam."

Uncle Sam. He swallowed. "I promised you it will be all right, Leo. *You'll* be all right. Do you trust me?"

Leo hesitated for a long moment, then slowly nodded.

Sam held out his hand to Rennie. "You guys want me to read you a story?" Leo acted scornful when he read aloud each night, but he'd seen the boy listening.

"I want Delaney to read," Rennie announced. She picked up two books from her bed. "These."

"Let's go ask her."

When Rennie ran to her with the books, Delaney smiled. But there was a shadow in her eyes. "I'd love to read to you, Rennie." She glanced at Leo. "Do you want to sit with us, Leo?"

"Rennie's probably upset. She needs me here."

He crowded in next to his sister, and Sam sat on the other end of the couch. Leo was paying as much attention to Delaney as Rennie was.

After the second book, Rennie asked for another. Delaney glanced at him.

He stood up. "It's bedtime," he said.

When he returned to the living room a little while later, Delaney was still on the couch. She'd drawn her legs up and wrapped her arms around them, and was resting her chin on her knees.

"Hey," he said softly as he sat next to her.

She tilted her head to face him. "This is a problem for you, isn't it?"

He didn't pretend to misunderstand. "Yeah, it is. I had no idea what being famous meant. No awareness of how the press hounded you."

"Don't you remember what it was like for Diesel?"

"No." He shifted away from her and stared out the window

into the darkness. "I was never around. You said Diesel barely mentioned me."

"I was being snarky when I said that. He missed you. He told me about his big brother who'd practically raised him. Who always protected him."

Didn't she realize he hadn't protected Diesel when it counted the most?

She smiled. "There was a time at school where one of the older kids tried to bully him. He said you kicked the kid's ass around the playground twice."

"He remembered that?" Diesel had been a scrawny kid with bright red hair and a swagger, trying to act as tough as his big brother.

"He remembered a lot of things, Sam."

The ticking of the kitchen clock counted out the seconds as memories spilled through his head.

"Is that why you stayed away from him?" she finally asked. "Because you couldn't handle the reporters and paparazzi?"

"I stayed away because I couldn't bear watching him destroy himself. I tried to get him clean and dried out, but he wouldn't let me help him. It was easier not to be around."

"You couldn't have saved him, Sam. He wouldn't let me help him, either." She studied the knees of her jeans as if they held the answer to everything. "That's why we wrote those songs and made those demos. I thought it would steer him in another direction. Instead, that's what killed him."

"What do you mean? How could those demos have killed him?"

When she lifted her head, her eyes shimmered. "He told Heather about the music. How excited he was, how it was going to take our career in another direction. He told her she had to go to rehab, and he was taking the kids."

Delaney wiped her face on her knee. "Heather got

hysterical. She said if he left her to be with me, she'd make sure he never saw Leo or Rennie again. She hired a shark lawyer who explained that Diesel's own drug use and infidelity would make him an unsuitable parent. A week later, he was dead."

Sam shifted closer to her. He'd never heard any of that. "Are you sure? I know Heather was out of control, but…"

"Yes, I'm sure. We were living together. After the kids were asleep every night, he'd leave their house and come to me." She watched him steadily. "He loved me, Sam. And I loved him. Enough that I was ready to leave the band. Leo and Rennie were everything to him. I couldn't bear to be the reason he lost them."

Speechless, he stared at her.

She slid off the couch, her eyes bruised. "I need to go."

"Wait." He grabbed her hand and tugged her back. "Don't leave. Give me a minute to get my mind around all of this."

She shook her hand free. "It was stupid of me to think I could be a part of Leo and Rennie's lives. A part of your life. It was stupid to fall in love with you," she whispered. "Diesel was your brother. He was my lover. I should have realized this would never work."

"What?" She thought she was in love with him? Panic rose inside him. This wasn't about *love*. He didn't do love anymore. Not since he'd failed Diesel. "Wait a minute. You can't be…"

She stood up and backed away. "Don't say it, Sam. I get to decide what I'm feeling, but I don't expect you to love me back. I always knew my relationship with Diesel would be a problem for you. You need to take care of the kids, anyway. Protect *them*." She edged toward the back door. "I'll keep you posted about the demos. Goodbye, Sam."

"Wait, Delaney. It's not Diesel. With everything that's happening, I never thought about falling in love with you."

"I understand." She paused at the kitchen door, quivering like a deer preparing to bolt. "You and the kids are leaving. This was always just a fling. I get it."

He'd hurt her. Badly. "That didn't come out right." He ran to the kitchen door. "Delaney, come back."

She didn't answer, and it was too dark to see. Twigs cracked in the distance, leaves crunched under her feet. The sounds grew fainter, then faded completely.

He stepped out the door to go after her, then heard Leo whimper in his sleep. The phone call from Heather must have brought back memories for him.

Sam needed to get this straightened out with Delaney.

But Leo needed him.

With one last look out the door, he closed it and turned away.

So MUCH FOR NEW beginnings.

"Together" hadn't lasted very long.

Delaney rolled over in bed the next morning and stared up at the ceiling. By this time, she should be in the kitchen, in her bathrobe, waiting for Sam.

No sexy games today.

Heather was getting out of the hospital soon. Sam and Leo and Rennie would go back to Miami.

She was staying in Otter Tail.

She crawled out of bed, her eyes gritty and barely open. Someone had knocked on her door an hour after she got home last night. Sam? One of the photographers? She hadn't looked.

She hadn't fallen asleep, either. She'd replayed her conversation with Sam over and over in her head.

I never thought about falling in love with you.

As the sun came up, she knew she didn't regret any of it.

Not confronting him about the reporters. Not talking about Diesel.

Not telling him she loved him.

She'd been walled off for three long years, refusing to feel anything. Refusing to live. She wasn't going back to that dark, cold place. She wouldn't hide her feelings anymore.

If telling him she loved him could scare him away, it was good to find out early. Easier to cut him out of her life before she fell any more deeply in love with him. Better a surgical incision now than a sloppy, jagged wound later on.

She started the coffee. It was going to be a long day.

DELANEY FOCUSED ON finishing the table and bed she'd been working on, wearing earplugs when she was using her machines, playing music at full blast when she wasn't. She'd promised delivery last weekend, and she was behind. Concentrating on work was good. Smoothing the wood, shaping it, forming it into furniture had always made her happy.

Maybe she couldn't be happy today. But she could be busy.

She'd locked the door, so she had no idea if any of the reporters knocked. She'd have to deal with them eventually. But not today.

Her phone was buzzing when she turned the music off. Was it Sam? She grabbed the phone and saw it was Paul. Swallowing her disappointment, she pressed the on button. "Hey, Paul."

"How are you doing, Delaney?"

"I'm fine. What's up?"

"I wanted you to know that it's okay if you don't come in to play tonight. Hank and Stu and I understand."

Oh, God, it was Friday. She'd forgotten all about the band. She thought about the reporters clustered at the end of her driveway. The ones who would show up at the Harp tonight. She'd told Sam she could deal with them. That she'd expected this.

Time to put her money where her mouth was.

"I'll be there, Paul."

"Are you sure?" he asked after a moment.

"Positive. See you tonight." Her hand shook as she turned off the phone, then she hesitated. Had Sam tried to call? She fumbled with the menu button and pulled up the missed-calls log.

Ten times. Starting early this morning.

She wanted to call him back. To hear his voice. Ask him to come to the Harp tonight. To stand with her when she faced the crowd.

Surgical incision. She turned off the power to the phone and headed back to the house.

Twenty minutes later, she stared at her computer screen, appalled. The pictures that the photographers had taken last night were already on the gossip sites. The kids were only shadowy faces in the windows, thank God. But Sam was clearly visible as he stood at her storm door.

Far worse was the shot of the two of them yesterday afternoon. She'd been right about the photographer hiding in front of the house when Sam arrived. In the photo, he was only holding her arm. But the expression on their faces was intimate. Private. The kind of look lovers would exchange.

Chantal's Mystery Lover? the headline screamed.

She slammed the laptop closed. She hadn't thought this could get worse. She'd been wrong.

SAM SAT IN THE CAR POOL line at school and watched kids pour out the door. Delaney hadn't answered her phone. He'd sneaked through the woods to her house and heard the hard rock shaking the barn, but the door was locked. He'd stood outside for a long time, trying to catch a glimpse of her through the window.

She probably wasn't dancing as she worked today.

The music never stopped, and eventually he walked back through the woods. Part of him was glad he hadn't been able to talk to her. What would he have said?

She loved him. The thought put a block of ice in his stomach.

Love had never been part of the equation. He thought she'd understood that. He cared about her, sure. Liked her a lot. She'd been great with Leo and Rennie. And the sex... the sex had ruined him for other women.

He'd get over it. He had to.

He didn't give a damn that she'd loved Diesel. He was glad, actually, that his brother had had her in his life. It sounded as if living with Heather had been hell.

Was he jealous? Of course he was. Who wouldn't be? But Diesel was dead and Sam was alive. Delaney said she'd put Diesel behind her. She'd said she loved *him*.

Sam had hurt her deeply. Now she had to face everything on her own. Everything he'd brought down on her head.

Desperation ratcheted up inside him, and an overwhelming need to take care of Delaney.

But those feelings couldn't be about love. They were about doing the right thing. About making sure she was safe.

He heard a sudden commotion behind him, and turned to see several people running toward the entrance of the school. Two of them held cameras.

Kids were pouring out of the building. The three men and a woman bumped into a young girl, knocking her down.

Sam scrambled out of the car and ran for the school door. Several teachers emerged, snatching the crying girl off the ground and herding the rest of the children back into the building.

"Get away from these children and off school property," an older woman said. She stood with her hands on her hips, glaring at the reporters. "Immediately."

Police sirens wailed in the distance. Sam pushed past the teacher. "They're after my kids," he said. "I need to get them."

"Wait. You can't go in the school."

"Try to stop me." He burst through the door and spotted Rennie's red hair behind some older children. She was clinging to Leo.

Sam snatched her up and held out his hand to Leo. "Let's go."

As they ran out the door, Leo flipped off the reporters. "Don't," Sam said in a low voice. "Ignore them."

"They scared Rennie," Leo said. One woman tried to edge closer, and Leo turned to her, snarling. She took a step backward.

"In the car," Sam said. "Quick."

They were barely buckled in when he took off. The four members of the press were running for their cars when the police cruisers showed up. Thank God. They wouldn't be able to follow him home.

As they left the town behind, he realized Rennie was sniffling behind him. "It's okay, Rennie. They're gone. You're safe."

"You saved us, Uncle Sam," she said.

"Of course I did. I won't let anyone hurt you."

He heard her fumbling with something. Suddenly, she stuck her head between the front seats. "That's because you love us, Uncle Sam. Right?" She smiled up at him. "I love you, too."

"Rennie, sit down and buckle your seat belt," he said sharply. He swerved to the shoulder of the road and stopped the car.

She patted his cheek. "You love us, right?"

It felt as if an arrow pierced his heart. But instead of pain, warmth spread through him. "Yes, Ren, I love you. Leo, too." He twisted around and lifted her back onto the upholstery. "But you can't take off your seat belt. Okay?"

He pulled onto the road again, watching the kids in the rearview mirror. *That's because you love us, Uncle Sam.*

He'd protected them because he loved them. Was that why he needed so badly to protect Delaney?

He hadn't figured it out by the time he turned into their driveway. As they walked to the house, Rennie said, "Who were those people, Uncle Sam?"

"They were bad people," Leo told her. "Don't worry about them, Ren. I won't let them get you."

Sam took Leo's hand. Surprisingly, the boy didn't snatch it away. "I'll make sure they don't bother either of you. My job, Leo. Remember?"

"They're not going away," Leo said. But he clung to Sam's hand.

"We will be, though. We're going back to Miami soon."

Rennie sat on the floor, her arms around Fluffy's neck. "Is Delaney coming?"

"No, sweetheart. She lives here. She has a business here."

"Then I want to live here, too." The dog barked, as if he agreed.

"No one asked you, Fluffy," Sam said. "Sorry, Ren. Your home is back in Miami. Mine, too."

Leo dropped Sam's hand and kicked at the bottom of the bookcase. "We're doing a unit on immigrants in social studies. I'm supposed to be a kid from Ireland. I can't leave yet. I already did all the research."

His nephew hadn't said anything about this project. Sam needed to ask both kids more questions about school. "We're not leaving tomorrow, Leo. I'm sure you'll have a chance to finish your project."

"I better." He scowled. "If I'm not there, my group will get marked down." He shoved his hands into his pockets, his cheeks flushed. "Do you think Delaney could show me how to play Dad's guitar before we leave?"

So Delaney had captivated Leo, too. "We can ask her." Sam put his hand on his nephew's shoulder. "You've been pretty rude to her. Do you think it's right to ask her for a favor?"

"She said she'd show me."

"I know." He watched the boy, waiting. Finally Leo shrugged.

"I guess she's not so bad."

"Are you going to tell her that?"

"Yeah." He kicked the bookcase again. "I'll apologize."

"I think that would be the right thing to do."

"Can I go over there now?"

"It's close to dinnertime. She's probably..."

It was Friday night. She played at the Harp on Fridays. Oh, God. What would happen to her there?

"Leo, I'm going to call Mike's mom across the road and ask her to watch you and Rennie for a little while. I have something to do."

"Is it about Delaney?" Leo asked.

"Yes, it's about Delaney. I think she might need some help."

CHAPTER TWENTY-ONE

WALKING INTO THE HARP that evening was one of the hardest things Delaney had ever done. Maddie would be there, and Quinn. Jen, too, probably. And a whole lot of other people who now knew who she'd been.

Clutching her drum bag to her chest, she took a deep breath, then opened the door.

The pub was already crowded. The tables and booths were filled, and people were two and three deep at the bar. Conversation and laughter drifted toward her, the sounds of people having fun.

Waiting for a show.

Keeping her head down, she turned to the front of the room and set the drums on the floor. Paul's guitar was propped in a stand, and the amps were in place.

The noise level dropped for a moment, and she knew people had noticed her. She turned around to face the crowd, and saw everyone staring at her. A few people waved and smiled, and as she waved back, the clamp on her chest eased a little. Either they hadn't heard yet or they didn't care. She hoped it was the second.

Then Paul appeared, pushing through the crowd. He scooped her into his arms and hugged her. "It's okay, Del. It's a five-day wonder. Good for you, facing them down. We're going to give them a hell of a show tonight."

"Thanks, Paul." She eased away. "How come you're so nonchalant about this?"

"I've known for a long time, Delaney." He tweaked a strand of her hair. "You think you could disguise that voice of yours from a musical genius like me? Those eyes? Your stage presence? Not a chance, babe." He hugged her again. "I'm damn lucky to have the opportunity to play with you."

"Paul." She stared at him. "Why didn't you ever say anything?"

He shrugged. "It was pretty clear you didn't want anyone to know who you were. I respect that. We all have secrets." He scowled. "We're going to have to deal with the reporters tonight, though."

She opened the vinyl bag that held her drums, feeling suddenly lighter. "I'll handle them."

As she put the drums together, she spotted Maddie making her way toward the front of the pub, a determined look in her eye. Delaney stood up slowly to face her.

Maddie stopped a few feet from Delaney. "I'm sorry," she said softly. "We were…we were horrible to you yesterday. Can you ever forgive me?"

"It's okay, Maddie." She shoved her hands in the pockets of her jeans. "I should have told you a long time ago. So we're even. Okay?"

Her friend shook her head. "No, it's not okay, and we're definitely not even. You needed our support, and we let you down. I couldn't sleep last night. I kept seeing your face as you pushed away from the table."

"I don't think it was my face that kept you awake." Delaney tried to smile, but it felt strained. "I blame junior there." She nodded at Maddie's belly.

"He or she didn't help."

"Don't worry about it," Delaney said.

She turned back to her drums, but Maddie caught her hand. "Do you want your coffee?"

Coffee was part of the ritual. She always drank coffee

when she played at the Harp so she didn't have to think about drinking vodka. She wasn't sure she needed it anymore, but it would make her feel as if it was a regular night. She needed something about this evening to be normal. "Sure. Thanks."

Someone touched her arm as she set up the bass drum, and she reached behind her for the coffee. "Thanks, Maddie."

"Delaney." Quinn's voice.

She set the coffee down and stood up to face him. "Hey, Quinn."

"Forgive me," he said in a low voice. "I wasn't judging you. I was surprised. Stunned, I guess, that Chantal had been performing here and I didn't realize it."

She nodded. "We see what we want to see."

He gripped her shoulders. "Are you okay? You didn't go out and buy a bottle after you left here, did you?"

Some people would resent that question, but she understood. Quinn had fought the same battles. He knew exactly how strong the temptation could be. She shrugged. "I did, actually. I'm an idiot. I didn't open it, though."

"Will you need it after tonight?"

"No." She smiled. "I put it away. For good, I hope."

"I kept that bottle of Jameson's on my shelf for a long time. It wasn't until Maddie that I was able to let it go. You should have called me." As soon as he spoke, he looked stricken. "You didn't feel as if you could, did you?"

"I phoned my sponsor. Don't beat yourself up."

He picked her coffee up from the floor and handed it to her, and the rich aroma grounded her. Reminded her that she'd done this every Friday for a long time. She could do it again.

Paul played a note on his guitar, too loud, and she glanced at him. He jerked his head at Quinn, and the message was clear—*want me to get rid of him?*

She smiled at Paul and shook her head.

"I have to give you credit, Delaney," Quinn said, as if he hadn't noticed the exchange with Paul. "You knew the place was going to be packed tonight. But you still showed up."

"It's what I do, Quinn." As she spoke, she realized that was true. She'd been trying to cleanse her life of all traces of Chantal. But Chantal was a part of her, and always would be. "I can be Chantal while I'm playing here," she said softly. "Then I can leave and be Delaney again. It took me a long time to realize that."

"You've got a gig here for as long as you want it." One side of his mouth quirked up. "Heck, I'll even kick up your pay."

Before he could leave, she touched his arm. "There'll be reporters." As she turned out of her driveway, she'd seen them scrambling for their cars. "Let me handle them."

"Are you sure?"

"Positive."

Stu and Hank showed up a few minutes later. Hank gave her a high five. "Coolest thing I've ever heard," he said happily. "I'm in a band with friggin' Chantal."

"Don't let it go to your head," Stu said, elbowing him. "You're still a lame-ass bass player. You doing okay, Delaney?"

"I'm fine, Stu. Thanks." She hugged him, then Hank, and finished setting up her drums. She felt steadier. More in control. This was going to be okay.

As long as she didn't think about Sam.

The first reporters began trickling in twenty minutes before the band was scheduled to begin playing. The bank of amplifiers and microphone stands and Paul's scowl kept them back for a little while. But as more of them packed into the pub, they pushed closer. One of them bumped an amp, knocking it over. Paul grabbed the microphone. "That's enough," he barked. "Back off, all of you."

Delaney took the microphone from him and stood there, waiting. The noise quieted as the crowd noticed her. There had to be at least twenty reporters in the pub. Several of them had videographers with them, cameras perched high on their shoulders. As she scanned the crowd, waiting for the buzz to die down, she saw Sam leaning against the bar, watching her.

He'd come here. For her.

Their gazes locked for a long moment. He straightened, then began elbowing his way through the packed room. As he got closer, she gripped the microphone and looked away.

"Thank you all for coming tonight." Her voice was too loud—mic feedback—and she moved it farther from her face. She heard the sound of beer splashing into a glass from behind the bar, and several people shuffled their feet. Otherwise, the room was silent.

"It's good to see so many friends here to support me. I appreciate each and every one of you, and I hope you enjoy our performance tonight. Paul and Stu and Hank are great musicians. It's been a privilege and an honor to play with them." She paused. "I hope I'm playing with them for a very long time."

Someone began clapping, then another person, and another. Soon the whole room was cheering. Jen and her husband, Walker, stood up in the middle of the crowd. Jen nodded at Delaney as she clapped.

The knot in Delaney's chest loosened a little. She finally smiled as she looked at her friends and neighbors. There were people in Otter Tail, she was sure, who would give her the cold shoulder.

But these people accepted her. She'd focus on them and ignore the others.

She glanced over at Sam and saw him clapping, too. She looked away quickly. "As for the gentlemen and ladies of the press...."

The cheering stopped, and she studied the group of reporters huddled together at the front of the room. Several of them were typing on their phones, but they looked up at her words. "You're welcome to stay tonight."

"Damn right we are," one of them yelled.

She smiled. "There are a few conditions. First of all, it'll cost each of you fifty dollars. That includes one beer, of course. Our bartender will be happy to recommend some local brews."

Some of the locals laughed, and the reporters looked stunned. From the back of the pack, one of them yelled, "You can't do that."

She was pretty sure it was the same guy. "Sure I can. This is a pub. Pubs have cover charges, and tonight's cover is fifty bucks. Our bartender is trying to make a living, and you're scaring away the paying customers. If you don't like it, you can leave.

"Second, there will be no pictures. And there will be no recording. If we catch anyone recording, your equipment will be confiscated and you'll be kicked out. Without your beer. If you stay, you keep your mouths shut and leave my friends alone. None of them want to talk to you."

She took a deep breath. "I'll answer all of your questions tomorrow. I'll ask the mayor and police chief to set up a press conference." She glanced at Quinn, and he nodded. "You can take all the pictures you want then. So as soon as you all pay your cover charges, we'll get started."

None of them left. The videographers took their cameras out to their trucks, then returned. They all paid Quinn and settled in.

Delaney glanced over at Sam again. He had a tiny smile on his face. When he caught her eye, he raised his beer to her.

She watched him for a moment and her control dissipated. Everything she wanted was in front of her, shimmering like an oasis in the desert. But when she reached out to take it, it slipped away like a mirage.

Not the time to think about it. She put Sam out of her head and watched Quinn accept money from the crowd around the bar. When he gave her a thumbs-up, she handed the microphone to Paul and sat down behind her drums. They'd come to see Chantal, and she would give them a hell of a show.

DELANEY WAS PUTTING ON a hell of a show.

Sam leaned against the bar, sipping on a glass of Fatty Boombalatty, a locally brewed Belgian pale ale Quinn had recommended. Delaney's arms flashed as she played her drums, her hands moving so fast they were a blur.

And her voice was stronger than he'd ever heard it. Rich. Full of emotion. Haunting.

Her hair was damp, and so was her tank top. When she moved her head, he saw the sweat sliding down her temple.

She was the strongest woman he'd ever known. She'd come in tonight and faced a roomful of people who knew the most intimate details of her life. She'd dealt with the reporters, then made them cough up some money if they wanted to stay and hear her play. Helping out the friends who owned the pub.

Friends who hadn't been there for her when she needed them.

Neither had he.

She'd told him she loved him, had bared herself in the most intimate way possible, and he'd freaked out. He'd left her alone to deal with a mess that he'd made.

It made him feel small. Contemptible.

Weak.

Maybe instead of love, all she felt now was pity.

After an hour, the band took a break. He tried to make his way toward her, but Delaney was mobbed by the audience. He stayed back and watched one person after another hug her, or pat her on the back, or take her hand.

Delaney's smile was dazzling. It lit the room.

It faded when she glanced at him.

Halfway through the second set, he noticed one of the reporters holding a digital recorder at his side. Sam shouldered his way past the patrons between them and backed the guy into the bar. "Hand it over."

The recorder disappeared into his pocket. "What are you talking about?"

Sam leaned closer. "I would love to pound the hell out of you. You have no idea how happy that would make me." He extended his palm. "Give it to me, or we'll discuss it outside."

"First amendment, buddy."

Sam smiled. "Outside now, *buddy.*"

The man stared at him for a moment, then slapped the recorder into Sam's hand. Sam slid it across the counter to Quinn.

As he turned away, he saw two more people shoving something into their pockets. He stepped in front of them and held out his hand without speaking. Both gave up their recorders.

By the time the band was ready for their second break, Sam had made his way to the front of the room. The music was too loud, thumping from the amp next to him, but he didn't care. He wasn't going to let her escape this time.

She saw him standing there, and leaned over to say

something to the lead guitarist. The guy glanced at Sam, then nodded. Delaney set her drumsticks on her lap and adjusted the microphone.

The audience stilled. Most of them had been here often enough that they knew what it meant.

The keyboard man played a few notes, then Delaney began to sing. When she got to the line "love was everything they said it would be," Sam tightened his grip on his beer and drained it in one long gulp. He felt like a total shit.

When the last "I'm leaving" faded away and she stood up to thunderous applause, Sam bulled his way through the crowd. Before she could slip past, he said, "Come outside with me, Delaney. Please."

She started to speak, but he grabbed her hand and pulled her through the crowd to the front door. Fresh air washed over them as they stepped out.

"What do you want, Sam?" She rubbed her hands up and down her arms. She was cold. She'd been sweating.

He took off his jacket and slung it over her shoulders. She hesitated, then huddled into it.

"That last song was for me, wasn't it?"

She drew the edges of his jacket closer. "It was about singing something I like. It's a beautiful song."

She'd meant it for him, and it had worked. The lyrics had been a punch to his gut. "You're incredible."

"Thank you. With all the press here, it'll be good publicity for the CD." She tilted her head as she studied him. "You said you needed to talk to me. What can I do for you, Sam?"

"You can forgive me for how I acted last night. What I said. I...you took me by surprise. I wasn't expecting you to tell me you loved me."

She didn't say anything. She just watched him with guarded eyes.

He shoved his hand through his hair. "I came over last night after the kids were asleep, but you didn't answer the door. I was awake all night, kicking myself."

"Sorry I disturbed your sleep. It won't happen again." He saw a flicker of pain in her aqua eyes.

"Don't say that." He grabbed her hand. "Please. Give me another chance."

"Another chance for what, Sam? More sex? Not going to happen. You were right to remind me I shouldn't have fallen in love with you. There's no future for us. I agreed to release the CDs because I wanted to get to know Leo and Rennie." She swallowed. "I thought we had more time, but..." She shrugged. "I know you'll take care of them." Her expression softened. "I've seen you with them, and I know they're loved. They'll be happy with you."

"I can move up here," he said desperately.

"And live in the snow?" She cupped his cheek, then let her hand fall away. "You'd last about a month. Besides, you wouldn't leave Leo and Rennie behind, and I wouldn't want you to."

"I'll figure something out. I swear, Delaney, I want another chance. I want to see what we could have together. I think...I think I could fall in love with you, too."

She smiled sadly. "It's not a chore you have to steel yourself for, Sam. It's either there or it's not." She stood on her toes and kissed him lightly. A goodbye. "You'll find someone, someday, and you'll know it's love."

She handed him his coat and turned to go into the pub. Before she could, a tall guy with dark blond hair stepped out. "Delaney?" He looked from her to Sam. "Are you okay? Jen sent me out to check on you."

"I'm fine, Walker. I was just heading back in."

The guy drew her to his side. "You told me once you'd

kick my ass if I hurt Jen." He studied Sam as if he were a bug in a collection. "Can I return the favor with this guy?"

Delaney hugged the stranger. "Thanks, Walker, but it's under control. If an ass-kicking is required, I'm more than capable of delivering it myself."

She disappeared inside, leaving Sam alone with the other man. The blond raised his eyebrows. "Maybe I should do it, anyway."

"Go ahead and try," Sam replied, balancing on the balls of his feet.

After a long moment, the guy shook his head. "Sounds too painful." He held out his hand. "Walker Barnes. You must be the infamous Sam."

He hesitated for a moment, then shook. "Sam McCabe."

"Delaney didn't look happy," Barnes said. "You responsible for that?"

"Yeah. I don't know how to fix it, either."

"That's the right answer." He sighed. "My wife and Maddie are sick about the way they hurt Delaney yesterday."

Sam wanted to tell Walker how bad it really was. That she'd bought a bottle of booze after their meeting. But it wasn't his fight. "They have to fix it with Delaney. Not me."

"They know it. But maybe I can do something for her in the meantime. I have a plan to get her out of here tonight without the press following her home, but I need some help. You interested?"

"Absolutely."

AFTER SHE'D SUNG THE LAST note of the last set, Delaney collapsed against the cool window behind her and exhaled. She was drained. Wrung out. She wasn't sure she could move.

Then she saw the crowd surging toward her. Except for Sam. He must have taken her at her word and left.

Swallowing her disappointment, she forced herself to stand up. Open the drum bag. Begin to take the set apart. When she finished, she could go home.

To her empty house and cold bed.

She'd squatted on the floor to take the bass drum off its stand when someone grasped her elbow. "Delaney, it's Jen. I'm so sorry. I'll give you a more thorough, detailed apology later, but right now you need to get out of here."

Delaney stood up and faced her friend. "Jen."

"Don't look at me like that," Jen begged. "Please."

"I'm exhausted, okay? I can't deal with this right now."

"I know. There's someone in the kitchen to take you home. He's got your coat. Give me your keys, and we'll drive your truck home later."

It took a moment to process the request. Jen wanted to help her avoid the reporters who were clustered around the front door. A gauntlet she'd have to pass to get home. Delaney dug in her purse and handed over the keys.

"By the time they all realize you're gone, you'll be home. Paul can take your drums apart. Right, Paul?"

"Yeah, Del, you get going. I'll put them in the bag and bring them to you tomorrow."

She didn't want to leave them behind, but she was swaying on her feet. And Jen was right. The members of the press were gathered at the front door like a pack of jackals.

"Take care of my babies, Paul," she said.

"Like they were my own," he assured her.

Jen wrapped an arm around her shoulders and steered her through the crowd. When one guy got too close, Jen threw an elbow.

When they reached the kitchen, her friend hugged her once. "We'll talk."

"Yeah." The adrenaline had all drained away, and Delaney could barely walk. The door wavered in front of her, and she leaned against it to push her way through. As she staggered forward, Sam stepped into view.

"Ready to go?"

CHAPTER TWENTY-TWO

"SAM." She stopped walking and stared at him. "I thought you left."

"Not without you." He helped her on with her coat, then slung an arm around her shoulders and steered her out the door. "Barnes and I worked it out. We're doing an end run around the press. Jen and Maddie are going to distract them while we get out of here."

"I can drive home."

"Of course you can. But they'd all be on your tail." The engine of his car was already running. He opened the door and waited for her to get in. Moments later, they were driving down County M.

"How do you feel?" he said.

"Wiped out." She laid her head against the seat back and closed her eyes. "I meant it, Sam. No sex." She still wanted him, though. In the car, she was sitting close enough to smell the leather of his coat, the scent of his shampoo, a hint of his aftershave.

"You're thinking about sex when you can barely sit up-right? Wow. That performance adrenaline must be a kick and a half."

She turned her head and opened her eyes. He was smiling. Teasing.

"No more sex, Sam." Her lack of sleep had turned off the filter between her head and her mouth, and she couldn't wrestle it back into place. "I want you. I thought about you tonight while I was drumming. I love you, but I can't do sex without love. Every time we made love, you'd take another piece of my heart. I wouldn't have any left by the time you leave."

He took her hand and twined their fingers together. In the darkness, with her eyes closed, she concentrated on his touch. His palm, rubbing against hers as the car vibrated. His mouth, as he pressed a kiss to the back of her hand, then the inside of her wrist. He lingered on her pulse, and she wondered if he felt it leap.

"I don't want it to be that way, Delaney."

"Me, either." She let go of his hand. "But it is."

She woke when the Jeep stopped. "Can you walk, or should I carry you in?" Sam asked.

"Walk," she mumbled.

He draped one of her arms over his shoulder and circled her waist with his. He steered her through the house, then took off her jacket, her shoes and socks, and her jeans. He eased her onto the bed and pulled up the covers.

"Bra, too," she said, reaching behind her. "Can't sleep in it."

He unfastened it through her tank top, then his hands disappeared. "You're on your own the rest of the way," he said in a hoarse voice.

She managed to pull her bra off and drop it on the floor, then snuggled into the pillow. Her last thought was that it smelled like Sam.

SHE ROLLED OVER in the middle of the night and felt the mattress shift next to her. Then an arm snaked around her chest and pulled her tight against a warm, solid body. "Sam," she whispered as she fell asleep again.

The next time she woke, something soft brushed against

her cheek, then tickled her nose. She twitched and tried to wipe it away. It touched her ear this time.

"Are you awake, Delaney?"

She opened her eyes and saw Rennie above her. One of her curls was trailing across Delaney's neck. "Rennie? What are you doing here?"

"Uncle Sam is making breakfast. It won't be very good," she confided. "But I want you to eat with me."

"Why are you in my house?" She sat up and looked around. This wasn't her bedroom. This was Sam's bed. Sam's house.

"This is our house, silly." Rennie ran out the door, yelling, "She's awake."

Sam murmured something Delaney couldn't hear, and a moment later he walked in the door. "Good morning." His hair was still tousled from sleep, and he wore a pair of flannel pants and an old Florida State T-shirt. "How are you feeling?"

"What am I doing here?" She yanked the sheet up and tucked it beneath her chin.

"I didn't want to leave you alone last night. I've never seen anyone so exhausted. So I brought you here instead."

"And slept with me? With the kids in the house?" She remembered feeling him against her. Soaking up his heat. Sleeping together like that had been almost as intimate as making love.

"I was on the couch by the time they woke up," he said softly. He sat down on the bed and leaned closer. The smell of peppermint toothpaste filled the space between them. "The other mornings when I've seen you, you've always been in a much better mood than this."

"Sex will do that." Clutching the sheet to her, she swung her legs over the side of the bed. "Where are my clothes?"

He reached behind him and handed her the jeans, her bra

neatly folded on top of it. She snatched it under the sheet, and he grinned. "My favorite part of your sleepover was when you asked me to take off your bra."

"Get out, Mr. Sunshine."

He stood up, laughing, and closed the door as he left the room.

What had happened? He wasn't acting like the man who'd run away from her two days ago as if his shirt was on fire. The man who'd panicked when she said she loved him.

Was he pretending that conversation had never taken place? He seemed relaxed. Calm. Happy she was here.

She was certain they hadn't made love last night. No matter how tired she'd been, she would have remembered that.

After throwing on her clothes, she ducked into the bathroom to freshen up, then stared at herself in the mirror. Her skin was pasty, her hair limp with dried sweat, and she had huge bags beneath her still-red eyes. Exactly the way she wanted her lover to see her in the morning.

Ex-lover, she told herself firmly.

She took one last look at herself and opened the bathroom door. If she was lucky, she wouldn't scare the kids.

Something was burning as she walked into the kitchen, and she saw smoke drifting up from the toaster. Leo stood next to Sam at the stove, pouring water into a frying pan and covering it with a lid. "That's how Rennie likes her eggs," he said to his uncle.

"Uh, hi," Delaney said, standing in the doorway.

Sam smiled. "Good morning. Have a seat and tell me how you like your eggs."

She shuddered. "I don't eat eggs."

"She needs coffee," Sam said to Leo. "Pour her a cup, will you?"

Leo set a mug of coffee in front of her, then hesitated. "Do you want some toast?"

"Thanks, Leo. That would be great." What she wanted was yogurt and fruit and the quiet of her house in the morning. But she was dying to know what this was all about, so she'd play along.

Leo threw the burned slices of toast in the garbage and put in two fresh pieces. White bread. She resisted rolling her eyes.

Rennie was sitting next to her, and she leaned closer. "We have a big breakfast on Saturdays. Uncle Sam doesn't know how to make eggs, though."

"That's okay," Delaney said faintly. "Toast is good."

She sipped her coffee and watched Sam put Rennie's eggs on a plate. Leo set her toast on a plate, too. "You want cinnamon toast?" he asked her.

She'd been Leo's age the last time she'd had that buttery, sugary concoction. "Yes, Leo, thanks. That sounds good."

"I make it for Rennie," he muttered.

She'd eaten her cinnamon toast and was on her second cup of coffee by the time everyone else finished eating. "What's this all about?" she asked Sam.

"All of what?"

"Bringing me here to sleep instead of my own house. You being all cheerful and bright in the morning. Eating breakfast like…" *Like a happy family.* She swallowed. "Like we do this every day."

"The kids have something they want to say."

Not Sam. The kids. She managed to smile at Leo and Rennie. "Yeah? What's that?"

Leo tore the crust of his toast into tiny pieces. "I'm sorry I was so mean to you," he muttered. "I called you a bad name."

"Yes, you did, and that was rude. It hurt my feelings. But

I understood. You were mad at me because you thought I hurt your mom and dad."

He stood up and took his plate to the sink. "You're not a...not that bad word. You're okay, I guess."

From Leo, that was high praise. "Thanks, Leo. I know it's hard to apologize. You're a great kid, and your dad would be so proud of you."

His shoulders relaxed and he scrubbed vigorously at the plate. "His guitar is sweet. Thanks for giving it to me."

"You want a quick lesson after breakfast? I don't know much, but I can show you how to tune it and play a few chords."

Leo looked over his shoulder. "Yeah? That would be awesome."

"Good." Delaney looked at Rennie. "What did you want to say?"

"That I love you," Rennie said promptly.

Delaney leaned over and hugged her, inhaling the scent of her hair. "I love you, too, sweetie."

"So you'll stay with us when we go back to Miami?" Rennie beamed at her.

Delaney froze for a second, then untangled herself from the little girl's arms. Sam hadn't asked, and he'd made it clear he never would. Even if he did, living in Miami with him would complicate his relationship with the kids. Heather would probably keep them away from him if Delaney was around.

"I can't do that, honey. I have to stay here. I'll miss you, though." She shoved away from the table. "Thanks for breakfast, everyone. Leo, when you're ready, bring the guitar over to my house. Just don't use the handle to carry it. It's broken and needs to be fixed. And come to the back door."

By the time she retrieved her jacket and purse from the bedroom, Sam was alone in the kitchen.

"I didn't put her up to it."

"I know you didn't." She reached for the door, and he opened it and stepped outside with her.

"Leo wanted to apologize. I thought it would be easier for him if Rennie had something to say, too. I had no idea she was going to ask you to come to Miami with us."

"Don't worry about it." Delaney started to leave, but he put his hand on her shoulder.

"Would you? Move to Miami?"

Her heart began to pound with hard, painful beats. This was what hope felt like. She turned slowly to face him. "Are you asking me to move with you?"

He let her go. "I have no right to ask you to make that sacrifice. Your business is here. Your friends. You've grown roots here."

So the answer was no. Just as well. The fact that she'd even consider moving was scary. "Right."

She headed for the trail through the woods. But she hadn't gotten far when she heard Sam behind her. "Wait, Delaney."

She turned to face him. He shoved his hands into his pockets, but didn't try to touch her. "I screwed up the other night. You scared me when you told me you loved me. I wasn't expecting that." He picked up a piece of bark from a white birch and crumbled it with his fingers. "It was my fault the press found you. I wanted to protect you, and you didn't need me to. I expected you to tell me I was a jerk. Not that you loved me."

She leaned against a tree and stared into the woods. Weak sunlight filtered through the branches, making patterns in the dirt. She'd taken a chance and laid her heart bare, and it had freaked him out. "You've made it clear you can't give me what I want from you, and I don't need you to protect me. I can take care of myself. So what exactly do you want from *me*, Sam?" she asked, watching the shadow of a bird on the ground.

He turned her to face him. "I need to sort things out. To figure out how I feel. We're leaving, but it could be a few weeks. I want to spend as much of that time as I can with you."

"I'd like some time, too," she said. "Time with the kids. I probably won't see them again after you leave." She loved Leo and Rennie, and not just because they were Diesel's children. She loved them for themselves—brave Leo, trying to be strong, and sweet Rennie.

"What about me?"

"I probably won't see you again, either." Her heart was crumbling into such tiny pieces that it would take a very long time to put it back together.

"That's not what I meant."

"I know what you meant. You want to come over in the morning again. I'm...I'm not sure I can do that."

"Then let me have time with you and the kids."

She wanted every last minute she could have with him. "I have that press conference today. Maybe tomorrow we can do something with them."

CHAPTER TWENTY-THREE

DELANEY SAT ON THE SMALL rise above the lake at Cave Point Park the next afternoon, enjoying the sunshine and unseasonable warmth as Sam squatted next to Rennie. The girl had been captivated by the sea glass they'd found. Leo had said it was lame, but he was searching for it, too. When he caught Delaney watching him, he said, "Rennie likes it."

He picked up a piece and examined it, turning it over carefully. Delaney scrambled down to look at it. It was blue and smooth around the edges. "That's a prize," she said lightly. "There aren't too many blue ones."

He stared at it for a moment, then handed it to her. "You take it, then. Rennie has lots."

The tiny piece of glass lay in her palm, dulled a little by the buffeting of the waves and the sand, sunlight sparkling off a tiny, clear corner. "Thank you, Leo. It's beautiful." More precious than the most valuable diamond. She put it into her pocket, checking to make sure there were no holes in her jeans.

"Maybe someone can make a necklace out of it or something," he said.

"Are you kidding?" She patted her pocket. "I'm not letting this out of my sight." She held his gaze. "It's far too valuable to trust to anyone else."

He blushed. "It's just a piece of glass."

"It's a lot more than that, Leo." She draped her arm across

his shoulders lightly. "Want me to show you my favorite cave?"

"Yeah." His face lit up. "Can we, like, go into it?"

"Absolutely."

As they started to walk away, Sam's phone began ringing. He glanced at the screen and froze. Then he motioned her over.

"It's Heather," he said in a low voice.

Sam watched Delaney, Leo and Rennie disappear down the shore, then he turned away. "How are you doing?" he said into the phone.

"I want my kids back. Immediately." Anger vibrated in her voice, but this wasn't Heather's usual shrill, screaming tantrum. Her voice was cold. Controlled.

Far more disturbing than her usual tirades.

"When are you getting out of the hospital?"

"I checked myself out today. This evening, actually."

"Really?" He moved closer to the low cliffs, trying to block the noise of the waves. "Did the doctor say you were ready to be released?"

"I don't give a damn what the doctor thinks. I saw the pictures."

Oh, God. She had internet access in the rehab unit? "What pictures?"

"Don't play dumb with me. I saw the pictures of you and her. She killed your brother, and you're f—"

"Heather, stop."

"I saw the other ones, too. The ones with Rennie. My baby!" She began to sob. "Walking down the street together, like it was her kid. She's taking my kids, and you're helping her."

Oh, my God. Someone had gotten a picture at the press conference. Sam and the kids had stayed at the back of the crowd, but as they were walking to the car, Rennie had run back to Delaney.

He gripped the phone tightly. "It's not what you think, Heather. Delaney had a press conference. She was talking about Diesel and the recordings they made. Rennie was excited to hear about her father."

"Cut the crap, Sam." His sister-in-law's voice was weary. "I know what I saw. Rennie wasn't running up to someone who talked about her father. She knows Chantal. I saw it in her face."

Heather was just as tragically flawed as Diesel had been. But it would be hard to see a picture of Rennie holding the hand of the woman Diesel had loved. "It doesn't matter, Heather. You're still her mother."

"That's right. I am. I revoked my power of attorney, so you don't have legal custody of them anymore. You bring them home in the next twenty-four hours, or I'll call the cops and tell them you abducted my kids."

Anger rose inside him in a huge, hot wave, sweeping away his pity. "Sorry, Heather, that's not going to happen. You go right ahead and call the cops—it'll only make you look like a fool. I'll get them back to Florida as soon as I can, but it's not going to happen tomorrow. Deal with it."

He snapped the phone closed, then stood staring at the small whitecaps on the lake. He shouldn't have taken the kids to Delaney's press conference. He should have been more careful.

He hadn't even thought about what would happen when they returned to Florida. Of course Rennie would tell her mother about Delaney. How had he ever imagined he'd keep this quiet?

And how had he imagined he could convince Delaney to move with him? Heather would never allow Leo and Rennie to spend time with her. He was sure Delaney had already figured that out.

Sam would have to leave her if he wanted to be part of his niece and nephew's life. She'd figured that out, too.

The three of them appeared around the curve of the cliff, and he forced himself to smile and wave. Delaney held tight to Rennie's hand and herded Leo away from the water. The sunlight made her hair glow, and she laughed as she listened to something Leo said.

Sam loved her, but he had to leave.

WHEN THEY GOT HOME from the lake, he put the kids to bed and called the next-door neighbor's teen daughter to stay with them. Then he hurried through the woods to Delaney's house. He'd told her about the phone call, that he had to leave. She'd told him to come over, and had given him the neighbor's phone number.

She must have been waiting in the kitchen, because as soon as he stepped onto the porch, she opened the door and held out her arms.

She whispered "I love you" when he slid inside her. She cried his name when she came. He tasted her tears as they lay tangled together on her bed, holding tightly to each other.

His throat swelled and his eyes burned, and he buried his face in her hair.

At midnight, he reluctantly pulled away. "I have to go," he said. "I told Tracey I'd be home by now."

Delaney slipped out of bed, her smooth, toned body pearl-white in the moonlight, and he pulled her into his arms one more time. "I'm not going to forget you, Delaney."

"I know," she whispered. She relaxed into his embrace for a long moment, then straightened. "I won't forget you, either."

FOUR DAYS LATER, Delaney stood outside the security gates at the Green Bay airport and tried to keep a smile on her face. Rennie was in her arms, and Leo was standing close, clutching his father's guitar case. Fluffy barked from his cage beside her.

"You can visit us, Delaney," Rennie said. "I'll show you my room."

"That sounds wonderful, sweetheart. I can't wait."

Sam swallowed and reached for Rennie. "We're going to miss our plane, guys. We have to go."

Rennie leaned out of Sam's arms and squeezed Delaney hard around the neck. "I'll send you more pictures for your 'frigerator."

"I'd like that," she managed to say.

Leo threw his arms around her and hugged her tightly, then stepped back. "Thanks again for the guitar. Uncle Sam said I could take lessons when we get back to Miami."

"I'll look forward to hearing you play it," she said, knowing that would never happen.

Sam set Rennie on the floor and wrapped his arms around Delaney. She felt him trembling, and she kissed him for a long moment. Then she whispered, "You're doing the right thing, Sam. I love you. Now go."

He captured her face in his palms and stared into her eyes. "I love you, Delaney. I'll be back."

He kissed her again, then turned and picked up Fluffy's cage and took Rennie's hand. They waved after they went through security, and she waved back, although she had trouble seeing them through the haze in her eyes. Moments later, they were gone.

DELANEY GUIDED ANOTHER piece of oak through the table saw, then stacked it carefully in a pile with the rest. She looked at the drawing on her workbench and picked up another piece of wood. The dresser she was building was a complicated design. She had to concentrate on every step. That was good. She needed something to fill her mind.

Sam had been gone for two days, and the pain was almost more than she could bear. He'd called the last two nights, and his voice made her ache. He was staying in Heather's house with Leo and Rennie, and he'd told her things were going well, but he sounded grim. Heather had pitched a fit, but he'd refused to leave.

Leo and Rennie missed Delaney, he said.

He missed her.

There was a huge hole in her heart, and she had no idea how to mend it. She'd searched for houses to rent in Miami, even though she knew it was a pipe dream. She couldn't move to Miami. Heather wouldn't allow her to have any contact with her kids. And Delaney couldn't force Sam to choose between them.

Her phone rang, and she leaped for it, then set it down when she looked at the caller ID. Jen.

Jen and Maddie had both called every day. While Sam was still here, Delaney had turned her phone off. After he left, she'd needed some time to regain her balance. She still felt too wobbly to talk to her friends.

She turned on the lathe, consulted the drawing again, and picked up a piece of wood. Work was her means of sanity right now. Work was escape. She adjusted the knobs of the machine and focused on making the facing of a drawer.

SEVERAL HOURS LATER, she was sitting in her darkening kitchen, drinking a cup of tea and watching the sunset over the woods, when she heard a car in her driveway. Probably not a reporter—most of them had left town when they realized there wasn't much of a story left to tell.

She peered out the window and saw a hugely pregnant

Maddie struggle out of the passenger side of Jen's SUV. Both of them headed toward her front door, determined looks on their faces.

Delaney turned on the lights in the house and opened the door. "Hi, guys." She took a deep breath. They were going to do this, whether she was ready or not. "Come on in."

Maddie tossed her coat onto the couch, then put her hands on Delaney's shoulders. "We know they're gone."

The sympathy in her expression, the distress in her eyes, were too much. Delaney covered her face with her hands, and all the tears she'd refused to shed streamed down her face. When her breath caught on a sob, Maddie pulled her into a hug.

She clung to her friends, sobbing, until she felt completely drained. The hard bump of Maddie's belly pressed against hers, and as she was sniffling and trying to gather her courage, she felt something flutter against her stomach.

She looked down in awe. "Was the kid just kicking me?"

"She was." Maddie let her go and smoothed her hand over her abdomen. "Clearly, she's going to be a soccer player."

"She? Do you know for sure?"

Her friend nodded. "I broke down and asked."

Delaney knuckled her eyes and grabbed a tissue from the box on the end table. Maddie and Quinn were having a daughter. Delaney thought about Rennie in Miami and struggled to smile. "That's great news. Names?"

"Not yet." Maddie linked an arm through hers. "We're not here to talk about me. The real estate agent told us Sam paid off his lease and turned in his keys. We figured you'd need some company."

Delaney struggled not to begin crying again. "He's been gone for two days."

"And you let him go?" Jen asked.

"I had to."

Maddie lowered herself to the couch, and Jen pulled a fancy gold box out of her huge purse. "We brought chocolate. Tell us what happened."

Delaney looked at her two friends. They'd both apologized for the way they'd reacted to the news that she was Chantal, but Delaney had been cool and distant the last time she'd seen them. She'd been ignoring their calls for almost a week. Still, they'd driven out to her house because they thought she needed them. They must have half expected she'd slam the door in their faces.

"Let me...let me get some tea," she said unsteadily. "Herbal for you, Maddie. Jen, what do you want?"

"Herbal is good."

Delaney was a little steadier by the time she set a pot of tea and three mugs on the coffee table. Jen pulled her onto the couch between them. "I've been pissed off at Walker for not pounding that guy when he had a chance. Tell us why we shouldn't go after him and cut out his heart?"

Delaney managed a sad smile. "Because he has two kids to take care of."

By the time she finished telling her friends about Heather and Leo and Rennie, they'd eaten half the box of chocolates and finished the tea. When Delaney's voice trailed off, Maddie said, "Well, that bites the big one."

Delaney sniffled. "You have such a way with words, Maddie. Must be because you're a reporter."

"This is so unfair," Jen said.

"No, it's not. I knew what the deal was—and this is exactly what I wanted. That's why I said I'd release the demos. I wanted to keep him here long enough to get to know Diesel's kids." Her stomach churning, she pushed the box of chocolates away. "I didn't plan on falling in love with him."

She gave the box another little shove. "I didn't think it was going to hurt this much."

"That's why we're here," Maddie said. "We know."

"Thank you," Delaney said quietly. "I should have answered your phone calls. I just…I couldn't talk to anyone. Especially you guys. You know me too well." She jumped up from the couch. "I knew you'd come out here, and that I'd cry. I hate to cry."

"We were afraid you were still angry with us," Jen said.

"No. I was never angry. I was hurt. I understood why you were shocked, but it still hurt."

"We have no excuses," Maddie said. "It's not like we're perfect ourselves."

Delaney smiled and felt some of her misery dissipate. She'd needed her friends. "You get a pass on being shocked. What were you supposed to do when you found out one of your friends was a notorious rocker who'd had a very public affair with a band member and been blamed for his death? I didn't expect you to say, 'Oh, that's nice, Del.'"

"'It's okay' would have been good, though," Jen said quietly. "So would 'it doesn't matter.' I'm so sorry."

"I am, too," Maddie said.

"I know you are. So let's forget about it, all right? I don't want things to be different between us."

"Oh, things are going to be different." Maddie leaned forward. "We have a source now for celebrity gossip, and we're going to mine it. We expect you to dish all the dirt."

Two days ago, Delaney hadn't thought she would ever laugh again. "Ask away."

CHAPTER TWENTY-FOUR

SAM PAUSED AT THE door of Rennie's bedroom, watching his niece sleeping. Fluffy was curled up at her back, his head on his paws. Heather had been appalled at the dog and had tried to get rid of him, but after Rennie's hysteria, Sam had taken Heather aside and explained. He'd told her how much Rennie loved the ugly mutt, and how attached they were.

Once she heard the story, Heather had agreed to let the dog stay. She was trying. He had to give her that. She'd clearly learned some things about herself in rehab.

He stopped at Leo's door, watching his nephew sleep, as well. The guitar case lay on the bed next to him. It was out of his sight only when he was in school. Every morning, before he got on the bus, he placed it carefully in Sam's office. Clearly, he knew what his mother's reaction would be if she found out where the guitar had come from. Or that it had belonged to Diesel.

Heather's nonrecognition of the guitar had told Sam all he needed to know about her relationship with his brother. Thank God Diesel had had Delaney in his life.

Delaney. Sam eased Leo's door closed and headed downstairs. It had been three weeks, and the ache hadn't gotten any better. He missed her more every day. As much as he loved talking to her and hearing her voice, he was beginning to dread the phone calls. They were a daily reminder of what he'd left behind.

As he reached the main floor, he smelled cigarette smoke

and heard Heather's voice. She had company, and Sam turned to go back upstairs.

"I can't, Tim." Heather's voice. "I have the kids."

The unknown Tim said something in a low voice.

"What am I supposed to do? They're my kids. I told Sam to bring them back."

She sounded weary. Worn down. Depressed.

Tim continued talking, but Sam had heard enough. He crept back up the stairs and sat in his office. For the first time in three weeks, hope stirred.

The next morning, after he'd seen Leo and Rennie onto the school bus, he wandered into the kitchen, poured himself a cup of coffee and sat down across from Heather. Her long blonde hair was tousled from sleep, and her eyes were sad.

"They're on the bus safely."

"Are you going to walk them to the bus stop when they're in high school?" she asked.

High school. That implied he'd be part of their lives permanently. His heart beat a little faster, but he said lightly, "God, no. They'd be totally humiliated."

Heather smiled. "Yeah, I forgot about hating your parents when you're that age."

"How is it going with you and the kids?" he asked. "Are you glad they're back here?"

"Of course I am." She grabbed her coffee and took a gulp. "They're my kids. I love them." She took another swallow, then stared into the mug. "I know I haven't been a good mother."

"You did the best you could."

"No, I didn't, Sam. I screwed up."

"At least you realize it. Leo and Rennie love you. They want a relationship with you. You can fix things if you really want to."

She nodded. "I do. I missed them while I was in the

hospital." Her eyes filled with tears. "I wanted to tell them I was sorry."

He looked at her hand, shaking slightly as she held the coffee. "You've still got a lot of work to do, don't you?"

"I need to go to AA meetings. And NA meetings. I'll be seeing a therapist twice a week."

Sam took a deep breath and let it out slowly. "Do you want me to take the kids? While you finish getting yourself straight?"

She stared at him for a long moment, then stood up and grabbed a container of yogurt out of the refrigerator. When she sat down, she stared down at the yogurt instead of him. "They're my kids. What kind of mother gives her kids away?"

"A mother who's overwhelmed. A mother who has a lot of problems she has to work through." He put his hand over hers. "A mother who wants what's best for them."

"They'll think I don't want them."

"I'll make sure they know you do. I love them, Heather, as if they're my own. They love me. Let me have custody of them while you get yourself sorted out."

"So you can take them back to Wisconsin? So Chantal can have them?" She stabbed the spoon into the yogurt cup.

"Yes, I want to go back to Wisconsin. But I think it would be good for Leo and Rennie, too. They had friends there. They were doing well in school. It's a different environment. Here, they're a celebrity's kids. In Wisconsin, they were just Leo and Rennie Adams. They could have a stable life."

"With you and Chantal." Her voice was sad. Defeated.

"With me and Delaney. She's changed, Heather. She knows how much she hurt you and the kids, and she really regrets that. She's wonderful with them."

"So she gets everything." Heather shoved the yogurt away, and it slid off the table and splattered on the floor. "First

Diesel, and now his kids. He loved her, Sam." She lifted her head, and her eyes were haunted. Full of pain. "He wanted to marry her. We'd been together forever, we had two kids, but he wouldn't marry me." Tears ran down her face. "Diesel told me they were going to get married."

"That must have hurt a lot." No wonder she'd been so needy. So desperate. So vengeful.

"You have no idea."

He reached across the table and took her hands. "Let me have temporary custody of them, Heather. I promise, no one else could love them more than I do. You'll see them often, as often as you want, while you're recovering. You have to get yourself straightened out before you can be a good parent."

A spark of hope flickered in her eyes, and sympathy washed through him. It hadn't been easy for Heather, either.

His voice was gentle. "Sometimes, doing the right thing for your kids means letting them go. I know it's hard. But make the right choice for Leo and Rennie."

DELANEY SANG THE LAST notes of "Learning to Fly," made a final drum flourish, then smiled as the crowd in the Harp cheered and clapped.

"Ready for a break?" Paul asked the band.

"Yeah, I need a beer," Hank said.

"Okay, fifteen minutes." Paul pointed at her. "You. Eat. Or you're going to embarrass yourself when your pants fall off in public."

"Yes, Mom," she said, setting down her drumsticks.

As she stood up to head into the kitchen, Paul stopped her. "Do you want to start out the next set with that song we worked on? The one you and Diesel did?"

"That would be great. The record company is looking forward to getting a little feedback."

Paul scowled. "How about you, Delaney? Do *you* want to sing that song in public?"

"Yeah, I do," she said. "It's time. I agreed to do publicity, and this is part of it. Might as well stir up a little interest in the CD." She smiled as she wove her way through the crowd and into the kitchen.

Singing a song she and Diesel had written and recorded wouldn't be painless, but she could do it. There would be some nostalgia, some regret, but it wouldn't turn her inside out. It wouldn't be wrenching. Not like the last four weeks had been.

She'd gone on with her life—made furniture, played at the Harp, hung out with her friends. If she had to force herself to smile, she made sure it didn't show. If she was distracted sometimes, she told her friends she was tired.

Eventually, the pain had to fade.

Eventually, she had to feel alive again.

It had gotten worse instead of better in the last week. Sam had seemed distracted. Rushed. Preoccupied. Every time she closed her phone, she'd felt hollow inside.

She'd known it would happen, but she hadn't figured it would start so soon. She'd thought she would see him once more, at least.

Maybe it was better this way. *Surgical incision.* A clean break was better for him and the kids.

And hell for her.

Glancing at the clock fifteen minutes later, she dumped the mostly untouched sandwich in the garbage and headed out of the kitchen. Second set. Diesel's song.

"Let's play something upbeat after the first one," she said to Paul.

"I've got the perfect choice," he said as he adjusted his

guitar. "How about 'I Get by with a Little Help From My Friends'?"

"Yeah," she said, giving him a hug. "That's perfect."

She nodded to Paul and leaned into her mic. "A lot of you know about the project I'm working on—getting some new songs that Diesel and I wrote ready to be released. We're going to sing one of them tonight. But please, no recording. That would make my record company very unhappy."

The crowd quieted, and she could almost see them leaning forward. Anticipating. She closed her eyes, had an image of Diesel smiling at her, and nodded to Paul.

The first notes of the intro settled her, and she began to sing. Paul joined her, and the music filled the pub. No one moved. No one talked. It was almost as if everyone was holding their breath.

As the last notes faded away, the room erupted into applause. People stamped their feet, cheered, whistled. Smiling, Delaney waited until everyone quieted. "Thank you," she said. "That song meant a lot to Diesel." It was the lullaby she'd hummed to Rennie. "And to me."

As they prepared for their next song, a child's voice rang out in the relative silence. "She sang my song!"

Rennie.

Delaney dropped her drumsticks on the floor and scrambled past the mic stands and the amplifiers. "Rennie?" She looked around, but after the bright stage lights, she couldn't see in the darkness.

A small shape ran toward her down the narrow aisle next to the bar. Delaney bent down, and Rennie jumped into her arms.

"Rennie." Delaney stroked her hair and inhaled her baby shampoo and little girl scent as she searched for Sam and Leo. Her eyes adjusted to the darkness, and she saw two more shapes hurrying toward her.

Leo reached her first. "Hey, Delaney," he said, wrapping his arms around her waist.

"Leo." She hugged him and kissed his head, then looked up. "Sam."

She let Rennie slide to the floor, and threw herself into his arms. He held her tight against him as he kissed her, and she felt tears on her face. His? Hers? She had no idea.

Dimly, she heard the people in the bar applauding and cheering. Then Paul's voice. "Well, folks, it looks as if we've lost our drummer for the rest of the night."

Delaney broke the kiss and leaned back to look at Sam. "What are you all doing here?"

Before he could say anything, Rennie piped up. "We're going to marry you and live in Otto Tail with you."

Delaney stared at her. Amid the laughter of the people sitting close to them, Leo said, "Rennie, you dope, Uncle Sam is supposed to say that."

More laughter broke out as Maddie pushed through the crowd and steered them toward the end of the bar. "Go in the office. We're all enjoying this, but you'd probably like a little privacy."

As the door clicked shut behind them, Delaney wrapped her arms around Sam again. "You're here. I can't believe you're actually here."

"I told you I'd come back. That I'd figure out a way." He kissed her again, and she lost herself in the taste of him, the feel of him.

The miracle of him.

"Why are they kissing so much?" Rennie asked.

"I don't know," Leo said. "It's pretty gross."

Sam laughed and eased away from her. "I'm very glad to see Delaney," he said. "I've missed her."

"That's lame, Uncle Sam. I missed her, too, but I'm not

going to slobber all over her." Leo made a face, and Delaney grabbed him and planted a big kiss on his cheek.

He wiped his sleeve across his face, but he was grinning.

"Tell me everything," she said, still holding on to Sam. "What's going on? What are you doing here?"

"We drove here," Leo said.

"It was raining in the mountains, and Uncle Sam said bad words," Rennie added.

Delaney looked at him, afraid to hope. "Are you really here to stay? For good?"

A shadow filled his eyes for a moment. "For now," he said quietly. He slid his fingers into the curve of her waist and tugged her closer. "Do you have to stay for the rest of the night? Or can we get out of here? The mutt is in the car."

For now? She grabbed her jacket and purse from the desk and gripped them tightly. "I think the guys can survive one night without me."

The band was finishing a song as they exited the office, and everyone in the crowd smiled as they walked toward the front of the pub. Before they left, she said to Paul, "Can you get my drums?"

"I'll bring them out tomorrow," he told her.

"Thanks."

The air outside was warm, but a sharp breeze blew in off the lake. "We'll follow you home," Sam said.

She watched the headlights behind her as she drove. They were steady. Strong. And they stayed close.

Sam pulled into her driveway right behind her. He had a carrier on his roof, and the back of the SUV was packed to the ceiling. Her heart began to pound. There was an awful lot of stuff in the Jeep for a quick visit.

"I called Myrtle and reserved a room at the Bide-a-Wee," Sam said in a low voice as the kids escorted Fluffy into the trees to take care of business. "We're not going to invade your privacy."

"Are you kidding me?" She held tight to his hand, as if he might try to escape. "You're not going anywhere. I have two small bedrooms upstairs that I don't use. The kids will be fine up there."

"Where am I supposed to sleep?" Sam asked.

"Later," she said as Leo, Rennie and the dog came running out of the woods.

An hour later, Rennie was drowsy and warm in a sleeping bag, but she clung to Delaney's hand. "Will you always kiss me good-night before I go to bed?" she asked, half-asleep."

Delaney's heart swelled. "You bet, sweetheart."

Rennie smiled. "Fluffy, too?"

The dog was curled against the child's back, watching Delaney. "Fluffy, too."

In the other bedroom, Leo was already asleep, one hand resting on the guitar case.

As soon as she and Sam were in the living room, he snatched her into his arms and pulled her onto the couch. "God, I thought they'd never go to bed."

She grinned as she burrowed closer. "You sound like a parent."

He stilled. "Before we left Florida, all I could think about was you. About getting in the car and driving north." He eased away from her and held her arms. "But I had a lot of time to think on that drive."

Delaney tensed. This was the "for now" part. He was having second thoughts. Recognizing the enormity of what he'd done. "It's okay, Sam." She tried to smile. "I understand. I've missed you, too. But I don't expect you to...to rearrange your whole life." As long as she had a little time with him. As long as she got to spend a few nights sleeping next to him.

He frowned. "You think I'm having second thoughts? That I want to turn around and go back to Florida? Nothing could be further from my mind."

"What's wrong, then?"

He slid his palms down her arms and twined his fingers with hers. "Before we left, I didn't think about what I'd be asking of you. What I'd be expecting you to take on. Rennie said we were going to marry you and live here with you, and that's exactly what I thought."

Some of the tension in Delaney's chest eased. "But...?"

"At some point, we'll have to go back to Miami. Heather is trying to recover. She let me take the kids for now, so she can focus on getting better. But eventually, she'll want them back.

"What do we do then?" His eyes clouded with worry. "Do you give up your business and move to Miami with us? Do we have a commuter marriage? I don't like either of those options, but I want to be part of Leo and Rennie's lives. I need to be."

"We'll have complicated lives," Delaney said. "Lots of people do, and they make it work. We can, too."

"It's not just that." He pulled her closer. "You're getting a ready-made family. And it wouldn't be an easy one. I'm still trying to figure it out. Neither of us has lived with kids. I have no idea what the hell I'm doing. On the way up here, I realized it's not fair to ask you to take all this on."

The fist around her heart relaxed. "Sam..."

"Don't say anything yet." He touched her mouth. "It's not as if these are kids who have had a normal life. They wanted to come here, wanted to be with you and me, but they had to leave their mother behind. I know you love them, but you'll never be their mother, Delaney, just like I'll never be their father. Can you do that? Can you watch the kids you love go back to a woman you have every reason to dislike?"

"Will it be easy with Heather? No, it won't. But we both love Leo and Rennie. We can figure it out as we go along."

She slid onto his lap and cupped his face in her hands. "All four of us will figure this out. Heather, too, when she's ready. I love you. I love Leo and Rennie. So, since you're obviously not going to ask me, I'll ask you. Will you marry me? Or do I have to kick your butt until you agree?"

His shoulders relaxed and he pulled her against him. "You're such a romantic, Delaney. How can I refuse an offer like that?"

She curled her arms around his neck. "Is that a yes? You're willing to give up the sun and the beach and the ocean to live in the frozen north? You're willing to take on a woman who's cranky in the morning, who loses herself in her work and forgets important stuff like eating? A woman who's going to be gone for big chunks of time to promote this new CD? Are you sure you can live like that?"

"Smart-ass," he murmured into her ear. "Don't you know there's nothing I want more? That I'd live anywhere with you? Do anything to have you as my wife?" He kissed her, and desire began to stir. "I love you, Delaney. When can we get married?"

"Soon." She shivered as his hand crept beneath her tank top. "Very soon."

"Here's the big question for the night—where am I supposed to sleep?"

She wriggled closer, luxuriating in the feel of his hand on her body. "How does the couch sound?"

"I don't think so." He cupped her breast.

She sucked in a breath. "A sleeping bag on the floor?" He touched her nipple, and she moaned into his mouth.

"Sounds very uncomfortable." He raised the thin cotton shirt and watched her as he rubbed his thumb over her skin. "Any other ideas?"

"I'm...I can't think." She closed her eyes. "Just don't stop."

"Never, Delaney." He lifted her off the couch and carried her to the bedroom.

A long time later, he smiled down at her. "I love you. Have I mentioned that?"

She twined her arms around his neck. "Say it again. I'll never get tired of hearing it."

EPILOGUE

CHRISTMAS MORNING. Delaney couldn't remember ever being this excited about it, even when she was a kid. The tiny, multicolored lights twinkled on the Christmas tree in her living room, and the scent of pine filled the air. Outside, dawn painted the sky pink and orange as she and Sam waited at the bottom of the stairs, listening to Leo and Rennie stir in their bedrooms.

She and Sam had gotten out of bed as soon as they heard movement above them. But instead of the expected charge of footsteps into the living room, rustling sounds and giggles drifted down.

She leaned into Sam. "What are they up to?"

"I have no idea." He peered up the stairs. "But I suspect it's related to all the whispering and closed doors recently."

Delaney glanced over her shoulder at the presents piled under the Christmas tree. "I wish they'd hurry up. I'm as excited as the kids."

He wrapped his arms around her. "I used to hate Christmas," he said softly.

She turned in his arms. "How come?"

"It was the last time I saw Diesel alive. The time I told him not to come to me for help anymore. And three months later, he died."

"He knew you loved him, Sam." She cupped his face in her hands. "He knew why you said what you did. You have to let it go."

Sam pressed his hand over hers, holding her palm to his cheek. "I like to think I'm making it up to him now. By standing in for him with his kids."

"They're happy," she said. "Loved. Secure. You love them as much as Diesel did. And you helped Heather get clean and sober. Diesel would be happy."

Before he could answer, a door on the second floor opened and Leo and Rennie ran down the stairs. Dressed in their pajamas, they rushed past Delaney and Sam and into the living room. Fluffy trailed them, wearing a huge red bow around his neck. He stopped every couple of steps and tried to scratch it off.

"Santa was here," Rennie squealed.

Leo rolled his eyes, and Delaney pulled him close. "Where did that sleigh bell come from? It wasn't there when we went to bed." She pointed to the dull silver bell suspended by a strip of leather from the front of the Christmas tree. "Rennie will be able to hear it. Will you?"

They'd read *The Polar Express* earlier in the week. Leo's glance shifted from the tree to Delaney. He looked uncertain. She rang the bell, and its clear sound filled the room.

Leo's eyes widened, and she saw the magic of the season there.

"That's what I thought," she said, hugging him.

She and Sam sat on the couch, their hands entwined, while the kids opened their presents. There were none from Heather, because they were all going to Miami tomorrow, and the kids would have their own Christmas with their mother. They'd spend the rest of their Christmas break with her, while Sam and Delaney had the honeymoon they'd postponed after their summer wedding and the flurry of publicity connected with the release of Delaney and Diesel's CD.

As Leo and Rennie opened boxes and unwrapped books, Sam grabbed a red ribbon from the debris on the floor. He looped it behind Delaney's ears and tied a bow on top of her head. "Here's my Christmas present," he said, kissing her. "All I want. You've made all my dreams come true."

She touched her stomach. Later, she'd give Sam his Christmas gift. One more dream was going to come true, as well.

After all the presents were opened, including the chew bone for Fluffy, Rennie nudged Leo. He nodded and pulled his guitar out from behind a chair. "Can I tell them?" Rennie said, bouncing up and down. "Please, Leo?"

"Yeah, you can tell them."

"Leo made a song for you," she said, her eyes shining. "A Christmas song. And I helped."

Delaney clutched Sam's hand. "You wrote a song, Leo? Really?"

He nodded, his cheeks flushed. "It's kind of stupid," he said, fiddling with the guitar strings.

"It is not," Rennie objected. "It's a good song."

Sam cleared his throat. "Can we hear it?"

Leo strummed a chord, then began to play and sing. "There once was a dog named Fluffy, a puppy who needed a home."

Rennie picked up Fluffy's front legs and made him dance. He snapped at the bow on his neck and almost fell over. Delaney grabbed Sam's hand and held on tightly.

"He was lost in the woods in the winter, a bad dog who wanted to roam."

The dog jumped away from Rennie and tried to eat a piece of green wrapping paper. Sam leaned forward and snatched it away from him.

"Then he found a new family to love him, they kept him and gave him a bath."

Delaney bit her lip as she tried to hold back the tears.

"And now they're one big happy family, except when he passes the gas."

Delaney laughed and cried at the same time, and dragged the boy into her arms. "Leo, that was wonderful." She scooped Rennie into her arms as well, and hugged both kids fiercely. Sam wrapped his arms around all of them.

"The last line is kind of stupid, but I couldn't think of a word to rhyme with fart," Leo said.

"I think it's a brilliant song." She leaned away from him. "Your dad would love it, too, and I know he heard it. He's smiling right now because he's so proud of both of you."

"I'm going to take my guitar to Miami and play it for Mom."

"That's a great idea," Sam said. "She'll love it."

Still holding on to Leo, Delaney leaned against Sam and pulled Rennie into her lap. The four of them looked at the room, the floor covered with torn wrapping paper and ribbons, presents in random piles. Fluffy was chewing on his rawhide bone.

Her family. She had never thought she'd be able to say those words, but all her dreams had come true.

She smiled at Sam. "What do you think of Christmas now?"

* * * * *

HARLEQUIN®
Super Romance®

COMING NEXT MONTH

Available December 7, 2010

HSRCNM1110

REQUEST YOUR FREE BOOKS!

2 FREE NOVELS PLUS 2 FREE GIFTS!

HARLEQUIN®

Super Romance®

Exciting, emotional, unexpected!

YES! Please send me 2 FREE Harlequin® Superromance® novels and my 2 FREE gifts (gifts are worth about $10). After receiving them, if I don't wish to receive any more books, I can return the shipping statement marked "cancel." If I don't cancel, I will receive 6 brand-new novels every month and be billed just $4.69 per book in the U.S. or $5.24 per book in Canada. That's a saving of at least 15% off the cover price! It's quite a bargain! Shipping and handling is just 50¢ per book.* I understand that accepting the 2 free books and gifts places me under no obligation to buy anything. I can always return a shipment and cancel at any time. Even if I never buy another book from Harlequin, the two free books and gifts are mine to keep forever.

135/336 HDN E5P4

Name _____ (PLEASE PRINT) _____

Address _____ Apt. # _____

City _____ State/Prov. _____ Zip/Postal Code _____

Signature (if under 18, a parent or guardian must sign)

Mail to the Harlequin Reader Service:
IN U.S.A.: P.O. Box 1867, Buffalo, NY 14240-1867
IN CANADA: P.O. Box 609, Fort Erie, Ontario L2A 5X3

Not valid for current subscribers to Harlequin Superromance books.

**Are you a current subscriber to Harlequin Superromance books
and want to receive the larger-print edition?
Call 1-800-873-8635 today!**

* Terms and prices subject to change without notice. Prices do not include applicable taxes. N.Y. residents add applicable sales tax. Canadian residents will be charged applicable provincial taxes and GST. Offer not valid in Quebec. This offer is limited to one order per household. All orders subject to approval. Credit or debit balances in a customer's account(s) may be offset by any other outstanding balance owed by or to the customer. Please allow 4 to 6 weeks for delivery. Offer available while quantities last.

Your Privacy: Harlequin Books is committed to protecting your privacy. Our Privacy Policy is available online at www.eHarlequin.com or upon request from the Reader Service. From time to time we make our lists of customers available to reputable third parties who may have a product or service of interest to you. If you would prefer we not share your name and address, please check here. ☐

Help us get it right—We strive for accurate, respectful and relevant communications. To clarify or modify your communication preferences, visit us at www.ReaderService.com/consumerchoice.

HSR10R

HARLEQUIN®

A Romance

FOR EVERY MOOD™

Spotlight on

Classic

Quintessential, modern love stories
that are romance at its finest.

See the next page
to enjoy a sneak peek from
the Harlequin® Romance series.

See below for a sneak peek from our classic
Harlequin® Romance® line.

Introducing DADDY BY CHRISTMAS by Patricia Thayer.

Mɪᴀ caught sight of Jarrett when he walked into the open lobby. It was hard not to notice the man. In a charcoal business suit with a crisp white shirt and striped tie covered by a dark trench coat, he looked more Wall Street than small-town Colorado.

Mia couldn't blame him for keeping his distance. He was probably tired of taking care of her.

Besides, why would a man like Jarrett McKane be interested in her? Why would he want to take on a woman expecting a baby? Yet he'd done so many things for her. He'd been there when she'd needed him most. How could she not care about a man like that?

Heart pounding in her ears, she walked up behind him. Jarrett turned to face her. "Did you get enough sleep last night?"

"Yes, thanks to you," she said, wondering if he'd thought about their kiss. Her gaze went to his mouth, then she quickly glanced away. "And thank you for not bringing up my meltdown."

Jarrett couldn't stop looking at Mia. Blue was definitely her color, bringing out the richness of her eyes.

"What meltdown?" he said, trying hard to focus on what she was saying. "You were just exhausted from lack of sleep and worried about your baby."

He couldn't help remembering how, during the night, he'd kept going in to watch her sleep. How strange was that? "I hope you got enough rest."

She nodded. "Plenty. And you're a good neighbor for

coming to my rescue."

He tensed. Neighbor? *What neighbor kisses you like I did?* "That's me, just the full-service landlord," he said, trying to keep the sarcasm out of his voice. He started to leave, but she put her hand on his arm.

"Jarrett, what I meant was you went beyond helping me." Her eyes searched his face. "I've asked far too much of you."

"Did you hear me complain?"

She shook her head. "You should. I feel like I've taken advantage."

"Like I said, I haven't minded."

"And I'm grateful for everything…"

Grasping her hand on his arm, Jarrett leaned forward. The memory of last night's kiss had him aching for another. "I didn't do it for your gratitude, Mia."

Gorgeous tycoon Jarrett McKane has never believed in Christmas—but he can't help being drawn to soon-to-be-mom Mia Saunders! Christmases past were spent alone…and now Jarrett may just have a fairy-tale ending for all his Christmases future!

Available December 2010, only from Harlequin® Romance®.

SPECIAL EDITION

USA TODAY BESTSELLING AUTHOR

MARIE FERRARELLA

BRINGS YOU ANOTHER HEARTWARMING STORY FROM

When Lilli McCall disappeared on him after he proposed, Kullen Manetti swore never to fall in love again. Eight years later Lilli is back in his life, threatening to break down all the walls he's put up to safeguard his heart.

UNWRAPPING THE PLAYBOY

Available December wherever books are sold.